CW00685144

If I Asked You to

Stay

Brianna Remus

ALSO BY BRIANNA REMUS

The Falling for You Trilogy

Dare to Fall

Dare to Need

Dare to Love

For anyone who's ever been left behind.
You're worth coming back for.

PROLOGUE

MELANIE BAXLEY

*G*irls *like me never get their happy ending*, I thought to myself as hot tears streamed down my face. Having been born into one of the wealthiest families in the Southeast, I had a single job to do. Marry a man equally or more rich than my father. It didn't matter that my father died from cirrhosis of the liver from his chronic binge drinking before I was even ten years old. I still had a mother to prove my worth to and she wouldn't be satisfied with me falling in love with a boy from the wrong side of town.

Strike that.

If I wasn't her only heiress to our family's fortune, she would knock me out cold for the sinful deed I had committed. Of course, she wouldn't lay a hand on me unless we were behind closed doors and she had full-coverage concealer on standby. It was one of her rules—family secrets stayed in the family.

And it was the only rule that had made me cry.

"What do you mean we're over?" Landon's bright blue eyes reflected every ounce of pain I was feeling.

When his palm met the side of my face, wiping my tears away, I thought for a second that I might not be strong enough to walk away from him. The only person I'd ever loved and the only person who loved every piece of me. No matter how fucked up those pieces might be.

The moment of doubt flickered away, nothing but dust in the wind as I recalled the reason I was leaving him. My mother's wrath. It was the only thing powerful enough to make me walk away from the boy I loved.

"There's no point in us dragging this out, Landon. We both know there's no future for us. My mother would never let me marry you and your parents hate me."

"We don't need them." His words were a plea that broke my heart. He grasped my hands in his, holding them up to his chest as his eyes searched my face for any hint of reprieve.

He wouldn't find any. Because as much as it pained me to let him go, the thought of my mother raking him over hot coals with her wretched thirst for vengeance on the boy who 'tainted' her daughter was something I would never be able to live with.

I yanked my hands from his. The flash of hurt in his eyes forced me to look away from him. I was losing my nerve and had to make this quick if I wanted to get out alive.

"Wake up, Landon! This"—I gestured erratically between us—"was never going to work. *We* were never going to work. This isn't some fairytale. We were always Romeo and Juliet— destined for failure from the start."

"You don't mean that, Mel." He tried to reach for my face again, but I swatted his hand away.

"I do," I sniffed. The tears flowing down my cheeks were a

betrayal of the words I spoke. He knew me better than anyone. I could see the denial written all over his face.

My stomach coiled into a tight knot. I knew what I had to say, even though every cell in my body fought against the words roaring in my mind. It was the only way he would let me go. And I needed him to let me go. For his sake and mine. I loved him too much to see him ruined by my mother.

"I'm a Baxley, Landon. And you're nothing but a boy from across the train tracks. It was fun. But you honestly didn't think that someone like you would ever end up with someone like me, did you?"

The light in his eyes that I had cherished beyond measure burned out. Like a swift blow of breath to a candle's flame, the only memory of the fire was a trail of black smoke. Fury started to smolder in those frost-blue irises and for the briefest moment, I was scared of what he was capable of.

"You're right, Melanie. You are a Baxley and I've been a fool to think you were anything more than a spoiled bitch looking for a pick-me-up because your shiny life got too boring."

It was a slap in the face and I deserved the sting that made my chest ache with regret.

He narrowed his gaze on me—assessing—before he turned around and walked out of my life forever.

When the image of his body disappeared in the dark of the night, I screamed through the sob that wracked my body. Landon was gone and he was never coming back and it was my fault. We would never get the chance to fulfill our promises to one another. Dreams whispered in the dark on passionate breaths—lost forever.

As I fell to my knees under the moonlit sky, my hand found its way to my lower belly where a flicker of life was nestled deep in my core. I had to protect Landon from my world.

And our baby, too.

CHAPTER ONE

WILLOW MAE

I wasn't supposed to be here. In fact, this was the last place on earth I wanted to be. Yet, somehow the universe had brought me to this exact place—the bane of my existence.

Pebble Brook Falls. A tiny little town nestled in the mountains of Northwest Georgia. With its picturesque views and sweet little downtown shops. Anyone passing through would see it as the perfect Southern town.

To me, it was anything but perfect, it was hell on earth. Filled with secrets and lies and too many skeletons to count. Though, they were buried deep enough that no one could see them—unless you knew exactly where to dig.

With a press of my finger on the small button embedded in the armrest of my car door, the window slowly rolled up. The old hunk of moving metal was falling apart and I was terrified the engine would give out on me any day now.

It didn't help that the air conditioning had stopped working halfway through my drive. I knew I was a hot mess, but I always preferred to not *be* hot. Spreading my elbows out wide, I did my best to prevent myself from sweating from the late summer heat.

That's the thing about trying to make your dreams work—you had to sacrifice luxury items like replacing the air conditioning in your beater car.

Thankfully, I pulled right into the parking lot of Sarah's Bakery before the first bead of sweat started to gather under my arms. Grabbing my small leather crossover from the passenger seat, I swung the purse strap over my head and stepped out of my car.

Holy hell it was *hot*.

In an attempt to save myself from turning into a puddle on the ground, I quickly hopped onto the sidewalk and sought shelter under the white awning of one of the downtown shops. The place looked abandoned as I gazed into the large glass windows. A sign on the door indicated the corner shop space was available for leasing. I rolled my eyes as I wondered who in their right mind would want to rent a space in downtown Pebble Brook Falls.

Then, I immediately reprimanded myself as I was reminded of Sarah. Her bakery was a few shops down and from what she'd told me over the past few years, it was incredibly successful. So much so that she was looking to hire a few new employees in the coming months. It probably helped that Sarah's parents were one of the most powerful couples in the town and everyone wanted to support their daughter—even if her parents didn't. Not that I would ever say that to her face. She worked her ass off, against all expectations that her family and society had for her. She made it work and no one could take that away from her.

The sticky air started to claw at my throat as I quickly

darted past a few more shops and stepped in front of Sarah's Bakery. Baby pink awnings shielded me from the sun and I couldn't help but smile as I saw my friend's name written in swirly cursive letters across the shop's dual windows.

She did it.

Despite all the pressure she had from her parents to become a lawyer or a doctor or to do some other mind-numbing profession, she fulfilled her dream of making sweet treats that brought others joy.

Not all professions required some grand purpose. Some things were simple. Created to bring a smile to your face, even when you're having a bad day. And that's exactly what Sarah's baked goods did.

Though I didn't have any parents who I was forced to impress, it was still difficult taking the entrepreneur route. Similarly to Sarah, I wanted to own a business—a fashion boutique. And by a fated turn of events, I was one giant leap closer to making that happen.

For the past ten years, I'd spent most of my time in restaurants and retail stores as I tried to teach myself everything I would need to know about cute Southern fashion and the nitty-gritty of running a business. It was hard work. And if I wasn't completely in love with it, there was no way I could spend twelve-hour work days busting my butt, only to come home and spend several more hours researching everything I needed to know to prepare myself to open my fashion boutique in Nashville.

I just needed to get this trip over with so I could move on with my life and finally take the next step toward making my dreams come true.

With a breathy sigh to myself, I swung open the glass door.

Goosebumps rose along my skin from the cold air conditioning blasting through the space. Sweet aromas tingled my nose as I took a deep breath in. Notes of chocolate, hazelnut, and other spices I couldn't quite place filled my soul with warmth.

"Willow!" Sarah's voice blasted through my thoughts of everything sugar and spice.

"Sarah!" I echoed her excitement as my heart fluttered from seeing my best friend for the first time in five years. We kept in contact several days a week, but between our work schedules and my unwillingness to come back to Pebble Brook Falls, years had passed since we'd last met up.

She wiped her hands on her apron as she dashed around the large glass display case that housed tantalizing treats that already had my mouth watering. Her tiny frame wrapped around me as she pulled me in for a tight hug. I wasn't normally one for affection, but it was hard not to make an exception for Sarah. She was the nicest person I'd ever met and she had a way of cracking through my prickly shell. Anyone who knew our personalities would think we couldn't be friends, but that was because they didn't get to see the sassy side of her that she held on reserve.

"I'm so glad you're here! How was the drive?"

"Traffic wasn't that bad since I left at three a.m. I just forgot how far off this place is from the highway."

She beamed at me and I couldn't help but feel my lips widen further.

"Yeah, we're definitely tucked away out here. But I'm glad the drive was smooth." She gestured toward one of the stools in front of the counter. "Here, take a seat while I wrap up some of these cookies."

Setting my purse on the counter, I hopped onto one of the white leather stools and peered over the case of sweet treats. Chocolate-drizzled croissants sat next to decadent donuts with various iced toppings that made my stomach growl. There were a few empty slots up top that I was sure she was planning to fill to the brim with her famous cookies. But it was the bottom tier of the case that had my eyes nearly bulging from my head. Row after row of perfect miniature cupcakes sat there, taunting me with their delicious swirls of icing and airy cake. Each line of cupcakes had a different color of icing with various toppings from bits of bacon to a cherry-red drizzle.

My head whipped up as I looked over at my friend and took in her slight frame. "So, um, are you going to tell me your secret on how you don't eat everything you bake? I can hardly sit this close to the case without feeling like I might impulsively throw myself into it and start stuffing my face."

Sarah's breathy laugh was a familiar sound to my ears as she said, "It was really hard at first, but when you've had more than one stomach ache from eating the batter straight from the bowl, you tend to learn your lesson."

I wasn't sure if I believed her, but I did my best to turn away from the case and focus on what she was working on.

"So, how're you feeling?"

My body immediately tightened at her question and I did my best to lower my shoulders and let some of the tension go —a practice I was still trying to master after all these years.

"Honestly"—I quickly pulled my hair back into a low ponytail—"I don't know how I feel. It's all so...bizarre."

Sarah put the spatula she was using to take cookies off the pan down on the counter. "Yeah, I guess it is bizarre isn't it?"

"I just can't believe after all this time and after everything they did that they decided to leave me the estate. I mean, my name was written into her will. Why not just give it to a local charity or one of their beloved family friends? It doesn't make sense."

"Well, I guess a lot of things people do don't make sense."

I half-chuckled. "Isn't that the truest statement of the year?"

Sarah's eyes rounded as she took me in. I was sure I was a strange sight to behold. The orphaned girl who never had a penny to her name was suddenly the wealthiest woman in town. Not that anyone but Sarah knew that yet. But I was sure the news would spread fast once the biddies got wind of it. Their gossip spread faster than wildfire in a drought.

I should have had a smile on my face or been dancing around Sarah's Bakery knowing that all my dreams were about to come true. By some luck of the draw my original title of heiress to the Baxley fortune was bestowed upon me once again. Even though it never should have been taken away from me in the first place, I should have been happy. Jumping for joy even. *Right?*

But all I felt was crippling anxiety that had me shaking to my core every time I thought about walking into that humongous house that was supposed to be where I grew up. Playing with my dolls under the large oak trees and dressing in the finest clothes that money could buy. Sipping sweet tea while I swung on that front porch swing as the summer clouds rolled by.

A childhood I was always meant to have and would never get the chance to live because it was stripped away by societal expectations and propriety.

"Willow?" Sarah's voice was like a bucket of ice water over my thoughts.

"Oh! Sorry, I got wrapped up in my head. What were you saying?"

Her lips formed a straight line. "You don't need to apologize. My mind would be a wrecking ball if I was going through what you're going through. Is there anything I can do to help?"

I shook my head. "No. You're already doing so much by letting me stay with you. Which I really appreciate by the way."

"Are you kidding? There's no way I would have let you stay in a hotel while you were here. It'll be like old times, except we won't have my parents checking in on us. We can drink wine and do face masks tonight if you'd like."

I smiled. "That sounds perfect."

"Let me just grab my spare set of house keys for you so you can go get settled into the guest room."

I silently chastised my stomach for growling again when I stole another glance at the pastries. I'd made myself a big breakfast before I took off from Nashville and there was no reason why I would be hungry right now. Other than the fact that Sarah's desserts were made to perfection and even though it had been years since I'd had one, my taste buds would never forget what they tasted like.

Thankfully, Sarah came back out of the kitchen just in time before I gave in to temptation and snagged one of the freshly baked cookies that were within arm's reach over the counter.

"Here you go!" She slid the key into my palm. "I stocked the fridge yesterday and there's plenty of coffee and tea in the coffee bar. Seriously, help yourself to anything in there, okay?"

I nodded and slipped the key into the back pocket of my purse. "Thank you again, Sarah. I owe you big time."

"Don't sweat it. It'll be nice to have some company. It can get lonely sometimes living by myself."

"I definitely know the feeling."

Sarah and I had worked hard to maintain a close friendship since high school. It was...difficult for me to make new friends. The people in Nashville were great, but it was a bustling city and I found it challenging to make friends in such a crowded place. I always felt like everyone was moving a million miles a minute and I was doing all I could just to keep up. It probably didn't help that I was often working two jobs and spending all my extra time researching business strategies for retail.

"I close the shop at five, so I should be home shortly after that and we can get our girls' night started."

"Perfect!" I did my best to sound enthusiastic through the lingering anxiety that kept clutching my throat. "Can't wait."

I grabbed my purse and swung off the stool, heading for the double glass doors. Just as I stretched my arm out to grab the handle Sarah called out to me, "Willow?"

"Yeah?" I tilted my head over my shoulder to find Sarah looking at me with a mischievous smile on her face. "What?"

She shook her head vehemently, though the smile on her lips only grew wider. "Never mind."

My brows pinched together. "Okay," I said, more as a question than a statement.

"I'll see you tonight."

"Sounds good."

As I swung the door open I thought I heard her say something under her breath, but I wasn't quite sure if she'd actually said something or if I was making things up in my head.

Air as hot as the Sahara desert rolled over me the second I stepped out of the bakery and for a moment I thought I might choke to death. I started fanning my face with my hand as I sucked in breath after breath like a heaving cow.

As I finally managed to start breathing normally again, I sent a silent prayer into the world that nothing too crazy would happen over the next two weeks. That I could get everything in order before I was scheduled to head back to Nashville where the heat was slightly less deadly and my dreams awaited.

Bark!

Bark! Bark!

"Um...where is that com—" I looked behind me, then forward again, and saw a pale yellow face covered in fur peeking around the corner at me. "Oh! Hi there, pup."

Kneeling, I reached my hand out in the dog's direction. "Come here, pup. Come on. It's okay. I won't hurt you."

With one more little yip, he turned the corner and started prancing toward me with a smile that melted my heart. He was a huge yellow labrador with a giant head and a toothy smile.

"That's such a good boy," I crooned as he let me rub the space behind his ears. "What're you doing out here all alone?"

It was still really early in the morning and there were hardly any people on the streets. Pebble Brook Falls residents always had a tendency to start the days slowly, so it wasn't surprising that most of the stores hadn't even opened yet.

Hmm, I wonder where his owner could be.

A deep blue collar was wrapped around his neck, but it didn't have any tags on it. "Well, that's not very helpful now, is it? Whenever we find your owner, buddy, I'm going to give him a piece of my mind."

I rose from my crouched position and said, "Okay, boy. Show me where you live."

Before I had a chance to follow, he darted back around the corner. "Hey!" I tried, calling after him, but by the time I made my way around the building he was gone.

CHAPTER TWO

"*I* seriously don't know how you wake up this early *every day*," I said through a long yawn as I poured coffee for Sarah and me. She laughed cheerfully and I rolled my eyes.

"I've always been a morning person. There's just something great about the brand-new start of a day. Don't you think?" She grabbed the cup of coffee I made her and blew over the steaming rim.

"No. I don't think. Probably because my brain doesn't even function properly until I've had at least two more cups of these." I raised my matching mug to hers and she clinked hers against mine from across the kitchen island.

We stood in silence for a few passing moments, each of us gently sipping on the steaming liquid. I relished in the warmth from the mug seeping into my hands. Thankfully for me, Sarah kept her house a cool sixty-eight degrees during the summertime, which was much appreciated given how I nearly melted into a puddle yesterday.

"What's on your agenda for the day?"

"Mmm"—I swallowed the sip I just took—"I think I might walk around downtown for a bit and work on some sketches at the park."

"That sounds fun!" she said in her much-too-chipper-for-this-early-in-the-morning tone. "Do you think you'll go look at the property before meeting with the lawyer?"

I know she didn't mean to do it, but I hated the way Sarah looked at me. Sadness and concern shone in her eyes and I wanted to do nothing more than wipe the look off her face—mostly because it made me feel embarrassed...and somewhat angry.

I didn't grow up with parents. Or any family really. And that was okay. I learned a long time ago that I didn't need to rely on anyone to get me where I wanted to be in the world. *I* was all I needed and I'd proved that to myself over the last ten years when I was thrust into the world without anyone to keep me accountable, teach me how to apply for jobs, or how to build a life for myself.

But that didn't mean I didn't take a punch to the gut every time someone looked at me like I was a wounded animal. Maybe it was that small part of me that still felt insecure for having been the child that her family didn't want that made me loathe the sympathetic look Sarah was giving me.

It wasn't her fault though. So I swallowed the bitterness rising in my throat and forced a smile.

"I don't really have any reason to look at the estate until I have the keys. So, I'll just wait until I get them from the lawyer."

"Let me know if you want me to go with you when you get them. I can have Stephanie cover me at the bakery."

Stephanie was Sarah's younger cousin. Home for the

summer between her spring and fall college semesters at Vanderbilt.

I set my mug on the counter. "Thanks. I'll keep you posted on that."

I wanted to say more. That I wasn't sure if I wanted anyone to be around when I walked into the house of the people who'd abandoned me. As soon as the news was out that I was back in town to claim the Baxley estate, there would be prying eyes everywhere. Even if it was just Sarah with me in the house, it would still feel like an invasion. It was messed up, but it was how my mind had worked for a long while. I preferred to do things alone.

With the tension rising every day that grew closer to the meeting with the lawyer, I wondered if I'd have the courage to go through with my plan at all despite how simple it was. Get in. Get out. With as little time spent here as possible and I'd deal with the rest later.

Sarah dumped the last splash of coffee from her mug into the sink and grabbed her purse from the center of the island.

"I have to get to the bakery to finish some of the cupcakes from last night. But I'll keep my phone on me if you need anything."

"Thanks, Sarah."

With a quick hug, she darted out the door and I was left alone in her kitchen. The bundle of nerves ignited by her sympathy grew heavier in my stomach. Deciding there was no sense in standing there with my feelings, I quickly got ready and headed out into the stifling summer heat.

"You have a nice day now, Willow. Stop by again before you leave," the woman behind the counter said to me as she handed me the vanilla ice cream cone, trails of the gooey sweetness already making their way down the sides and onto the thin napkin. Mrs. Sheehan had been the clerk at the ice cream parlor since I was a child. She always gave me an extra scoop and I was forever indebted to her.

"Thanks," I said quickly before I started licking the sides. "I'll definitely be back again."

Before I could reach the door to leave, three teenage girls barrelled in, their arms linked together as they giggled to themselves about something I couldn't quite hear.

When they nearly ran into me, they stopped abruptly, taking me in with their bright wide eyes. The middle one with long blonde hair and a splattering of freckles across her face peered at my white sundress and nude wedges.

"I love your outfit!" she exclaimed, melting my iron heart.

"Thank you," I smiled at her despite myself. The people in Nashville were friendly, but it was still a big city where most people were consumed with themselves and hardly looked up from their phones. I'd forgotten just how friendly the residents of Pebble Brook Falls were and it scraped against my nerves in a strange way.

An introvert by nature, it was always difficult for me to navigate the Southern hospitalities. Everyone knew everything about everyone and you couldn't turn a corner without seeing someone you knew. The worst part was that it was always difficult to tell if someone was being genuinely nice to you or if they were hiding their disapproval behind a graceful facade.

When I looked at the young girls in front of me, I stomped out the insecurities that tried to blossom from my past. They were sweet and I just needed to get over myself even if it did leave me feeling unsettled.

Winding my way past the three young girls and out of the ice cream parlor, I found myself walking through the little downtown park that was so small it didn't require a name. Memories flitted through my mind as I roamed over the bright green grass until I landed right in front of the famous oak tree that was older than the town itself. Every year, all the residents of Pebble Brook Falls would gather under the tree for the Summer Festival, listening to the cover band selected for that year, sipping on sweet tea, and munching on funnel cakes.

It was one of the only outings we had at the orphanage. Ms. Mosely would gather us all into the shortened school bus donated by the town and bring us to the festival.

I wonder if it's still here, I thought to myself as I circled the tree, my eyes shifting to the lower portion of the trunk.

"Oh my gosh!" I covered my mouth with my hands as nostalgia hit me square in the chest.

We'd gotten in a ton of trouble for it when Ms. Mosely found out, but sure enough, there they were. All the names of the kids from the *Hope for All* orphanage carved into the ancient oak—stamped in time forever. I remembered it like it was yesterday, the youngest of us circled around, their backs to the tree making sure no one was looking as we each took a turn carving our names into the tree.

19

Noah. Olivia. Benny. William. Zach. Jordan.

Mist clouded my vision as I ran my fingertips over each name, wondering where they all ended up. Hoping they were happy and had found a place in the world where they were wanted.

My heart sank through my chest as I rounded the curve of the tree to find my own initials embedded in the bark...right next to the initials JM.

Johnny Moore.

A pang reverberated through my heart, breaking away pieces of the walls I'd built miles high. More memories flooded my mind and I was suddenly overwhelmed with all the emotions from my teenage years. Butterflies soaring through my stomach from the slightest touch of his skin against my own. Deep rivets against tan skin next to his pink lips. Dark brown eyes that held a burning curiosity to discover more—to discover *me*. A goodbye kiss that would leave me breathless and utterly empty. Void of anything good.

It took years for me to recover from the depth of my despair, but I did it. And now—under this giant oak tree—I was reminded of how fragile my strength was when it came to *him*. With a stroke of my fingertip, the tears lining my eyes disappeared and I forced myself to look away from the small jagged heart that encircled our initials.

Just as my head turned, I was met with bright golden eyes looking up at me.

"Hey there, buddy! It's you again!" My spirits immediately lifted as the big pup wagged his tail at the sound of my voice.

Bark!

Kneeling, I looked around and there didn't seem to be anyone looking for their dog. A few kids played over on the playground, each of their mothers watching over them closely.

The dog let out another yip as he walked toward me, nuzzling his face against my hands. A wide smile pulled against his cheeks as he leaned into my scratches.

"Are you going to let me follow you this time or are you just going to run off again?"

He tilted his head back and forth as though he understood every word coming out of my mouth. With an agreeable bark, he turned around and started toward the side street.

Brushing off my knees, I stood and watched him trot off. My sketches could wait. There was no way I could let him get away again without finding his owner and telling them just how far away from home their dog had gotten.

As I marched on behind him, something far back in the recesses of my mind nagged at me. Maybe I was crazy, but I had a strange feeling that I wasn't exactly going to like where this big pup was taking me.

CHAPTER THREE

I was sweaty and out of breath after the big pup led me all over downtown until he finally stopped right outside of a large building with light blue paneled siding. *Far Away Archery* was written on a wooden sign hanging from the edge of the roof in bright red letters.

Bark!

"Is that where your owner is, buddy?" He was wagging his tail harder and harder as he inched toward the back edge of the building, looking at me over his shoulder every few steps like he wanted me to follow him.

Gravel crunched under my feet as I made my way up the building's driveway and off toward the side where the dog was. When I got a few feet away from him, he darted off with a single bark and disappeared behind the building.

"Hey! Where are you going?" I yelled after him as I turned the corner.

"There you are, Asher. Did you have a good adventure, boy?" A deep voice, smooth as velvet sounded in my ears as my eyes met the dog and his alleged owner. The man's face was shielded behind the large dog as he was crouched down, giving him chest rubs.

"You really should keep him on a—"

Oh no. No, no, no. This cannot be happening right now, I thought as the man rose from his knees and I was face to face with none other than Johnny Moore.

He wasn't supposed to be *here.* He was supposed to be somewhere far far away so that I would never have to see him again.

Squeezing my eyes shut, I prayed that I would see another face when I opened them. But as I cracked one eye open and then the other, I knew the fates were not on my side today because Johnny Moore was still standing in front of me and he was—quite literally—the last person on earth I wanted to see.

"Hi, Lo." His old nickname for me rolled off his tongue effortlessly, sending shivers up my spine and straight to my heart.

My mouth popped open to respond, but nothing came out. Instead, I stood there looking like a fish out of water as I took him in. He was still *him,* but different. Changed. He was no longer the tall gangly boy who left ten years ago for the military. Thick forearms spilled out of his rolled-up flannel sleeves and his chest flexed with each movement he made under his white t-shirt. My mouth went dry as my stomach fluttered, filling with butterflies that hadn't flown for years.

I took a step forward, though I had no idea where I was going, and before I knew it, I was tripping over thin air stumbling forward like an unstoppable stampede. Arms flailing wide in an attempt to stop myself from face-planting, I watched myself in slow motion make a total and complete fool of myself right in front of *him*.

Grassy earth barreled towards my face with unparalleled speed and just as I was sure my nose was going to crunch into the dirt, I felt strong arms grip my waist. My breath whooshed from my lungs in a violent explosion that nearly had me seeing stars.

"Whoa there. I've got you," Johnny said as he slowly righted my body.

I clung to him with shaky hands as I sucked in a lungful of air. I shouldn't have done it, but I found myself peering up at his rich brown eyes that I knew better than my own. It was a mistake because the moment I noticed his full lips tilt into a wide smile, my heart stammered in my chest and I flung myself out of his arms, nearly landing on my bottom in the process.

Johnny's arms were outstretched, ready to catch me again if I fell. Heat burned my cheeks as I tugged my top down and combed my fingers through my hair.

Dizziness flooded my brain as I sucked in too much air, completely flabbergasted by the whole situation.

"You good?" His large hands dove into his jeans pockets and I couldn't help but stare at his wide chest again. Johnny had always been much taller than me, but I didn't remember him being so...big.

His head dipped, forcing me to look from the flexing muscles under his shirt to his face. Which, honestly, wasn't any better for stopping the swarm of butterflies assaulting every inch of my stomach. When he'd left all those years ago, I was sure there was no way he could have been any more handsome. There wasn't a man in the world who compared to him in my mind. But—somehow—he'd one-upped himself in the looks department. With his strong jawline and chiseled cheekbones, he looked like an All-American model straight from a Calvin Klein advertisement.

"Yeah"—I brushed off the non-existent dirt from my shirt and shorts—"I'm good."

Averting my gaze, I looked down at the big pup who was sitting right next to Johnny looking pleased with himself. Like he knew exactly what he was doing when he guided me all the way from the park to the very man I wanted nothing to do with. I glared at him, making a mental note to never trust another four-legged animal again.

Keeping my gaze locked on the golden retriever I remembered why I had followed him in the first place.

"Do you know who he belongs to?" I asked, finally turning my attention back to Johnny. Which was a major mistake because his dimple started to reveal itself as his lips pulled back to the right with that lopsided grin that had always made me weak in the knees.

No, I scolded myself.

I will no longer fall victim to Johnny's allure. He left you, remember?

I stood up a little taller as I tried to shove down the swarm of butterflies that continued to attack me every time my eyes met his.

"He's my service dog. His name is Asher." Johnny bent over and gave the dog a pat on the head and the pup gratefully licked his forearm.

"Well, you should really keep him in a fenced yard or something. I mean he made it all the way downtown. He could have been hit by a car or som—"

As Johnny straightened, he stepped into my space and I was suddenly very aware of just how large he'd gotten. The man towered over me and I gulped as I tried *very* hard not to look at his chest again.

Breathe. He's just a guy. You've seen plenty of guys.

Yeah. No. There was not a single male specimen on the planet who looked like him and my body was starting to react against my better judgment.

All it took was a single finger under my chin tilting my head back so I was forced to look at him. The one touch of the pad of his fingertip against my skin had me shivering. My body reeled for more contact as flickers of memories darted across my mind. A time, so long ago I wasn't sure it was even real, and yet the images of us together were so vivid I knew they were true.

"Is that really what you're going to say to me right now?" His voice lowered an octave. Something else that was new to this version of him.

The smell of warm cedar wrapped around me like a familiar blanket. Some things hadn't changed.

"I…" My mouth popped open and closed like the words I wanted to say to him couldn't quite make their way from the neurons in my brain.

He smirked and that damn dimple taunted me. All I could think about was kissing the space between his dimple and lips —right on the edge of his mouth where I knew his skin was soft and sensitive.

But then, the one memory I wanted to eradicate from my

mind more than anything else, appeared. Tears had streamed down my face in a violent downpour of anguish that day. All I could see was Johnny's back as he walked away. His black duffle bag strung over his shoulder, making his lanky form tilt to the side. The skin of my forehead still burning where he planted a final kiss, the light brush of his lips like a tattoo ingrained onto my heart forever.

I stepped away from him, watching his hand fall from my face back to his side. Where it belonged.

"Lo?"

His voice broke through my thoughts, bringing me back to the present where I was certainly being laughed at by the cosmic forces that brought us both home to Pebble Brook Falls.

Exasperated by the series of events that brought me to this very moment I said, "What else would I say to you?"

He took a step toward me again, crowding my space. His jaw tilted low as he looked at me and that damn dimple appeared again. Taunting me.

"How about, how're you doing, Johnny? It's been a long time. What're you up to nowadays?"

The scent of cedar swarmed my senses and my mind threatened to catapult me back in time once again. To faraway places that I had no interest in going to.

"Umm...I..." My voice was small and breathy as the corner of his mouth ticked up. He knew what his closeness was doing to me. What it had always done to me.

Bastard!

Heat swam through my veins as the pent-up anger I'd felt for him over the past twelve years took hold. Grounding me. I didn't want to do this anymore. Not with him. It took long enough to get over him the first time and now that I was face-to-face with him again, I wasn't going to let our past distract me from my purpose of coming back to our hometown.

In and out. That was the job. Two weeks and everything would be wrapped up and I could make my way back to Nashville where I belonged.

Squaring my shoulders, I took another step back and said, "I have to go."

When his brows drew inward, I stamped down the part of me that wanted to know why that look told me he didn't want me to go. Through the barrage of thoughts running through my mind, I—somehow—found the strength to turn away from him. My legs pumping as I ran and ran, all the way to Sarah's Bakery.

"Holy shit," I cursed, sliding down the glass door of Sarah's Bakery, my legs shaking beneath me so violently I doubted they would hold me up much longer.

"Mm-mm." Someone cleared their throat and I looked up to find that Sarah was not alone in her bakery. More than half a dozen patrons had their necks craned, gawking at me. One elderly woman, in particular, had a scowl on her face that made me want to crawl away and find a hole to die in. The moment I realized the faces belonged to many people I knew, I silently cursed myself for being so stupid. And that's when the whispers started. Their unified murmurs felt like a snake crawling over my skin.

I finally found Sarah's eyes and smirking mouth. She nodded toward her kitchen. With my shoulders rolled forward, I put one wobbly foot in front of the other as I passed by all the onlookers, making my way to her kitchen.

Thankfully, the kitchen wall shielded me from all the prying eyes as I found her stool and plopped down on it, giving my legs a much needed respite. I was *not* a runner and I was equally impressed and shocked that my legs didn't spontaneously fly off of my body from that sprint.

A few long minutes ticked by before Sarah burst through the kitchen, eyes round and a smile as wide as Texas plastered on her lips.

"I think you might have pissed off Mrs. Grotemyer," she snickered.

I rolled my eyes. "At least I gave them something different to talk about."

Sarah peered over her shoulder toward the front of the store, likely making sure no other patrons needed her for a few minutes before she made her way further into the kitchen and leaned against the metal counter in front of me.

With arched brows, she tilted her head at me. "So, are you going to explain what just happened?"

I crossed my arms over my chest. "Are *you* going to explain why you didn't tell me that Johnny Moore is back in town?"

When she swallowed hard I asked, "How could you not tell me, Sarah?"

Her words came out in a rush, arms flailing as she paced the floor before me. "Every time you talked about coming back to Pebble Brook Falls you sounded like it was going to be the death of you. I know this town holds a lot of difficult memories for you and honestly, I was worried if you knew he was here that you wouldn't come at all. I didn't want anything to get in the way of you doing what you need to do to make your dreams happen, Willow. I know it's not ideal circumstances, but you deserve every penny from that family."

My shoulders drooped in defeat. There was no way I could be mad at her for that.

"And," her voice grew higher. "I might have been a little selfish in not wanting him to chase you off because I miss having my best friend in town."

I looked up at her. Her small arms were stretched in front of her body, making her shoulders round forward as she looked at me, shyly.

Rising on my unstable legs, I hugged my friend and said, "I'm not mad at you, Sarah. I don't think I ever could be mad at you. Especially after that award-winning speech." We both laughed.

"I think I was just shocked from seeing him after all these years." Heat crept up my neck and into my cheeks. I tried to steel my nerves, but the second I thought about Johnny and the way his muscular body moved to catch me, there was no stopping the physical reaction that took hold of me.

"Where did you see him?"

"Long story short, there was a dog in the park who looked like he had run away from home. So I followed him and he led me to this large warehouse-looking building and Johnny was there."

Sarah chewed on her top lip. "He opened up an archery store about three years ago. It's been pretty successful with all the hunters around here. And he teaches lessons to children with special needs a few times a month as part of their activity plan."

The thought of Johnny teaching children shot me back through time when he would teach all the younger kids in the orphanage how to defend themselves against the bullies who were always ripe with meanness. Being a parentless child was hell enough, but having other children bully you because of that fact made life a lot harder. Johnny was the protector of those kids and to hear he still carried his love of children hit me in a way I wasn't expecting.

"So, what did he say?"

My head snapped up as she asked the question, breaking my daydream of moments passed.

"Umm...well..."

"Oh my God," she teased, crossing one arm over the other. "He still gets to you, doesn't he?"

I shifted back and forth on my feet. "No!" I blurted.

"Oh! He *so* does. I mean, who wouldn't melt at the sight of him? He was always a good-looking guy when we were growing up, but now he's flat out gorgeous."

My eyes widened as my mouth popped open. "He is *not* gorgeous. I mean, he's handsome. Sure. But gorgeous? No way."

"Uh-huh. Whatever you say, Willow." Sarah nodded her chin toward me in a mocking gesture and I knew she didn't believe a single word that came out of my mouth.

"Whatever." I tugged at the hem of my t-shirt. "Can we just be done talking about him?"

Her right eyebrow rose toward her hairline. "We can be done talking about him if you help me pour some bags of flour into the mixers."

"Deal," I said, a little too quickly.

We spent the rest of the afternoon in her bakery's kitchen.

Sarah updated me on all the town gossip I'd missed since we met up last and I tried to stay present with the conversation. But when silence descended between us, all I could think about was strong hands against my skin and the soothing scent of cedar wood.

CHAPTER FOUR

I worked my bottom lip, reading the labels of all *four* flour bags over and over again trying to figure out which one Sarah meant for me to get.

Bread flour. Almond flour. Unbleached flour. Bleached flour.

Seeing as how most of my baking came from a plastic bag or cardboard box with all the ingredients already mixed together, I was severely unequipped to handle such a task. But I couldn't head back to the bakery without getting the right one because Sarah was already starting to prepare all the sweet treats she'd be selling at the Summer Festival this weekend and I didn't want to put her behind. She was busy enough running the bakery by herself and now she was having to bake double her normal amount. When I left her, she was elbow-deep in her mixers, looking like a mad woman.

Acknowledging defeat, I reached for my phone from my back pocket, ready to scour the internet for research on which flour was the right one.

"Need some help?"

I nearly jumped out of my skin at the sound of Johnny's voice. My phone tumbled right out of my hand and skittered across the tile floor. Johnny reached down and picked it up. I avoided looking up at him as he extended my phone toward me. Careful not to touch his fingers, I grabbed my phone and looked it over for any damage. Thankfully, it survived my clumsiness.

"You really shouldn't sneak up on people like that, you know," I murmured. Still refusing to look at him.

His laugh ran over my body like a warm wave. I couldn't help it as I finally tilted my head back to find his handsome face bright with humor. And that damn dimple only made his lips look that much more kissable.

Get it together, Willow. There will be absolutely no *more thinking about his lips.*

We both shifted our attention to the bags of flour on the shelf. "I take it Sarah has recruited you into helping her bake for the Summer Festival."

I swallowed hard, trying my best to focus on the words he said instead of how deep his voice had gotten since we last saw each other all those years ago.

"Yeah," I managed to say. "She's been baking up a storm since last night. When I left her this morning, I was a little worried I'd come back to find she'd drowned in all the sugar and flour. I don't think I've ever seen someone work as hard as she does."

He chuckled. "I'm glad she finally went after her dream. Especially since she had to fight her family tooth and nail the entire way."

I nodded in acknowledgment of Sarah's tumultuous journey to success. Having also come from one of the most wealthy families in Georgia, Sarah was considered Southern royalty. And with that title came a certain expectation. The men were urged to become a lawyer, doctors, or politicians and the women were groomed to find a rich husband. Though their parents would often settle for them also pursuing a 'worthy' career. Sarah and her brother had been chained to a certain fate from birth and when she decided to break the mold and create a business of her own, neither one of her parents took kindly to it.

"Exactly. Which is why I really don't want to choose the wrong one and put her even more behind."

Johnny took a small step toward me that anyone else looking at us probably wouldn't have even registered, but my body reacted instantly sending heat straight to my core. Old instincts to reach for his hand nearly took hold of me. But I narrowed my focus on the flour bags, once again, chastising myself that Johnny Moore was totally and completely off limits for the sake of my survival.

"Twelve more days," I whispered to myself.

"What was that?"

My cheeks flushed wickedly as I shook my head. "Nothing." Desperate to change the subject I gestured toward the shelf. "She mentioned making her famous chocolate chip cookies and some chocolate croissants. I thought about just grabbing all the boxes of chocolate chip cookie mix from Betty Crocker, but Sarah would have a conniption if I came back with that."

Johnny's deep laugh rumbled from his chest and I couldn't help but notice how he seemed to laugh a lot more over the past two days than he ever did when we were younger. I wondered if maybe a woman had softened him over time and

I immediately regretted the thought as jealousy flickered to life in my chest.

"All-purpose flour tends to do the trick for most things. If we were in Europe I'd recommend using pastry flour for the croissants, but it's not the best to use in the States." He reached for the bags and started loading them into my cart. "Did she mention how many bags she needs?"

"Um"—I reached for the bags next to him—"ten, I think."

We loaded my cart in silence, filling it nearly to the brim with all-purpose flour.

Wiping my hands together to get the remnants of flour off I asked, "How did you know about the flour?"

His brown eyes met mine as he piled the last bag into the cart. "When I was deployed to Afghanistan for a year, I picked up baking as a hobby. There wasn't as much at my disposal as there is here in terms of ingredients. But it kept things interesting, trying to find Middle-Eastern alternatives. A nice distraction from the hard days."

My mind wandered with all the questions I wanted to ask him about his time in the Marines and his experiences overseas. But I clamped my mouth shut. Going down that road with him would only lead to one place.

With all the bags loaded, we were left in an awkward silence that made me itch to run away.

"Well, thanks for all your help. I should get going so Sarah isn't waiting on me to get started."

The smile he gave me nearly sent me to my knees. It was the same smile he'd given me all the years we grew up together and somehow it was different—more masculine, more knowing, more *him*.

"It was good to see you again, Lo."

The way his nickname for me rolled off his tongue was almost my undoing. All I could manage was a "Mmhm," before I attempted to scanter off with the cart. Only the cart barely moved under the weight of all the flour.

"Want some help with that?"His tone was edging on the side of amused and it took every ounce of my willpower not to turn around and glare at him.

"Nope," I grunted, pushing the cart with all my strength. "I can manage." Thankfully, the wheels started to turn and I was able to make my way down the aisle. I felt the heat of his gaze on me with every step I took and I wanted to know what he was thinking after the second time I ran away from him. But as much as I felt the urge to look over my shoulder at him, I stayed forward and put all my focus on getting the cart to the checkout line.

After what felt like thirty minutes of pushing an obnoxiously large amount of flour to the checkout counter, I finally made it. As I stared at the black conveyor belt, I was struck with the sudden realization that I was going to have to unpack every single bag onto the damn belt.

"Shit."

"Honey, don't worry. I can come around and scan them." The elderly woman running the cashier stared at me over her thick-rimmed glasses that were about to fall off the tip of her nose. I was so damn flustered I couldn't even think straight.

"I can help her out, Ms. Annabell."

My heart plummeted straight through my stomach. Why wouldn't he just go away?

Turning around slowly to find Johnny right in front of me, my neck craned back as I looked up at him. His closeness made my throat go dry immediately.

When did he get so damn tall, too?

"It's an old system,"—Ms. Annabell waved her scanner in the air—"so we will have to scan each one to track inventory."

With a devilish grin that made my heart soar from the floor through the ceiling, Johnny moved around me and started maneuvering the bags of flour so Ms. Annabell could scan them. I couldn't help but notice how Ms. Annabell stared intensely at Johnny like he was the most beautiful thing she'd ever seen. When I followed the older woman's gaze to find the muscles of his biceps and forearms flexing against his sun-kissed skin, I knew exactly how she felt. Completely stricken by the godly specimen of a man that he was. I wondered if Ms. Annabell was telling the truth about the old grocery store's system or if she just wanted to prolong being around Johnny.

It almost wasn't fair how gorgeous he was. But certain parts of my body that remembered how it felt to have those muscles bare and flush against my skin made me feel thankful for just how damn good-looking he was.

No.

We are not thinking about his muscles—or other unmentionable body parts—against our skin. Get it together, Willow.

Zipping my thighs together to ward off the pulsing sensation that was innately building the longer I stared at him, I tried to distract myself by being useful. He had moved most of the bags around as I reached for a few on the cart's lower shelf.

With the last bag scanned, Johnny turned to me and asked, "Want me to help you out?"

"Isn't that the bagger's line?"

A flash of emotion flickered across his face, but he'd always been a master of keeping his true feelings at bay. It was there one second and gone the next, replaced with his knowing smile.

"I've been a lot of things in my life, Lo. I don't mind being a bagger-boy today."

"Oh just take him up on his offer, sweety. It's not like you can load all these bags into your car yourself."

I glared at Ms. Annabell and she raised an eyebrow at me as though she were saying, "Don't even try me, little girl."

Crossing my arms I turned back toward Johnny. "Fine."

After paying for the flour with the cash Sarah gave me, Johnny helped me push the cart out to my car. We loaded the trunk in silence and after he shut the hatchback we stood there, staring at one another.

"Go out for coffee with me tomorrow morning."

"What?"

"Go out to coffee with me tomorrow morning," he repeated as he reached up toward my face, tucking a strand of my loose hair behind my ear. A trail of fire burned from my cheekbone to the back of my ear where his fingertips brushed against my skin. Every fiber of my being was aware of his movements as he slowly shifted toward me.

For the briefest moment, we were no longer standing outside of a grocery store with a pile of flour inside of my trunk. The background of the dark gray parking lot faded away, replaced by waves of tall brown grass gently blowing in the early spring breeze. We'd run away from Ms. Mosely for the afternoon and found ourselves in the abandoned field off of Sunflower Drive in the middle of the night. For as long as I lived, I'd never forget the way the stars glimmered in the sky that night or how Johnny stole the very breath from my lungs with our first kiss.

I'd never forget it. No matter how badly I wanted to.

"I..." Lost in the distant memories of us, I couldn't quite get the words I wanted to say out of my brain—which included an emphatic *no*.

His eyes shone with life as he brought his hand back from the side of my face and buried it deep in the pocket of his jeans. "Why don't I just answer for you? Tomorrow, eight o'clock, at The Roasted Bean."

"Ummm," I stammered again, completely unable to speak the single two-letter word that bounced around in my brain.

Was that because I wanted to go to coffee with him?

No.

Don't be ridiculous. You do not want to go to coffee with Johnny Moore.

I continued to stare at him. Utterly silent.

With a quick nod of his head, signifying that he had won completely, he said, "See you in the morning, Lo."

When he turned around to leave, I gaped at his back like a fish out of water. Was I seriously going to have coffee with the one human on this entire planet that made me stumble over my words as though lightning had fried my brain of any and all ability to speak on my own behalf?

"Shit, shit, shit."

No. I was not going to have coffee with Johnny Moore. When the sun rose in the morning, he would be all alone at The Roasted Bean while I lay snug in Sarah's guest bed. That would show him to make decisions for me.

CHAPTER FIVE

"So you agreed to have coffee with Johnny?"

I threw my flour-covered hands in the air, completely exasperated. "No! I did not agree to have coffee with Johnny."

Sarah pulled her hands up in mock defense. "I'm sorry. I'm just a little confused. He said to meet you at The Roasted Bean at eight tomorrow and then walked away. But you didn't actually agree to meet him there?"

"Exactly."

"Well, are you going to go?" Her right eyebrow arched toward her hairline.

"Yes," I blurted out. "No!" I covered my face with my hands. "Ugh! I don't know."

Sarah giggled as she grabbed a dish towel and ran it under the facet before tossing it to me.

"You might want to wipe the flour from your face before you walk out in public. You know how easily rumors start in this town."

I snorted. "Yeah. All it will take is for some old bidi to see that I have white residue on my face and the whole town will think I've resorted to cocaine to cure my woes."

I scrubbed hard at my face making sure the flour was dissolved from every nook and cranny. Even though ten years had passed since we were all in high school, the sting of rumors being spread about me burned just as hot now as it had back then. That was the thing about small towns. When your high school class had all of one-hundred students in it, everyone knew everyone. And rumors flew faster than a jet. I'd fallen victim to the rumor mill on several occasions. Mostly because being an orphan made me an easy target and teenagers were generally just assholes.

But the last thing I wanted to deal with was the Pebble Brook Falls rumor mill. Especially when I was only going to be here for two weeks.

"He's even more good-looking now than he was in high school."

I dragged the cloth down my forehead and over my eyes until it was resting just above my cheekbones so I could see Sarah's wide grin.

"Who?" I asked, even though I already knew the answer.

"Johnny."

I threw the used towel at her face and she caught it, cackling at me like a wild hyena.

"I suppose if you like that sort of…look…that he has, then sure. He's good-looking."

Sarah's eyes turned to slits as she studied me. "You mean the six foot three height. The strong chiseled jawline with his full plush lips. Oh! And his humongous biceps and how his back muscles ripple when he pulls a bowstring back. There's also—"

"Okay! Okay!" I threw my hand out, palm up, to stop any more of her antics. "Yes. Johnny is hot. But that still doesn't change...Wait. When did *you* see his back muscles ripple?"

"He runs an archery camp once a month for children with special needs. One time, they were practicing down at the park," she replied matter-of-factly. "Johnny has always been yours and always will be yours. I have no interest in touching him with a ten-foot pole." She gave me a look as though my mere thought of her with Johnny was offensive to her character.

The tension in my shoulders immediately melted away. Even though I had no intention of ever touching Johnny again, I still didn't want the image of him and my best girl-friend together. Only because it would be weird and not at all related to the raging jealousy that flickered to life any time I thought about him with any other woman.

"In all seriousness, Willow, I think you should meet with him. If anything, it would be good for you two to catch up. You were so close when we were younger. It would be a shame to let all that history go to waste."

The real shame was that he walked away from me and everything I thought we could have been. At sixteen, I had no idea how to get a hold of someone in the military and he never wrote to me. Not once. The ache in my chest still lingered as I thought back to that younger version of myself. The one who waited by the front door every day when Ms. Mosely brought the mail in. My heart plummeted every time she shook her head at me.

But I didn't say any of that to Sarah. Two years of waiting for him were long enough before I aged out of the system and was forced to make it on my own. And I did. It was hard and lonely, but I made it work. Letting the young, idealistic future of being with Johnny fade away, I focused on making myself better. Forged new dreams and busted my ass making them come true. And by some stroke of luck, they were going to come true faster than I ever thought possible.

Though, it still felt like I was cheating the system by taking the Baxley's money. I had to tell myself over and over that I deserved it. After everything those people did to me, I could take what was owed and move on even if it still felt wrong.

I blew out a harsh breath. "Maybe you're right. It would be good for both of us to move forward." I twirled a strand of hair between my fingers. "He seems different, you know."

"How do you mean?" Sarah asked over her shoulder as she started pouring chocolate chips into two of the large mixers.

My blonde strands fell through my fingers as I rubbed my arms up and down to stow away the chills that coursed my skin at the thought of him. "When we were younger he had this tendency to question himself. He always asked me if the decisions he made or wanted to make were the right ones. It was almost like he was afraid of screwing up or making one bad move that would impact the rest of his life."

Sarah's joking smile from earlier faded as she set the bag of chocolate on the counter. "As much as I love Pebble Brook Falls, it can be a damning place for anyone who makes a mistake. Not only because the entire town will find out, but a lot of people here have rigid views. One wrong move and it can stick with you for a really long time."

I nodded, not wanting to think about my birth mother even though she fit into the category of making a long-lasting mistake—*me*. It didn't matter how much money the Baxleys had. Some secrets clawed their way from the grave with a vengeance. And once the entire town found out that the most beloved daughter and heiress of the Baxley fortune had gotten herself pregnant as an unwed teenager, the Southern equivalent to the Rothchilds' name was soiled. Even when Melanie Baxley died in a mysterious boating accident at the tender age of twenty-nine, the town still talked about her teenage pregnancy as though she were the anti-Christ. Or at least that's what I was told by Sarah's parents.

It still frazzled my mind how accepting Sarah's parents had been of me, given my status in the world. Yet, they couldn't accept that their daughter had decided to make a living for herself instead of pursuing marriage as a means of raking in money.

As much as I loved the deep south, there were some customs in all cultures that simply needed to be eradicated.

"I guess it makes sense that he would have been mindful of his decisions given that his parents were both alcoholics and drug addicts. He always said he would do anything not to end up like them." I shrugged, careful not to let my mind wander too much to the distant past.

"Maybe that's why he went into the military."

My eyes shot up to meet Sarah's. While she didn't know the extent of the agony I'd felt when he walked away from me that day, she knew that his absence had turned me into a shell of who I was before he left.

"I'm sorry," she murmured. "I shouldn't have brought it up."

I pinched the bridge of my nose. "No, it's okay. I'm over it now."

I totally was not over it.

"But you said he was different. What did you mean by that?"

I dropped my hand from my face and sighed. "He seems more sure of himself. Like he knows exactly who he is and all the things he's capable of, despite what people might think or say about him. It's almost like he's grown into himself. Not just physically, but mentally. The few times I've seen him, there hasn't been a trickle of the self-doubt that used to plague him."

"Wow."

"What?" I asked earnestly.

"You've thought a lot about him, haven't you?"

I snorted. "Pshh. No. I just knew him really well and now he seems different. That's all."

"Mmhmm." Sarah gave me a look that said she was not at all convinced of my charades.

"Fine. I'll go."

Sarah let out a squeal that rivaled a newborn piglet as she clapped her hands vigorously.

"I love *love*!" she shouted as she ran over to me, taking me in a tight embrace.

"Whoa, whoa, whoa." I gently pushed her off me. "No one said anything about love, Sarah. This is just two old friends having coffee together to catch up. Nothing more and nothing less."

"Well, I think it's the start of something that was never meant to end in the first place." She winked at me. A hopeless romantic since we were children, Sarah always rooted for epic love stories.

As I watched my best friend cheerfully prance around her bakery's kitchen talking endlessly about which outfit I should wear, I couldn't help but feel saddened by the fact that Johnny and I would never have an ever-lasting love story. It took years for me to come to that realization and stow away the hurt he'd caused. As badly as I had wanted a forever with him, he had walked away from me—from *us*.

And that was a clear enough message that he didn't see a future with me.

CHAPTER SIX

There was no stopping my hands from shaking as I walked along the sidewalk toward The Roasted Bean coffee shop where I was supposed to meet Johnny. I hated that my body reacted this way every time I thought of him. I chalked it up to the residual effects of our past. He was my first...for everything. It was only natural for my body to remember how it had once felt to be loved by him. Consumed by the passion that stole my breath away every time he would kiss the tender spot along my shoulder. Or when my skin was ignited by his flame the night we decided to give everything to one another.

I would never forget the way the moonlight reflected in his eyes that night as we bared our souls to each other under the starlit sky. I stopped walking as the barrage of memories seized my thoughts. My pulse quickened as I closed my eyes, the sensation of his rough hands roaming my body was still as present today as it had been that night. His trail of kisses felt like a brand on my soul.

He'd ruined me for all others after that. The two years

after he left were like living in a black hole. It wasn't until I turned eighteen myself and was forced to survive on my own that the anger settled in.

I gave and he took. *Everything.*

I was still angry. But seeing him for the first time in twelve years ignited something deep within me that hadn't sparked in a very long time. Something that felt like *home.*

Urging on the side of self-preservation, I stomped out all feelings—good and bad—related to Johnny Moore. Opening my eyes once again, I let the bright morning sun chase away any last nerves before I finally stepped through the door of the coffee shop.

Johnny wasn't hard to miss even though the small space was filled to the brim with patrons. Some were sitting at the petite wooden tables, while others gathered in groups, standing throughout the shop. Several pairs of eyes slid over to me. Some were friendly, while others were assessing. The atmosphere was buzzing with life, mimicking my racing heartbeat as Johnny rose from his chair and made his way over to me.

I stood there like a deer caught in headlights as he enveloped me in a hug. Damnit, why did he smell so good? My body instantly reacted, melting against the familiarity of him, all the while immensely alert to just how manly he had become. Where his chest and waist had been slight from him shooting up like a beanstalk, he was now filled out and muscular in ways that made my mouth water with a desire to see just how ripped he was under his flannel.

When he let me go, guiding us back to the table he'd chosen, I tried not to stare at his taut ass in his Levi's jeans.

Focus, Willow. Remember, we are not here to gawk or feel *anything.*

When we sat down, he sprawled himself out, legs stretched out wide, his arms draped casually over the back of the chair. He looked like a Southern king, overwhelming a throne that was much too small for him.

Ugh. Who was I kidding trying to defend myself against the innate reactions I had toward him? I was completely helpless against him and there wasn't a damn thing I could do about it.

"How've you been, Lo?" A question that should have been easy to answer if anyone else had asked me.

The things that came to mind when he asked me that question included, "Oh. I've been so great Johnny. Ever since you left me I haven't been pining after your memory at all. Spending countless nights wondering why you never wrote. How you could make such profound promises to me and then toss me to the side the moment you were free. So yeah. Overall, I've been dandy. How about you?"

But I didn't say any of those things. Instead, I awkwardly said, "I've been good. I, um, actually started looking into opening a small fashion boutique. I've always loved fashion and I think it's a good fit for me long-term."

"I remember." He smiled and that devilish dimple made its appearance. My mouth instantly twitched with the need to press my lips against it. Flattening my palms against the top of my thighs, I willed thoughts of kissing any part of Johnny out of my mind.

"Your favorite Christmas present from Ms. Mosely was the packet of needles and ten spools of thread. It wasn't much, but you used to sew cool patterns into your jeans and t-shirts."

My heart warmed at the memory. And the fact that he remembered that.

"Yeah," I chuckled. "It took about three weeks for my thumb to heal from all the times I'd pricked it with the needle."

I almost bled out the week after Christmas from how much sewing I did. My thumb paid the consequence. So much so, I was surprised it didn't fall off from the blood loss. Every night before we went to sleep, Johnny would kiss my thumb to make it feel better in the morning. And it always did.

My cheeks flushed at the thought of his lips pressed against my skin.

"I think it's really great that you've taken your passion and turned it into something."

"Thank you," I blushed, casting my gaze downward because it was too much to bear when his eyes sparkled with pride. Despite his leaving me, I knew that he was genuinely happy for me. He always fought for the underdogs of the world and even though the blood running through my veins was blue with Southern royalty, my upbringing was anything but.

"What about you?" I asked, trying to change the subject away from me. "How did you get into archery?"

He took a long sip of his black coffee before settling back into his chair. I settled my eyes on his, being careful not to ogle at his broad chest.

Seriously, when did I become such a muscle fiend?

"When I was in the Marines, I discovered that I was a pretty good shot. I went through training to become a sniper.

In a lot of ways, it was peaceful. The process itself is so meticulous, it requires you to be calm and patient. After I was discharged, I had a hard time adjusting to civilian life. Everything felt chaotic and out of sorts. One of my buddies from my platoon mentioned archery being helpful for him when he got out. It only took about a month and I was hooked. Everything else started taking shape after that."

"Wow," I hummed quietly. "Sounds like everything fell into place for you."

"I wouldn't quite say that." His shoulders immediately drew upward as he adjusted himself in his seat. The edges of his face grew sharper and for the first time, I noticed the stress he must have carried with him from his time in the service. Years of wear and tear on his soul. But he hid it well because, after the briefest moment, any tells of his distress were gone.

"Four deployments aren't exactly kind to a person—mentally or physically. It took a lot of work for me to get back to a sense of normal. And I wouldn't even call it getting back to normal. More like I had to find a new way of living."

Just as I was about to ask about how he built his business from the ground up, a sauntering figure caught my eye behind Johnny. My stomach immediately turned sour as I recognized the curvy brunette who had a mischievous grin on her face, similar to that of the Cheshire cat.

Melody. Freaking. Carnelle.

Ugh.

Did this seriously have to be happening right now?

Melody Carnelle had been our high school's 'it girl' and infamous flirt. Her parents owned some of the best dressage horses in the South and she let everyone know it. Melody had always been the kind of person who relished making others suffer. The ultimate bully, I couldn't even keep track of the number of times she would break into my locker and fill it with opened tampons and pads, smelly old food, and dirt. One time—unfortunately for me—she even managed to fill it with chocolate pudding so it looked like diarrhea was seeping out the vents.

Originally I thought that Johnny was the one person on earth I would never want to see again. But I had been mistaken. Melody Carnelle was certainly number one on that list.

Johnny's face tilted, his brows scrunching together as he noticed the look on my face. But just as he was about to turn around to see what had made me so upset, Melody clasped her freshly manicured hands over his eyes and bent down low next to his ear. I purposefully turned away so my eyes didn't have to be assaulted by her large breasts, which I was certain were spilling out of her dress on purpose.

"Guess who?" she whispered in a sing-song voice that was like nails on a chalkboard. My stomach churned, acid building in the back of my throat.

What the hell was going on here?

Johnny had always protected all the children at the orphanage, me included. Melody Carnelle was one of the many people he protected me from and now he was smiling as she wrapped her too-skinny fingers around the front of his face, grazing his cheeks with her thumbs.

My head was going to explode.

I couldn't help but watch—my mouth slightly ajar—as Johnny gently peeled her fingers away and tilted his head back to look up at her.

"Hey, Melody!" he chuckled. "I thought you were supposed to be out of town this week."

Um, how the hell would he know her work schedule?

Unless...

"Daddy decided to change his plans because we have a potential buyer for one of the new foals." Her deep Southern twang raked against my nerves as her long fingers traced over Johnny's large shoulders, giving them a tight squeeze as though she suddenly became a masseuse and no one else was around.

My skin grew hotter by the second and if I didn't get out of here, I was going to burst into flames.

In a flurry of hurt, anger, confusion, and embarrassing jealousy, I jumped out of my seat and dashed toward the door.

This was literally my worst nightmare. Not only did he break his promise and leave me jilted for over a freaking decade, but he decided to fraternize with the enemy. Ugh! Images of Melody in his arms, trailing her long fingers through his hair threatened my sanity as I barreled down the sidewalk to God only knew where.

"Lo!" Johnny's voice echoed from somewhere behind me, but I kept walking. Trying to put as much distance between us as possible.

But his strides were much larger than mine and he caught up to me easily, gently taking hold of my arm until I stopped walking.

"Why do you keep running away from me, Lo?"

With a tenderness that nearly brought tears to my eyes, Johnny captured my chin between his thumb and forefinger, tilting my head back so I was forced to look at him. But I was quickly reminded that just mere seconds ago, another woman had her hands all over him. And that woman just happened to be the person who made my life a living hell for four years.

I shook my head out of his grasp for fear that if I let him touch me for too long, I might give in to the swarm of butterflies that attacked me any time his skin brushed against mine.

The moment our connection was lost I felt the heat of my anger flood back in.

"Are you seriously with her?" I seethed.

He swayed backward. Just an inch, but enough for me to notice that my words had made an impact.

"Melody?" He snorted. "You're kidding, right?"

My hands found their way to my hips as I hissed, "No, Johnny. I'm not kidding. I just can't believe that someone like you would ever consider dating such a snake in the grass."

His lips formed a solid line and I could tell I hit a nerve. But I didn't care. I was fuming. And I had absolutely no right to. I was nothing to Johnny. He was a free man who could do whatever he pleased, even if it pissed me off. I needed to let it all go before it ruined me and everything I was working toward.

He had left me. And that was that. Nothing more and nothing less to it.

"Forget I said anything." I waved my hand through the air. "What you do and who you do it with isn't my business."

I turned to walk away—my heart in my throat—and I got all of about two steps before he said, "Stop!" The command in his tone stilled me at the same time that every single inch of my body sparked to life.

Boots on cement sounded from behind me and I could feel his presence even though he wasn't touching me. Like two magnets drawn to one another, the air vibrated with energy between us. Neither one of us was willing to give that final inch. I knew I had my reasons, but I couldn't help but wonder what his were.

Air filled my lungs as he leaned down next to my ear, the bristle of his stubble tickling the delicate skin of my cheek.

"Why do you keep running away from me?" His voice was low, still laced with authority that had my pulse quickening and my lips twitching to meet his, even though I couldn't see him. I knew what he tasted like. Remnants of mint and something totally and completely *him.*

"Because it's what we do," I breathed. My chest rising and falling in quick succession.

Squeezing my eyes shut I gathered all the anger I felt for him and let it stomp out the desire that pooled at my core. As I opened my eyes, I took a step forward and another and another, until I could no longer feel him behind me.

There was no reason for me to assume that he felt anything as I walked away. But some part of me knew I had just made him hurt. And that same part of me enjoyed it.

CHAPTER SEVEN

"*A*re you sure they left me everything?"

The lawyer—well, I guess he was *my* lawyer now—nodded. Sitting across from me, behind his large mahogany desk, Mr. Anderson was every bit the portrait of Southern money. His wavy black hair was peppered with white just above his ears giving him a distinguished look of a gentleman. Although, I was savvy enough to know a shark when I saw one and the fact that he'd worked for my biological grandmother told me he was deadly.

"Yes, it's all outlined here." He gestured toward the stack of papers that I assumed was my grandmother's will. His black and gold fountain pen reflected the natural light streaming in from the window behind him. Another tell of his opulent status.

"Why would they do that?"

"Do what?" His face didn't move as he asked me the question. Likely due to the botox in his perfectly sculpted face.

"Leave me everything when they didn't even want me."

He answered, "Guilt? Shame? I think it's a little late to ask now, don't you think?"

My eyebrows shot up at his candid remark. So different from what most people in this town would have said. Maybe that's why my grandmother had hired him. A straight shooter like him had no interest in scheming behind his clients' backs.

Setting his pen down, he grabbed a small silk bag off his desk and emptied it into the palm of his hand. A single silver key rested against his skin as he leaned forward, handing it to me. His skin was dry against my fingertips as I plucked it from his grasp.

"The estate is yours now. We just have a few more things to wrap up during our next meeting."

Examining the house key, my mouth suddenly went dry. For most of my life, I'd only owned the shirt on my back and I wouldn't have even had that if it weren't for the generosity of those who donated to the orphanage. Now I had the key to a multi-million dollar estate between my fingertips.

I wanted to puke.

"What am I supposed to do with it?"

The slightest tilt of Mr. Anderson's lips told me he was laughing at me in his head. To him, I probably looked every bit the orphaned girl lost in a sea of wealth just because of the blood that ran through my veins.

"You can do whatever you would like. You can move in, sell it, or turn it into a wedding venue. It's yours now, so only you can make that decision." Interlacing his fingers, he set his hands on top of his desk. "We will get all of the accounts in order during the next meeting." With a quick glance at his watch, I knew my time was up.

"Thanks, Mr. Anderson."

He just gave me a quick nod before turning his attention to his computer.

I tossed the key into my small purse like it wasn't the key to an estate that would fund every dream I'd ever had and then I walked out of Mr. Anderson's office.

"Gross. Melody Carnelle? Are you sure you were seeing correctly?" Sarah's face was twisted with a disgusted look. She always had a habit of seeing the good in pretty much everyone. But Melody Carnelle was public enemy number one when it came to Sarah and me.

"Yup." I swallowed a giant gulp of the red wine I'd bought on my way back to Sarah's place after I'd left Mr. Anderson's office.

"That woman has more Botox in her body than an entire army of puffer fish and she's not even thirty."

"Well, Johnny seemed pretty impressed with all of her assets." My stomach tightened as I thought about her hands running all over his masculine shoulders. "Even though she does have bird claws for fingers."

Sarah almost spewed her wine at me and I couldn't help but laugh as red liquid dribbled down her chin. She darted for the sink and spit out the wine before it stained her pristine white countertops.

"I never thought that he would go after someone like her. I mean, she's everything that's wrong with our entitled generation. She's never lifted a finger to work, she spends all of her trust fund on clothes and purses, and she uses guys like they're disposable face wipes. Use it once and throw it away."

Sarah finished wiping her face with the dish towel and sat down on her stool.

"I'm not exactly sure what you saw at the coffee shop, Willow. But I know he hasn't dated anyone since he moved back to Pebble Brook Falls."

I rolled my eyes at her and crossed my arms and she giggled at me.

"You know that Melody has always tried to stir the pot. I'm sure that once she saw you two sitting there, she wanted nothing more than to make you think something had happened between them. And Johnny's different now. You said it yourself. He probably wasn't even thinking about what she was like in high school toward you."

"I'm not even sure Melody recognized me. But you made my point, Sarah." I ran my hands through my hair, tugging slightly at the roots from frustration. "I shouldn't care this much. It was over twelve years ago when we made the promise to one another, and I've moved on. I'm trying to open up a boutique in Nashville for Christ's sake. I just thought that maybe—" I cut myself off before I let the truth come out that I'd hidden for so long.

Sarah reached across the island, rubbing my arm up and down. "You thought what, Willow?"

I looked up at her. Brown eyes shone with concern. My friend of over twenty years. The one person in my life who had always been there despite every societal reason that told us we should never have been friends to begin with. I could trust her. I *had* to trust her. The fatigue of going through so much alone over the past several years had taken its toll.

"I thought that maybe one day, Johnny and I would meet each other again and everything would be like it once was. He would recognize his mistake in leaving me and I would be willing to forgive him. And then..." I rubbed at the ache growing in my chest from the revelation I was making. "And then he would finally choose me over whatever it was that made him want to leave me."

Tears gathered in my eyes. A weakness that only seemed to arise when I thought of Johnny.

"Oh, Willow." Sarah took me into her arms, hugging me fiercely, which only made the tears fall harder.

"Shhh," she crooned as she ran her hand up and down my back.

The emotions I'd been holding back for a very long time poured out of me. The sadness of losing the only person I'd ever known as family, the confusion of his broken promise, and the heartache that settled way beyond my body and buried itself deep within my soul.

After what felt like an eternity, I pulled away from Sarah's arms and wiped the dried saltiness from my cheeks. She rubbed the side of my arm, her large brown eyes filled with concern.

"I'm okay," I sniffled.

"I know you are." Her smile was small. "Sometimes we just need to get all the emotions out of us before we can move forward."

I sucked in a long, deep breath as I nodded. Sarah reached for another bottle of red wine from her wine rack and poured us two large glasses. We stood there for several minutes, slowly sipping on the wine. And in that moment I was incredibly thankful for my friend. I'd purposefully spent my adult life alone, focusing on my future and trying to make something of myself. There was little time to form friendships along the way. But I was always able to come back to Sarah, even when we'd gone months without talking at all, we were able to pick up right where we left off. Despite everything feeling like it was out of control, Sarah was my ever-steady rock. A constant in my life that brought some sense to the world and I was so grateful for that.

Setting the long-stem wine glass down, I reached for my purse on the island and took out the small silver key that packed a big punch, and slid it across the table to her.

Her brows rose into her hairline as she audibly gulped down her mouthful of wine. Picking up the key, she inspected it, just as I had when Mr. Anderson handed it to me earlier.

"Holy shit," she whispered, as though the tiny metal thing were cursed. "So, it's really yours now."

"Yup."

She set the key back on the counter and asked, "How do you feel?"

I blew out a long breath. "Weird. Terrified." I took another sip of wine. "When I was little, I always wondered what they were like—my mom and grandma. I wondered what I did wrong for them to not want me. But once it came out that I was just the product of a teenage love affair only to be stowed away and hidden like a skeleton in the closet, everything changed. I felt this strange desire to prove them wrong somehow. I wanted to show them that I was a Baxley too. The same blood in their veins ran through mine and that should have been enough for them to want me."

Sarah shook her head slightly, lost in thought, before she

said, "It was so strange what happened to your bio mom. It doesn't make sense."

When I was ten years old, the truth of who I was was revealed in a scandalous news article after my biological mother's death. Someone in the elite social circle discovered the truth and reported it to all the major news outlets. It didn't take long for the scandal of one of Southern royalty's darling daughters and her surprise teen pregnancy to take the nation by storm. It felt so strange that her death was almost masked by the revelation of her having a child out of wedlock.

I remembered when Johnny and I had snuck into Ms. Mosely's office where the only TV was and we watched the news story unfold. I was too young to fully understand everything, but it didn't take a rocket scientist for people to figure out that I was the only child in the orphanage who was old enough to be Melanie Baxley's daughter.

And then the rumor mill started flying...in *elementary school*. Fellow classmates overheard their parents talking about the scandal and of course, my name got brought up. So I had gone from the orphan who had no idea who her family was to the orphan who had been abandoned by the Baxleys. Tossed aside like last season's Hermès bag.

And then Melanie died.

Even though I didn't know her and even though she left me in the orphanage to save her family's name, I felt the loss as though I had spent every day with her by my side.

"Yeah," I whispered, so low I wasn't sure if Sarah even heard me.

A few minutes ticked by, the silence dragging on as old emotions erupted within me.

"Do you know what you're going to do with it all yet?" Sarah broke the silence and I was thankful for it.

"Nope," I sighed. "I don't have a freaking clue."

"I'm here to talk it out if you need to."

"Thanks, Sarah." I forced a smile on my lips.

I knew that coming back to Pebble Brook Falls was going to be hard. It was the price I had to pay if I wanted to take this opportunity to make my dreams come true. But nothing could have prepared me for everything that awaited me here.

I suddenly felt very tired and all I wanted to do was curl up in a warm blanket and sleep this nightmare away.

CHAPTER EIGHT

I didn't sleep a wink last night and the attitude I was projecting onto my wardrobe strewn across Sarah's guest bedroom was a sure sign that today was going to be torture. No amount of coffee could cure the irritability I felt.

And it was all Johnny's fault.

What little sleep I got was plagued with dreams of him. That stupid wide smile that displayed the dimple on the right side of his cheek. His dumb, overly large biceps that flexed beneath his flannel shirts. And the memories of his skin against mine as he rolled his hips into me, sending me off the edge of oblivion only to follow me all the way down.

Heat singed my core and I clamped my thighs tight to fend off the aching desire that my traitorous body released.

"I *hate* him," I screeched, throwing a frilly white top as hard as I could, only for it to slowly fall to the floor a foot away from me.

"Whoa!"

I whirled around to find Sarah standing in the doorway to

the room, a large to-go mug of coffee in her hand and her eyes wide with humor.

"You okay in here?" She giggled as she took in the mess I'd made, my clothes and makeup products covering the entire bed and most of the floor.

"I'm fine," I grumbled as I snatched a light pink top off the ground and pulled it over my head.

"Yeah, you look it."

I glared at Sarah the moment my head peeped through the opening of the shirt.

"I have to head out to grab the pop-up tent from Malcolm. Meet you there?"

I grabbed my car keys and purse off the bedside table that had somehow evaded my attack. "Yup. I'm going to make a cup of coffee and then I'll be leaving."

"Okay." She turned to leave then stopped, peering over her shoulder at me. With a nod toward my mess, she said, "You might want to take some deep breaths before coming."

I stuck my tongue out at her and her laugh faded as she walked down the hallway and out the door.

With a sweet Southern smile screwed onto my face, I made my way down the sidewalk. Savory smells already wafted through the air as I drew closer to the Summer Festival area where all the town's vendors were busy cooking up a storm and setting their booths up. The sun had barely crested over the distant mountains and there was a touch of coolness to the air.

I was about to round the street corner when I realized I was right next to the empty storefront I'd noticed the first day I arrived. It somehow looked different today and then I noticed that the lights were turned on inside. Leaning toward the glass, I brought my hand up over the top of my eyes to shield the sun's glare. The interior walls were paneled with white-washed wood and the entire back wall shone with pearlescent backsplash. It was gorgeous and my mind immediately ran away with ideas of clothing and jewelry placement for a fashion boutique.

The entire layout came so quickly it surprised me.

My phone vibrated in my back pocket, interrupting my thoughts. I grabbed it and saw that it was a text from Sarah asking if I was okay and if I was still going to make it. I started around the corner, leaving as I typed out a quick reply that I'd be there in a few minutes.

The park and downtown streets were brimming with people. As I made my way through the growing crowd, several people spoke out to me.

"Hi, Willow!"

"Glad to see you're back in town, Willow."

"So great to see you!"

Some of them were people I'd known from high school and a few others were parents of the children I'd known. It didn't take long for the forced smile I'd been wearing to turn into a real one. Everyone was mingling. Patrons helped vendors finish setting up, while the vendors were offering people free food or whatever goodies they had in exchange for the help. The scene was the perfect picture of Southern hospitality and it warmed my heart to see so many people helping out their neighbors.

"There you are!" Sarah called to me as I finally found her tent.

"Wow, Sarah! This looks fantastic." I pulled my purse off my shoulder, ready to do whatever she needed.

A pale pink banner hung from the front of the white tent, displaying her bakery's name in swirly white lettering. The table was covered with a cloth of the same pink color and on top of that was a miniature display case where she was already stacking up pastries from her large Yeti cooler.

"What do you need?"

She pointed to another display case behind her and said, "Can you put that on the other side of the table and start filling it with the cupcakes? They're in the other cooler, over there."

I stored my purse and to-go coffee cup under the table and got to work lining up a variety of Sarah's best-selling cupcakes. Before long, I was basked in a cloud of sweetness, my mouth watering for just a small bite of one of the tasty treats.

My stomach grumbled even though I wasn't actually hungry. "I seriously don't know how you don't eat everything you bake. I feel like I'm being tortured right now," I grumbled.

"Eh, you get used to it after a while. Plus, the more I eat the less money I make," Sarah chuckled.

I raised my eyebrows with a nod. "Good point."

"So, do you think your parents will stop by today?" I asked cautiously.

Sarah's shoulders immediately drew closer to her ears, but

she continued to work, loading more items into the case. "They haven't made it to the festival since I paid for my first booth a few years ago."

"Damn. I didn't realize things were that bad. I'm sorry, Sarah."

She straightened, wiping her hands on her pink apron. "Yeah, it sucks. But I've had to learn that not everyone will jump on the support train and I have to be okay with that."

Sarah had a lot more grace than me. Though I knew from our previous conversations that she endured her own trial of hurt when her parents threw a fit about her opening the bakery.

"Well, they're missing out."

She gave me a smile that didn't quite reach her eyes.

A few minutes later and the booth was ready for business. Sarah and I sat back in our chairs, people-watching the entire town of Pebble Brook Falls as they made their way around the Summer Festival. It didn't take long for people to notice Sarah's bakery items and in about ten minutes, she had a line longer than any other vendor. We worked in tandem. Sarah boxed the baked goods and I took the money and re-stocked the miniature display cases.

I was so lost in the process that I didn't even notice Johnny walk up to the side of the tent until he said, "Hey, Lo."

My breath hitched as I took him in from head to toe. He was wearing a deep blue flannel over a bright white t-shirt. And his jeans hugged him in all the right places—so much so that there was no hiding my blush as my gaze raked over his manhood. Steel-toed boots covered his feet and the entire ensemble made him look like a sexy lumberjack. I almost didn't notice Asher sitting tall next to him, his tongue lolling out of the side of his mouth.

Forcing myself to look away, I took the five-dollar bill from the woman in front of me and said, "Hi."

He laughed. The sound was a deep rumble that left its mark on me. Heat crawled up my neck.

"I find it interesting that you've become a woman of so few words. I didn't expect that from you at all."

I snorted, his remark immediately fueling the anger I'd felt for him since last night. I envisioned myself grabbing one of the decadent cupcakes and throwing it straight at his stupid sexy face. Then I remembered where we were and just how many people were watching.

Though I didn't look directly at him, I could see him move closer out of the corner of my eye.

"Can we talk?" His voice lowered. That sultry Southern accent sent chills over my skin.

I glanced at Sarah who was still packing up boxes for her patrons, but she looked up at me and shot me a wink. She knew exactly what was happening.

I finally looked at Johnny again, which was a mistake because his eyes captivated me. The usually dark brown of his irises had turned a bright hue of honey from the early morning sun reflecting in them.

Damnit.

"I'm kinda busy at the moment."

"It's okay, Willow. I got this." Sarah nodded toward Johnny. "Go talk."

"No." I shook my head. "I'm not leaving you here all by yourself when I promised to help."

"Go!" she urged with a half-laugh. "I do this stuff by myself all the time. I'll be fine."

I glanced back at Johnny and my heart leaped into my throat.

Looking back to Sarah I said, "Fine. But if you need me just text me. I'll have my phone with me."

"Deal." She smirked and I knew there was no way she was going to text me.

I grabbed my purse and let Johnny lead us out toward the crowd with Asher prancing between us.

Once we neared the edge of the park Johnny said, "I'm sorry about yesterday."

"Why are you sorry?"

His hands disappeared in his jean's pockets and I wondered if he was nervous.

"After I thought about it, I realized that it's probably been a while since you've seen Melody. I remember that she wasn't the nicest person to you in high school."

"That's an understatement," I chided.

He grasped my arm, stopping me from walking forward. "I feel like you've been pissed off from the moment you saw me. What's going on, Lo?"

The way his brows knitted together and his lips tilted downward had me thinking he was genuinely concerned. My mouth popped open and I almost told him everything. How it didn't matter that I'd been chasing a dream for the past ten years because all I could think about was him. Or that when Melody touched him, I wanted to rip her hair out. And that I felt completely weirded out when it came to my bio family and the insane amount of money that was about to be handed over to me.

But that young girl he left behind—the one who was hurt and angry—won out. *The stubborn little brat.*

So I settled for, "To be honest, I just have a lot going on in my life right now and it's made me on edge. I'm sorry for taking it out on you."

His expression shifted to one of disappointment. I twirled the ends of my hair around my fingers, trying not to think about what that meant.

We continued walking as he said, "Is it anything I can help with?"

A strangled laugh escaped from my lips. "Unfortunately not. This one's all on me."

He nodded. No hint of the smile he normally wore.

We continued to stroll away from the Summer Festival until we ended up on a side street with bright white houses that were older than the town square. I remembered that during the holidays the houses were decorated with perfectly placed twinkle lights, highlighting the edges of the roofs and front porches. Johnny and I would run away from the orphanage at night and meet Sarah and some of our friends down here to see all the lights and the first snowfall. I laughed to myself as I remembered all the snowball fights we used to have and the look on Johnny's face when I turned on him, smacking him square in the face with a ball of snow.

"What're you thinking about?" he asked, looking at me sidelong.

I smiled as more childhood memories played out in my mind. "Just how we used to get into *so* much trouble."

He chuckled. "Yeah. We did do a lot of that. My favorite was probably when we switched out sugar for salt and Ms.

Mosely used it in her coffee. The look on her face was priceless."

"Oh yeah!" I laughed deeply. "It was totally worth the three weeks of being grounded."

"Not that we ever abided by her grounding rules anyway." His eyes darkened as he looked over at me and there was no hiding the blush that crept over my cheeks. I turned my face to the side, hoping he wouldn't notice.

When he stopped walking I turned to face him. He took a step into my space, crowding my senses in a way that made it impossible to think. The world stopped moving as he brought his palm to my cheek, stroking my skin with his thumb.

"You're so beautiful when you blush. I've always loved how your cheeks turn pink like an early morning sunrise made just for me. " His voice was raspy. I leaned into his touch, closing my eyes so I could savor every single second.

I heard his breathing increase and it was a song that matched my heartbeat. One that we had danced to countless times before when the only thing that mattered was being together and the promise that was shared when our bodies became one.

My eyes fluttered open and I saw the pain of our past etched into his irises. And something more—weariness, perhaps of what the world had almost turned him into. Fatigue from the burden he carried of being the product of such damaged souls. And the weight of witnessing the under-belly of the world while fighting in a war.

It was all there, laid bare for me to see—like he *needed* me to see it. All I wanted to tell him was that I'd been here. This entire time, waiting for him to let me in again. Confused at how we had been each other's everything, only for him to walk away, deciding to do it all alone.

Why, I wanted to scream. Why leave me? Leave *us?*

My chest tightened with such brutal force, I could hardly breathe. I took a step back, his hand dropping from my face. Everything he'd revealed in that one look was gone in an instant. Locked—once again—behind a door that I didn't have a key to.

Bark!

I nearly jumped out of my skin as Asher made his presence known, traipsing across a lawn of grass toward one of the large white houses. I tugged at the hem of my top, feeling overwhelmed with everything that just transpired and not quite sure what to do or say next.

When Johnny started walking toward the house that Asher had run up to I shifted my attention to the old estate.

"Shouldn't you try to keep him off other people's lawns?" The words came out before I even realized what I was saying, my mind was such a jumbled mess.

Johnny looked at me over his shoulder. The mask of his playful smile was back in place. "Seeing as how it's *his* lawn, I think we're good."

I stood there, dumbfounded on the sidewalk as Johnny continued up toward the house. Asher pranced around on the front porch, sticking his nose between the various flower pots searching for some unfortunate little creature to terrorize. In front of the white porch was a garden bed filled with deep red roses in full blossom, their deep green leaves a gorgeous contrast to the brightness of the house. Two large cylinder columns framed the entryway and the large porch wrapped the entirety of the house.

It was beautiful.

And it also happened to be the exact house that I always said I wanted growing up. When we would pass along this street on our adventures, we always stopped at this house and I would rattle on about my dreams of one day owning it—or something like it.

As Johnny stood on the top step of the porch, he turned to look at me. Asher pranced at his side, wanting to play desperately. The scene before me shook me to my core. It was a dream I'd wanted for so long and yet, I felt like it was behind a thick shield of impenetrable glass.

Johnny on one side and me on the other.

CHAPTER NINE

*G*ravel crunched under my feet as I walked up the short path to Johnny's front porch. A giant honey bee buzzed past my face, landing on one of the puffy roses. As I took in the front of the house, I noticed that the shutters were painted a light gray, the perfect offset to the bright white. He'd done a beautiful job renovating it from what it looked like when we were kids. But then again, I hadn't seen the house in ten years, so maybe someone else was responsible for the additions.

He must have remembered that this was the one, right? Why did he buy it? Was it out of spite?

Oh God, I hoped not.

I rolled my eyes at myself because I was likely making a way bigger deal out of the situation than I needed to. The man bought a house—as normal people do when they become adults—and he just happened to buy this one.

The exact house that I dreamed of living in one day.

I blew out an exasperated breath as I neared the steps.

"What do you think? A pretty decent upgrade from the orphanage, huh?"

And we were back to playing the game we seemed to have started. I smirked. "Definitely the perfect setup to woo women." I gestured toward Asher. "The perfect dog. The perfect house. I'm surprised you don't have a line of women waiting at your doorstep at all times."

His gaze sharpened on me. "A line of women isn't what I want, Lo." An almost imperceptible shake of his head had me clamping my mouth shut.

"Come sit with me." He nodded his chin toward the porch swing that hung to the left of his front door.

Butterflies flickered to life in my chest as I sat on the swing next to him, our legs so close they almost touched. He flexed his foot back and forth to swing us while my feet didn't even touch the ground. We sat there in silence for a few minutes and it reminded me of all the times we would sit together as teenagers—never feeling pressure to say something because having him close was enough.

I quickly realized that it was enough in this moment too. My racing mind was calm, I could hear birds chirping in the woods that lined the sides of his property, and I could feel the heat of the sun every time we swung forward. It was…peaceful. I tried to rack my brain for the last time I felt this way and came up short.

"I've never brought anyone here before." Johnny slid his gaze to me and my heart swelled.

"Really?"

He nodded as he looked over his front yard again, a distant look on his face.

I thought that was all he was going to say, but after a few

moments he continued, "I haven't dated anyone either." When he looked back at me his eyes were a golden yellow, like the tip of a smoldering flame. That same heat flooded my body as I licked my lips.

So many questions roamed through my mind, but there was only one that truly mattered. "Since you've been back home?"

He shook his head, never taking those golden-brown eyes off me. "Since I left."

My eyebrows shot up, my heart stammered like a herd of wild horses chasing the horizon.

"Neither have I," I admitted and it was his turn to look surprised.

When he leaned toward me, a rush of excitement flooded my veins and as his fingers brushed my hair behind my ear I became that young girl again. A girl—so in love—that it didn't matter that my family had abandoned me, or that every day at school felt like torture with the constant bullying, or that I had no idea how I was going to make things work for myself when I phased out. None of it mattered because I had *him* and he was all I needed. And I loved him with every stitch of my being, so much that I physically hurt when he wasn't around.

All of it came back to me in a rush and as much as it pained me to know that he walked away, I didn't care. I wanted him back and damn if I wouldn't do absolutely anything to have him.

"Tell me the truth." He traced the bottom of my ear to the edge of my jaw with the pad of his finger, the light touch shot thrills all throughout my body.

"What truth?" I breathed.

His eyes flicked to my lips for a moment and I wondered if

he wanted to kiss me as badly as I needed him to. A flare of disappointment sparked when he looked back into my eyes.

"Why do you keep running away from me?"

I sighed deeply, letting my shoulders fall with my breath and Johnny let his fingers fall from my face. I sat back on the wooden swing with a thud, frustration falling over me like a wet blanket.

I didn't want to talk about this. All I wanted to do was feel. Let myself be washed away by the moment with him because I knew that it was fleeting and I wanted something to savor when I left Pebble Brook Falls. But he kept pushing me every time we saw each other.

"I don't know, Johnny." I crossed my arms and stared out toward his front lawn.

He huffed, irritated. "I think you do know. You just don't want to tell me."

"And why should I?" I screeched, much louder than I intended, but his poking around was scraping against my nerves and I was shot.

I immediately regretted my outburst as I saw him flinch, though he refused to back down.

"I think we owe that to one another, don't we? Truth." His once bright irises had dulled as he narrowed his eyes at me.

"You seriously want to talk about truth? What about broken promises, Johnny? You keep asking me why I am running away from you when you've never told me why you —" I clamped my mouth shut, refusing to go there with him.

His voice was dangerously low as he said, "Why I what, Lo?"

The words threatened to spill from my lips, but I sealed them shut. Completely unwilling to share any more with him.

This was the man who had promised me the world—yes, we had been teenagers at the time, but he was the only thing I had and he walked away from me. Knowing his actions would leave me in a pile of rubble that I'd be forced to clean up by myself.

"I don't want to do this right now. Not with you." I stood up from the bench so quickly, I stumbled over Asher who'd made the floor beneath the swing his naptime spot. Asher darted forward and Johnny's strong hand caught my wrist before I fell.

In one swift motion, I went from teetering toward the wood planks of his porch to being firmly pressed against his chest. A strong, calm heartbeat ticked in his chest and for a moment I just rested my cheek against him. Listening to the steady rhythm of his heart. The sound was soothing as I tried to steel my breath.

His large hand pressed into the center of my back, bringing our bodies even closer together. It felt foreign and familiar all at the same time. The smell of fresh cedar wood had always been uniquely his, but the size of his grown body encapsulating my own was a change from the lanky frame he'd had as a teen. I decided I liked this version of him more.

"Why do you keep fighting me?" he growled against my hair as he tucked his chin and pressed his cheek against the top of my head.

When I wriggled in his grasp, he tightened his arms around me and I became acutely aware of every inch of my body that was touching his. Especially my upper thigh that grazed his flexing length—giving away the arousal he felt from our contact.

Tilting my head back, I looked up at him. His square jaw

was tense, and those brown eyes were a well of emotions that I didn't understand. His nostrils flared as he breathed in deeply.

"Memories," I whispered.

When his brows furrowed slightly I said, "Memories are why I keep fighting you."

His hands stilled at my hips. I wanted to say so much more, but every time my lips parted to speak, a wall shot up and I was speechless.

I could see that same wall shielding Johnny.

He may have changed in a lot of ways, but he was still the same boy I fell in love with. The boy who had been my best friend—my family. His tells hadn't altered.

Like the way his eyes grew distant when he was thinking deeply. Or the way he clenched his teeth when he wanted to say something but knew better. How his shoulders lifted when he felt insecure or worried. And now—the way every angle of his face hardened to stone told me there were secrets he was hiding. Words he was unwilling to share.

I stepped back and he let me go. The moment was completely broken as an overwhelming sadness consumed the space between us.

"I wish things were different, Lo. This"—he gestured between us—"doesn't feel right. It's not who we are."

The threat of tears started to build up behind my eyes and I blinked them away. "It's been so long, Johnny. I don't think we even know what is right and what's wrong anymore." I laughed through my sniffles. "I mean come on. It's been over ten years since we saw each other. There's no way we could expect for things to be the same between us."

He took a step forward and I put a hand up, his eyes

growing wide as they flicked back and forth between my open palm and my face.

"Please don't make this any harder than it needs to be, Johnny."

"I just want to know you, Lo," he pleaded and his words broke my heart wide open. "I want to hear all about your adventures. What brought you back to Pebble Brook Falls. What your dreams are. I want to know them all, just like I always have."

"There's not much to know." I shrugged as tears spilled down my face. "I'm just a girl from a small town who's trying to make something of herself. Simple as that." The words were ashen lies on my tongue.

"We both know there's nothing simple about you." He took another step forward and I let him. Because the truth was that I wanted to tell him everything he wanted to know. My body craved his touch and the longer I looked at him, the more I wanted to fall into his warm embrace.

But my mind was a jumbled mess of the past and present. The sullen look on his face was a reminder of *that* day. And my heart couldn't take being broken by him again. I wouldn't survive it and after everything I'd been through, I deserved to survive.

"I'm so sorry, Johnny," I whispered through my tears. "I have to go."

I wished he chased after me as I walked off his front porch steps.

But he didn't.

And somehow, that broke my heart all over again.

CHAPTER TEN

Sarah had sold out of her inventory early, which was perfect because she was able to accompany me to the George Strait cover band concert. I desperately needed a distraction from my thoughts of Johnny and I wasn't ready to be alone yet. The town hired out a cover band for every Summer Festival and most of the time they did a pretty decent job of picking out solid bands from what I remembered. This year was no exception.

It seemed like the entire town had made it out to see the George Strait impersonator and I didn't blame them. He was pretty damn good. Everyone was pushed up close to the stage, dancing and singing along like it was actually the king of country who was performing.

Just in front of Sarah and I was a father twirling around his little girl as she laughed and laughed, the biggest smile pulling on her chubby cheeks. And next to them, an older couple swayed together, only having eyes for one another as though they were eighteen again.

It was one of the things I loved most about the Summer

Festival. It brought the old and young alike to a common place where everyone got along and the only intention was to have a good time.

I was trying really hard to do just that and to forget about everything that happened at Johnny's house. But the stupid man wouldn't stop plaguing my thoughts as I looked through the crowd over and over again, secretly hoping to see his face. Every time I peered through the sea of people and came up empty, my heart sank.

Sarah bumped me with her hip as she mouthed, "Are you okay?" I could hardly hear her over the music.

I nodded and smiled, doing my best to assure her that I was fine. Even though I was feeling the complete opposite of okay, I didn't want her to worry.

The moment I got out of Johnny's eyesight was the same moment that I regretted walking away from him. It was also the exact moment when I realized just how crazy I'd become. The emotional whiplash I was giving myself was worse than being in a five-car pileup on the highway. One second I was giving in to the reactions my body had toward him and the next, I was denying myself any sense of what I clearly wanted. And that was to be close to him.

All the lust and attraction to his stupid hotness aside, I missed my best friend—the boy I got into trouble with, told all my secrets to, and went on adventures with. Johnny was such a huge part of my life and I'd missed that more than anything. I didn't understand why I couldn't let shit go. He had always been a good person and if he had a reason for walking away, then it had to be a good one. *Right?*

It was the question I'd asked myself too many times to count over the past twelve years. It was also the same question I couldn't bring myself to ask him every time I saw him.

Probably because I'm too chicken-shit to hear the answer.

The crowd around me cheered as the band transitioned from playing *Write This Down* to *Every Little Honky Tonk Bar*. People threw their hands in the air, most holding some variation of light beer as their bodies twisted and grooved to the upbeat song.

An elderly man decked out in worn Wrangler jeans and a camel-colored cowboy hat bowed in front of Sarah, extending his hand toward her. She brought her hand up to her mouth as she giggled before taking his. He whisked her away—as quickly as he could move—and soon they were lost to the crowd. I wondered what his story was. If he was maybe a widower whose wife made him promise that he would live out his last years with joy in his heart. Or maybe he'd always been a rolling stone, never stopping long enough to set down roots.

The crowd parted slightly and I was able to see Sarah as the older man twirled her around, her movements slow, making sure that he could keep up. My heart warmed at the sight of them—like a grandpa with his granddaughter. His wrinkled eyes glittered with humor as her head was tilted back, mouth open wide with laughter. Two strangers with a lifetime separating them and somehow they found common ground on this day—a love for dancing. I wondered if this ever happened in the big cities, or if the scene before me was a gem only to be found in small towns.

It was moments like this that made me thankful to have grown up in Pebble Brook Falls where life was slow and filled with purpose. Sure, I didn't always have the easiest time given my circumstances, but there were always good people around me. Like Mrs. Sheehan at the local ice cream parlor who always added an extra scoop to my cone when Ms. Mosely wasn't looking. Or my third-grade teacher, Ms. Katz, who lived up to her name by fostering all the stray kittens when the shelter ran out of room. Even Ms. Mosely—despite all her faults—had a huge impact on my well-being simply by being willing to take me in.

None of those people were forced to be kind to those less fortunate than them. It was simply in their nature to do good. And knowing them made me want to be better...even if I wasn't here to stay. I'd take all the lessons they gave me and bring them with me to Nashville.

Everyone around me cheered again at the end of the song and I clapped right along with them, as though I were still a part of them and I hadn't spent all of my twenties running away. A strange feeling fluttered in my chest and I quickly realized that I was happy to be back in Pebble Brook Falls. Even if my initial thoughts of coming back were of pure disdain, the past few days had reminded me of everything I loved about the small town.

And then the guitar player struck the chord for the next song and I immediately wanted to run away from the pit that grew in my stomach.

Carrying Your Love With Me was *our* song. The one we used to dance to in the middle of the abandoned field off Sunflower Drive as the summer sun sank far below the western mountains. The lyrics were a promise that no matter where we went, our love would remain and somehow we would always find our way back to one another. Sorrow snaked its way through me with each passing beat. I wanted to get as far away from the sound of that song as possible, yet my feet wouldn't move. They kept me firmly planted just like the giant oak tree that had our initials carved into it.

"I wrote to you every single week that I was away."

I gasped as Johnny's voice sounded from behind me, just loud enough to break through the music and the crowd. I stilled, thinking I must have conjured his voice from the agony gripping my heart and then I felt him. His presence had always been so tangible for me, it was like a force that only I could feel, even if I couldn't see him.

Tears burned my eyes as I turned around slowly.

There he was. The same pain I felt reflected in the way his eyes shone, the shadows on the planes of his face, and the defeated look of his rounded shoulders.

He took a step forward and my breath hitched.

"I wrote to you, Lo. Every single chance I had, I wrote to you." Another step forward. "I told you about my training and how my sergeant was an asshole. I told you how scared I was that I'd made a terrible decision. And then, how I started to make friends and things got a little better."

One more step and he was standing toe to toe with me, his chest nearly brushing against mine. "I told you everything, Lo. But I never heard from you. Not once." His shoulders sagged a little more. "Why didn't you write back to me?"

He wrote to me. The entire time I thought he'd left without a word and he'd written to me.

I stood there, dumbfounded by his admission while he eagerly searched my face, waiting for an answer.

"I never got them," I replied. "I never knew you wrote to me, Johnny."

A muscle ticked in his jaw. He was angry and rightfully so.

I couldn't imagine how he felt as each week passed by. Continuing to etch his feelings onto paper over and over, only to receive nothing in return. It must have been heartbreaking for him to feel that rejection after everything we'd shared. Just as I had felt abandoned by him, without knowing that he'd actually been there for me all along.

I reached for his hands. They were so large, they covered mine completely and I let the warmth of him spread through me.

"I would have written to you. If I had known you wanted to hear from me at all, I would have found a way to write to you, Johnny. But I thought—" I cut myself off, bowing my head.

He slipped a hand from mine and grasped my chin, tilting my head back so I was looking at him. "You thought what?"

I closed my eyes and slowly opened them, still not believing this moment was real. "I thought you wanted to leave me behind.

"Lo." My name was a pang of regret on his tongue as he closed the small space between us, winding his arms around me until I was snug against him. He brought his hand to the back of my head and stroked my hair just as he had done the day he said goodbye. The parallels between this moment and that one were startling to me. It felt like I was being transported back and forth through time, trying my best to grasp onto something that might last longer than a fleeting second.

So I held him tighter. There was still so much I didn't know about that time. So many questions left unanswered. But I didn't care.

Johnny's arms wrapped around me was like getting into a warm bed after playing in the snow all day. A safe haven to recover, no matter what came my way. The ache I'd felt in my chest after leaving his house dissipated, replaced with a sense of ease that was slowly melding into desire.

"This is our song," he whispered against my ear and the feel of his breath sent tingles down my neck.

I couldn't speak, so I simply nodded against his chest, unwilling to let go of him for fear that I might never get the chance to hold him like this again.

"Dance with me?" A question that had played out in my mind countless times over the years as I relived so many memories of him asking me to dance—at homecoming, his prom, in the middle of summer rainstorms, and under the moonlight in the field. Every time, the answer was the same. And this time would be no different.

"Yes."

With that single word, I felt his body shift against mine. The hand that graced the back of my head trailed down my spine, leaving a fire in its wake before it settled at the small of my back. The fingertips of his other hand grazed the bare skin of my shoulder and arm as they traveled to my palm. Our fingers interlaced before he brought our hands together, resting them on his chest.

And when his hips moved to the easy melody of our song, mine fell in sync with his, just as they had time and time again. I rested my head on his chest, letting him lead us through the throng of people. Their faces blurred as I closed my eyes.

A soft rumble came from his chest as he started to hum the last lyrics of the song. As the final strum of the guitar rang out, it felt like a closing note to a chapter we'd never finished until now. At the same time, he brought me closer and his gesture was the seed of a brand new beginning. One that I hoped I could watch grow.

I stomped out the little flicker of remembrance that I didn't come back home for Johnny, no matter how badly I wanted to stay for him.

CHAPTER ELEVEN

"*H*ey, girl!" I shouted over the music to Sarah who had somehow gotten so close to the stage, I thought my eardrums might burst from the speakers. When she turned around and saw me, she threw her arms around my neck, giving me a sweaty hug.

"Hey!" she drew out the word in a drunken slur and we both giggled.

"Are you okay to get home by yourself tonight?"

"Yeah! I'll take an Uber home and get my car in the morning."

"You sure?" I asked.

"Yup!"

"Okay, good. I'll see you in the morning." I gave her a kiss on the cheek and as I went to leave she grabbed my arm, spinning me around to face her again.

"Who're you going home with, Little Missy?" Sarah waggled her eyebrows at me.

I rolled my eyes playfully. "We'll talk about it tomorrow."

"Make sure to wrap it nice and good."

"Sarah!" I gaped at her and she went into a fit of laughter, barrelling over as she clutched her stomach.

"Remind me to never let you drink beer again."

She finally caught her breath and said, "Mmm. I think I'll pass on reminding you of that."

"Goodnight!" I said mockingly as I waved at her over my shoulder.

She went right back to dancing as she yelled the lyrics of *Write This Down* to the lead singer who knelt down at the edge of the stage, giving her all the attention she hoped for.

I gulped as I saw Johnny standing in the crowd. A circle had formed around him as though he were such a powerful force, no one wanted to get too close. Not that anyone in this town would admit that Johnny Moore—the kid from the wrong side of the tracks—could impact them in such a way.

When I broke through the circle to stand by his side, he smiled down at me and said, "She's in rare form tonight." He jutted his chin toward Sarah.

I glanced at her over my shoulder and saw that she was now holding hands with the young George Strait look-alike as they sang to one another. I couldn't help the laugh that burst from me.

"Yeah." I nodded. "She's going to regret this one in the morning."

"Is she good to stay here by herself?" he asked, and it felt like old times. While Johnny had often been the one causing chaos in our little friend group, he was also the one to make sure we were always safe. He'd done the same thing for all the younger kids in the orphanage.

Protection. It was the one thing he always said he was good at offering others.

I wondered if that was why he decided to go into the military. To fulfill that part of himself.

"She's taking an Uber home, so she'll be safe."

"Good." When he looked at me again, his eyes shone with excitement that felt contagious as butterflies swarmed my insides and a tingle of nervousness crawled over my skin. "Ready?"

"Mmhmm," was all I could get out as his gaze pierced right through me.

He snaked his arm around me, tucking me close as he navigated us through the crowd and out toward the parking lot. I leaned into him harder than I wanted to admit, but it felt so damn good to feel him next to me after all this time. It didn't hurt that as I put my right hand against his abdomen as we walked, I could feel every single ripple of muscle beneath his thin t-shirt.

My mouth watered and my lips twitched to press gentle kisses along every smooth peak and valley of his stomach. I wanted to see what the military and years of hard work had forged him into.

Before my mind could get too carried away, we arrived at his truck. Which happened to be the sexiest and most masculine piece of vehicular machinery I'd ever seen in my life...and I normally didn't give a shit about cars.

Warm notes of leather and cinnamon hit my nose as Johnny opened the passenger door. Shocks of awareness coursed through me as he grasped my hips and lifted me into the truck. I thought he was going to shut the door, but instead, he stepped onto the undercarriage rail, leaned over me, and grabbed the seatbelt. His closeness made me dizzy with desire. I opened and closed my hands as I tried to ward off the need to reach out and touch him.

I gasped quietly as his hands brushed against my hip, deliciously close to my throbbing center as he buckled me in. When he grabbed the part of the strap that stretched across my chest and tightened it, I nearly burst from the heat that pulsed between us.

"Gotta keep my precious cargo safe," he said, his voice husky and low as he dipped his head so our lips were nearly touching. I closed my eyes, so ready to feel his lips press against mine. But he only flashed me a devilish smirk before he stepped off the rail and closed the door.

"Fuck," I moaned as I bucked against the seatbelt that I wanted nothing more than to rip off so I could climb into his lap and take what I wanted.

As soon as he opened his door, I quieted down and clamped my legs together to soothe the growing ache between them.

The headlights flicked on as the engine roared to life. Its loud hum matched my body's as I watched Johnny's forearm flex from turning the wheel.

Damnit. Why is he so sexy? And why the hell am I so turned on by a truck?

I stored the questions in the back of my mind to sort through later and turned my attention to the road ahead of us.

"Where are we going?"

Johnny slid his gaze over to me and said, "You'll figure it out in just a few minutes."

I crossed my arms. I hated surprises, or anything that

slightly resembled a surprise and he knew that. Or at least, I hoped he remembered that.

But he was right. It didn't take long before the familiar streets jogged my memory and I realized he was taking me to our special place—the old abandoned field off Sunflower Drive.

Happy memories floated through my mind of us running through the field in the middle of summer with popsicle stains on our fingers and not a care in the world to burden our souls. We were wild and free. Two best friends who grew into more—so much more. That field was our safe haven. The place we ran off to when Ms. Mosely brought the hammer down. A sanctuary where we felt safe enough to whisper our biggest dreams and deepest desires. It was where we fell in love and where I grew to hate him for leaving me.

It was just a field. And yet, it held more meaning than any other place in the world. And I would be leaving it all behind in a little over a week. My heart sank as his truck rolled to a stop. We'd arrived and I silently made a promise to myself that I would let it all go, just for tonight. Let myself live in the moment like I used to, without fear of what tomorrow would bring.

Johnny turned the key back in the ignition so that the radio was still on, but the engine turned off. Then he slid out of his seat and made his way to my side, opening the large door.

I reached for the buckle of the seat belt and he grabbed my thigh.

I looked at him, his eyes blazing and he said, "Let me."

My hands immediately dropped from the buckle as he took his time sliding his hands across the lower edge of the belt. I sucked in a sharp breath of air when his fingers met the middle, only a few inches above my throbbing sex.

And then he laughed. The bastard actually laughed a deep throaty chuckle that was both the best and most irritating sound ever to grace my ears.

I shoved at him and he didn't budge an inch. "You bastard!"

He laughed even harder. "Darlin' we both know I'm so much worse than a bastard."

I went to unbuckle myself, my body completely flushed from his touch, but he grabbed my hand as soon as it pressed against the small red button.

"I'm not ready to let you go yet, Lo." All humor had left him. His head dipped low as he closed his eyes, sucking in a deep breath. He looked wounded and it pulled at my heart in a way that only his suffering could.

I slid my free hand against the side of his neck, letting my thumb brush the side of his strong jaw. He sighed, pushing his face further into my palm.

"I'm right here, Johnny. I'm not going anywhere." The half-truth fluttered from my lips before I even knew what I was saying.

He opened his eyes, meeting mine and for the longest moment, I thought he might kiss me. His lips were a mere inch from mine, my hand still cradling his cheek. Then, the snap of my seatbelt buckle sounded between us, and the moment was lost. Johnny leaned back, letting the strap sink back to its holder and he helped me out of the truck, letting the door stay open so we could hear the soft hum of the radio.

He interlaced his fingers with mine as we walked out into the tall grass. I took in my surroundings, noticing that nothing had changed in the old field. It was a perfect picture, stuck in a time capsule from our past. The tall puffs of pampas grass flitted in the late night breeze, their tall stalks painted in silver from the moonlight.

As we grew closer to the center of the field, Johnny stopped, pulled me toward him, and wrapped his arms around me. We looked up at the bright full moon together, the moment bringing a flood of memories with it. All the times we gazed up at the cratered surface, asking questions that would never be answered. Two wide-eyed souls craving for freedom, only to be stuck in a meadow as their means of escape. Little did we know that we'd each have our own adventures, separate from one another, despite the promise we made.

"When you kept running away from me, I never got the chance to ask you why you came back." Johnny rubbed his knuckles along the center of my back, setting my skin ablaze. At the same time, ice ran through my veins at the thought of telling him the truth.

Johnny was the only person who knew how much pain I was in after finding out that my mother had only been a few short miles from me my entire childhood. And once her mysterious death landed in all the papers and I had to mourn the loss of her all over again, it took a lot of time to move forward and gain my strength back. It didn't help that Adeline Baxley—my biological grandmother—still refused to take me in after my mother's death.

I remembered the first time I'd seen Adeline Baxley after I knew her blood ran through my veins. I was fourteen years old, pushing little Noah in a swing at the park downtown. It was during one of our outings at the orphanage and it was always clear that we were the children left behind. Our clothes never fit quite right and there were far too many of us for Ms. Mosely to manage, so Johnny and I took up a lot of those responsibilities.

Adeline was walking on the nearby sidewalk with another woman who looked her age. They were both so clean, their clothes perfectly pressed and there wasn't a stitch of dirt on their handbags. It was almost like they glowed; they were so clean. I stared at her as I continued to push Noah in the swing and when she finally saw me, she paused, taking me in as her lips pulled down heavily. And when she turned back to her friend as though I were nothing but a sore sight for her eyes, I promised myself that I would never enter into their world.

Johnny knew about that promise and some part of me didn't want him to know that I'd come to collect the fortune that was waiting for me after Adeline died. I didn't want him to be disappointed in me or think I was taking the easy road.

So I pushed all of that down, burying it deep as I said, "It doesn't matter. I'm here...with you. That's all I care about."

He searched my face as though he didn't quite believe that it didn't matter.

"Okay," was his only response as he pulled me down into his lap and I was thankful he didn't push the subject further.

But as I leaned against his chest, a peaceful quiet settling around us, he said, "You've never been good at keeping secrets from me, Lo. Time may have passed between us, but there are some things that will never change."

I swallowed hard, my pulse quickening. "You're right. A lot of time has passed between us. Maybe you don't know me at all anymore."

His lips grazed my ear, sending a shiver through me. "Oh,

darlin'. I'm the only one who knows you better than you know yourself. Don't try to play that game with me."

"Maybe I just don't want to tell you," I retorted.

His laugh was deep as it vibrated against my back. "Or maybe you're just too scared."

I elbowed him in the stomach but his thick muscles didn't move. He laughed again, this time pulling me closer where my back was flush against his chest, his large arms wrapped around my front so we were both facing forward.

A few seconds ticked by before I whispered, "I don't want anything to complicate this moment with you, Johnny. Can we have one night where our lives aren't getting in the way of what we want?"

He was silent and after a while, I wondered if he was going to say anything at all. Then I felt his chest rise on a breath. "I would give you all of eternity if you never left my arms again." He pressed a kiss to my temple that had my heart skipping a beat.

I wanted to tell him that I would have stayed in his arms forever if he hadn't left me. But I shut that thought out because I didn't want the doubt to sink in like it always did when memories of that day haunted me.

A conversation for another time. Even if I was leaving, we could surely still talk. Maybe try to figure something out.

"I'd always hoped this moment would happen." Johnny's husky voice broke through my thoughts.

I leaned my head into the crook between his shoulder and peck so I could look up at him. "What do you mean?"

He grasped my chin between his thumb and pointer finger. "That we would find one another again. And that I would have the chance to hold you. To...make things right."

His words were like a balm to my insecurities that had festered for so long.

Did he care about me? Had he ever even loved me? Questions that were my constant companion since the day he left for the military. A decision made so quickly, it hadn't made sense.

Though I still didn't know why he chose to break our promise, he was here now. Telling me everything I wanted to hear. If it had been any other man speaking those words, I wouldn't have believed them. I would have thought it was some ploy to coax me into giving them what they wanted. But it wasn't another man. It was Johnny. For some reason— maybe it was even a stupid reason—I believed him.

So I opened my heart and said, "I did too. Every single day since you left I hoped that fate would bring you back to me. Even when I was..." My words trailed off because I still wasn't ready to go there. To tell him just how much he'd broken me.

His hand slid to the side of my neck where he rubbed his thumb up and down the column of my throat.

"When you what?"

"I..."

"Tell me," he coaxed, his lips falling dangerously close to mine.

"No."

His chuckle was raspy as his chest moved up and down beneath me. "You win this one, Lo. But one day you will tell me." There was no mistaking the command in his tone.

"What if I don't want to?" I breathed.

His lips brushed against mine, stealing my breath in the wake of his gentle caress. "You'll tell me. Because you won't be able to stop yourself."

And then his lips were on mine. There was nothing tender

about his kiss as I opened for him, letting his tongue search my mouth with greedy need. I threaded my fingers through his hair, pulling him down, closer to me. His arms grasped my middle, sliding me up his chest so he had greater access.

The thrill of having him was like an electric current pulsing through my body over and over again. With each brush of his tongue against mine, I felt like I was going to explode from all the sensations taking over my body. The groan that escaped him vibrated against my tongue, sending more shockwaves through me. All the pain and regret of missing him were gone, replaced with a desperate need that was old and new. It was the kind of kiss that shattered worlds because you would do literally anything to feel it again.

As we came up for air, the stark realization that there was no way in hell I could give him up again hit me like a giant yellow school bus. Johnny Moore had always been mine and I wasn't going to let him walk away from me ever again.

CHAPTER TWELVE

*J*ohnny brushed his fingers up and down my arm as we lay together in the field—my head rested against the crook of his chest and shoulder, my leg draping over his. We were a tangled mess of limbs and as we watched the moon slowly descend upon the westward mountains, I silently prayed for time to stop so I could stay in this moment forever.

"What was it like being in the military?" I felt this urgent need to catch up on so much missed time. Countless questions flowed through my mind and I wanted to ask them all. I knew the military was a big part of his journey that led him to where he was today. After he said he'd written to me about his experiences, I couldn't help but wonder what all those letters contained.

His chest rose and fell as he took in a deep breath and then exhaled. "It was one of the hardest things I've ever done. Just the simple nature of having to do what someone else says without question was a huge adjustment. Not just during our trainings, but there were times when I was overseas when we would receive an order that didn't make much sense to us. But it wasn't our job to question the authorities. It was our job to be the boots on the ground and follow orders.

"My first sergeant was a complete ass. He did everything he could to make other members of our platoon feel like shit just to make himself feel more like a man."

That man sounded a lot like Melody Carnelle. There was no reason for her to step on other people as she tried to climb the social ladder. She had everything a person needed to be successful in whatever venture she pursued—her wealthy family made sure of that. That didn't stop her from being a total and complete troll though. Maybe some people were just hardwired to enjoy others' suffering.

I snuggled against Johnny's side, relishing his warmth as he continued, "Thankfully, I was reassigned to another base so I didn't have to deploy with him."

"Were you scared?"

He was silent for a few moments before answering, "Not nearly as scared as I should have been." His voice sounded distant, like the words he spoke were more a thought to himself than a statement to me.

"When you're young and surrounded by other people who joined the military to fight for our country, there's a sense of valor that gets twisted into overconfidence. Every day we were fueled by our disdain for the enemy and you top that off with our fellow Marines and commanding officers drilling into our minds that we were there to do one thing—destroy terrorist organizations from the inside out—and we started to believe we were invincible.

"The truth is that no human is invincible, especially not against bullets and IEDs. So many of my brothers and sisters died overseas and bearing witness to those tragedies straightened me up real quick. It doesn't matter if you're front lines or sitting behind a computer analyzing intel. War changes a person."

As he spoke, his body was tense against me. I could tell how difficult it was for him to go back to that place in his mind. We were all haunted by something. It didn't matter what those problems looked like to other people. How big or small others might perceive them to be. Pain is pain. And when I looked up at him, I could see the suffering etched into the lines on his face and the slight tinge of purple under his eyes that likely meant he spent most nights with little sleep.

"I'm so sorry you lost people, Johnny. And"—I sucked in a deep breath—"I'm sorry that humans are conditioned to want to hurt one another. And that you were exposed to all of that at such a young age. No one should have to see humans murder other humans. Even if it is for a justifiable reason."

"I think the worst part isn't what happens in the middle of war. It's what comes after."

"What do you mean?"

He reached for my hand, pulling it across his chest and settling it beneath his. The gesture warmed my heart, breaking down another foot of the walls I'd built around it.

"When you're in the military you're surrounded by structure and a team of people with the same agenda or goal. You might not get along with everyone, but there's still a sense of comradery and universality because we all have a similar purpose. When you discharge, or leave the military, there's a pretty intense adjustment period back to civilian life."

"Did you have a hard time adjusting?" It was strange. This pull I felt to learn about his time away from me and the very thing that made him break our promise. While the sting of his decision was still there—and I feared it would *always* be there—I still wanted to know. Maybe it was because there were new pieces of him that I hadn't discovered yet. And I wanted to know everything about this man. Not just because I once had, but because there was a whisper of something deep inside me. Nudging me toward a path that felt hopeful and full of wild possibilities that I hadn't let myself dream about since he walked away.

I shifted my attention back to him as he answered, "During my last deployment, we got called out for a night raid. It was the peak of the war and shit was turning upside down. We were losing people left and right, and at the same time we'd never been so close to snuffing out the enemy." Johnny's words were quick and clipped with anxiety. I wanted to tell him that he didn't have to talk about it anymore, but as soon as I opened my mouth, he continued, "We got some intel on a house that was supposed to have one of our targets inside. But we knew something was off the moment we got in. Nothing looked out of the ordinary based on our prior missions, but it was a feeling. The air was so thick with it, it was hard to breathe."

My pulse quickened with every word he spoke. The simple telling of his experience was like living on the edge of a knife. I couldn't even fathom what it must have been like for him to actually live it.

"I was third in our formation as we cleared every room. There was one door left that we hadn't opened yet. It was the last one at the end of the hallway and the second Kevin's hand twisted the handle, I knew something was off." He gulped hard but edged forward. "There was a woman in the room. It was hard to see at first with the vest covering her chest, but she was pregnant. Her thumb pressed hard against the small triggering device in her hand.

"Kevin and Bradley tried to calm her down, but as soon as Bradley started talking to her it was clear she was panicked. I yelled at them to get back, to get the fuck away from her. But it was too late. She let go of the trigger and the entire building almost came down with her. If Kevin and Bradley hadn't been in front of me, shielding me from the blast, I wouldn't be here."

Tears crawled down my face. My chest squeezed as I rolled onto my side so I could hold him tighter and I was so thankful he let me as his body shuddered with each breath he inhaled.

"It took a long time to understand that their deaths weren't my fault." The way his voice cracked sent a shiver of cold straight to my heart. I wanted to say that there was no way something like that could ever be his fault. But it wasn't my place to make such statements. I'd never been in his shoes and I didn't want to say something that might make it worse for him. So I just squeezed his hand to show that I was here with him, listening for as long as he wanted me to.

"I started to see a psychologist when I got back. There was a lot of shame around it while I was in the service, but when I started to notice that I was drinking a lot more than I should, I decided to seek help."

I sat up, leaning on my hand planted firmly in the grass next to him. "I'm really glad you caught it early, Johnny."

He lifted a palm to my cheek and said, "Me too, Lo. It was really fucking close, but I caught it."

There was a hint of something unreadable that flashed in his eyes. Addiction had already cost Johnny a lot in his short lifetime. With a crack-addicted mother and an alcoholic father, it was a miracle he survived long enough to be placed in the *Hope for All* orphanage. His parents had grown up on the west side of Pebble Brook Falls where money was scarce and the intergenerational trauma was abundant. If not for the orphanage, Johnny likely would have ended up neglected, or worse. And the thought that his time in war almost pushed him to that edge had my mind reeling.

I grasped his large hand in mine and brought it to my lips, pressing gentle kisses to each of his knuckles. He watched me with hooded eyes that tracked my every movement. The air was thick between us. Tension buzzed and I thought he might pull me down to kiss him again as his lips parted.

But instead, he said, "I've missed this so much."

I knew what he meant because I felt it too, but I still wanted him to say it out loud. "What did you miss?"

The tilt of his lips revealed his dimple, nestled deep against the edge of his mouth. Even after all these years, he still knew me so well.

"I've missed *you*, Lo. I've missed the way the moonlight turns your blonde hair silver. How your tiny button nose scrunches when you're frustrated. And the way your blue eyes light up every time you see a furry animal." His gaze dipped to my mouth, an intense smoldering burned in his irises. "And the way you always taste of sweet nectar when you open up for me."

The pad of his thumb scorched me as he slid it over my bottom lip. When he pulled down slightly, the hunger I felt for him intensified. When we made love for the first time, it was tender and innocent. Neither one of us had a clue of what to do. And though neither one of us had been with anyone else, I still knew things would be different if we crossed that line now. Johnny was no longer a gangly teenager. He was a man in every sense of the word. And I wanted to see just what those twelve years of experience could do.

I swallowed hard as the nerves set in and before I even knew what I was saying I broke the moment. "How did you find Asher?"

Oh my God. Am I seriously asking about his dog *right now?*

Yes. Yes, I was.

He bowed his head with a giant smile on his face. "You're killing me, Lo."

"What?! You said you missed how I love furry animals." I rolled my eyes playfully.

"That I did."

I rubbed my open palms along the top of my thighs to keep my hands from shaking. While it was painfully clear that my assumptions about Johnny abandoning me were all wrong, there were still a lot of questions I wanted answered. Too much time had passed and too much hurt was experienced for me to move forward without fully clearing the air. As badly as I wanted to give in to the demands my body was making, I had to be smart about this. There was too much at stake for me to go into any kind of future with him blind. And I wasn't even sure if a future was what he wanted.

Knowing more about Asher wasn't exactly on the high-priority list, but it was still a piece of his seemingly complicated puzzle.

Johnny leaned back on his hands and I sat next to him cross-legged with my right hand resting on his abdomen.

"It was more like Asher found me."

I tilted my head in question.

"It was about a month after I moved back to Pebble Brook Falls. It was a strange time because I'd finished my therapy for PTSD and wrapped up the first contracting job I had in Texas after being discharged. There wasn't a plan after that, but I had this feeling that I needed to come home. So I packed up my little apartment in Houston and came back. One day I was out strolling through the park and I heard this little whine behind me. I turned around and Asher was sitting right there, not even twenty pounds yet."

"He was just a puppy when you found him?"

Johnny nodded. "I posted fliers across town and no one claimed him. I wasn't really in a position to take on such a big responsibility, but the day I tried to take him to the Humane Society I took one look at him and knew there was no way I could leave him behind. When he was about a year old, I put him through the service dog training myself. But he's retired now. Living a life of luxury."

His words struck through me like a lightning rod. I tried to stomp out the burst of emotions that flooded my chest, but there was no helping it. It didn't matter that Johnny had been in a much different place when he found Asher than when he left me for the military. Or that the military itself probably instilled values in him that he didn't have before.

Never leave your comrades behind.

The only things I understood about the military were what Johnny had just told me and its core value that was spoken across the country.

It wasn't fair for me to hold this against him anymore. Especially when I wasn't even brave enough to ask why he felt the need to leave when I was only two years behind him. But I couldn't help but think of how if he'd waited, we could have been together all this time.

"Where did you just go?" A deep river formed between his brows.

I forced a smile onto my face as the pit in my stomach continued to grow. "Nowhere."

"I can see it all over your face. Tell me," he urged, his eyes narrowing with concern.

"I was just thinking about the two years after you left and how much I wished I would have found an Asher during that time." The half-truth slid off my tongue easier than I expected.

The crease between his eyes lessened slightly as my response seemed to pacify him. I just hoped he couldn't hear the raging of my heart as it banged against my ribcage.

"I should have been there." The rasp of his voice scraped over my skin as the air grew heavy around us.

I can't go there. Too much hurt. Too many years. Questions upon questions never asked. And never answered. I didn't want tonight to be ruined by ghosts of our past. I wanted to forget those years without him had even existed at all.

"Johnny, it's fine," was all I could manage to say. The words I spoke were in direct conflict with the feelings in my heart. But it didn't matter. I wasn't willing to go there with him. I… couldn't go there with him.

"It's not fine, Lo. I left and—"

"Please"—I gripped his t-shirt in my hands as I squeezed my eyes shut—"don't. I…I can't talk about this right now."

His voice was stern just like it used to get when he was trying to convince me of something he felt was really important. "We're going to have to talk about it sometime."

"No, we're not!" I screeched and Johnny flinched. I lowered my voice and tried to reason with him. "Some things are better left in the past. There's no reason to open old wounds just for the sake of opening them."

The muscles in his face were stone and he was somehow still breathtakingly beautiful—even though I could tell he was fuming beneath his frigid exterior. Flames of determination danced in his eyes and I was sure he was going to continue pushing me.

So, I said, "I asked you for tonight, Johnny. Can you at least give me that before we both try and ruin it?" I felt like I couldn't breathe. Every word was heavy on my tongue.

We stared at one another for what felt like an eternity. Neither one of us was willing to give an inch. We were nothing but stubborn assholes, damned from the start. And somehow fate decided to bring us back together to torture us —or to watch us rip each other apart. It didn't matter if a hundred years had passed, we were still capable of destroying one another more than anyone else could possibly imagine.

"Come here." He stretched his arms toward me and though the same fight burned in his eyes, his gesture was a peace offering. One that I was willing to take.

The feel of his sturdy body wrapped around mine brought me more comfort than I wanted to admit. His heat seeped through my skin, landing deep in my bones. He held me tight, like he was afraid to let go and I hoped he never would.

"We're going to have to fix this at some point, Lo. We can't run away from it."

I didn't have the guts to say that him running away was the very reason I wasn't willing to go there with him.

So I settled for saying, "Okay," as I tightened my hold around his waist.

That little voice in the back of my mind reminded me that there was always the option to seek retribution. But that was the devil's game to play and when you sought out revenge, it was easy to get burned.

CHAPTER THIRTEEN

My mind was a literal cluster fuck. And my body was going through withdrawals from being away from Johnny for more than five hours. He let me get away with avoiding the conversation that I was sure was going to be the end of me. Judging by his pushiness, I knew he wouldn't drop it. If I wanted to continue seeing him, I was going to have to talk about the fact that his leaving me left an imprint on my heart for over a decade.

And the thought of that conversation made me want to puke. *Totally embarrassing.*

Forget that he still had no idea why I'd come back to Pebble Brook Falls and that despite our reconnection, I had every intention of leaving for Nashville in about a week.

Ugh. How did I get myself into this mess? I asked myself. Then I remembered how Johnny's chest would flex under his white t-shirt and how his dimple made my heart sing every time he smiled and the way my entire body tingled when I was in his arms. All it took was a few days and I was in deep. There was no denying that the feelings I had for Johnny when we were younger never dissipated, despite the anger I'd felt towards him for leaving me. He was my person—he always had been and I was quickly coming to terms with the fact that he likely always would be.

My knees bobbed up and down. It was freezing in Mr. Anderson's office, but a coat of sweat covered my neck, trickling down my back. Everything was supposed to be finalized today. I still hadn't gone up to the estate even though the key was nestled in the inside pocket of my purse.

The last time we met, Mr. Anderson said the estate was mine and I was free to do whatever I wanted with it. But it felt like a closet full of skeletons that I didn't want to open. The moment my eyes landed on Adeline Baxley in the park all those years ago was the same moment I realized that my biological grandmother was as wicked as they came. And that day made me wonder what it had been like for my mother to be raised by such a person. Was she just as wicked? Did she silence herself to stay within her mother's good graces? Was she a rebel?

Did she love me?

I wished—more than anything—that I could have talked to her just one time. To hear her voice. Even if she told me that leaving me was the best decision she ever made, I still wanted to hear what she sounded like. Google had become a spiral of detrimental curiosity the two years after Johnny left. Without him around to keep me company, I spent a lot of time researching my mother on the library computers, trying to find anything I could about her life and potential clues as to why she gave me up.

Looking at her photos was like staring into a mirror. She had the same blonde hair with a slight curl that framed her heart-shaped face. The bright blue of her eyes matched my own. The only difference was our noses—where hers was sharper, mine was rounded like a small button. A trait I likely inherited from my father. Who also happened to be a mystery, even more so than my mother.

After my mother's death and the revelation that I was her child came to light, rumors sparked around town as to who my father might have been. The rich kids in school started placing bets, yelling out their bids during lunchtime. Although Johnny's fists had put an end to the bidding war real quick, the sting of those days had taken a long time to heal. And not quite as long as the wounds from others calling my mother a whore and that she deserved to die.

I didn't know her. But that didn't stop me from loving her. Even if she didn't love me back.

Mr. Anderson's door swung open and I was forcefully snapped back to the present. As I rose from the chair on shaky legs, I looked toward the open door and immediately stilled.

Johnny. Except he didn't look like himself. My gaze raked over his body, noting the nuances of his attire that had my mouth watering. A pale green button-down enhanced the yellow flecks of his eyes, making them appear like freshly poured honey. And the silver-gray slacks showed off his tailored waist. As my eyes dipped further, a scarlet blush crept over my face from his obviously large member pressing firmly against the zipper of his slacks. He could have worn a burlap sack and he'd still have trouble hiding just how endowed he was.

"What're you doing here?" I muttered.

His smile made my heartbeat thunder through my veins.

"Mr. Anderson is the only decent lawyer in town and I needed some advice on expanding my store."

"Oh."

He took a step toward me and his brows furrowed. "Wait. Why are *you* here?"

I felt my nose scrunch. "I, uh—"

"Ms. Baxley, I have another appointment after yours and I don't want to get behind schedule today. We should get started." Mr. Anderson interrupted me and my stomach immediately coiled, but I couldn't take my eyes off of Johnny.

Confusion swept over him. "Ms. Baxley? Since when do you use your birth mother's last name?"

"Um—"

"Ms. Baxley." Mr. Anderson's firm tone raked over my nerves and I wanted to yell at him, to tell him to shut up and just give me a minute to fix what was about to be very broken between Johnny and I.

But I wasn't some boisterous New Yorker who laid everything out in the open for everyone to see. I was raised in the South where we kept our mouths shut and swept our feelings under the rug.

"I'm sorry, Johnny. I have to go." The look on his face almost cleaved me in two as I left him in the lobby and followed Mr. Anderson into his office.

The meeting was quick and efficient. Fifteen minutes tops, even though I was sure Adeline's estate was likely paying for a full hour.

Everything was officially mine.

The entire twenty-acre estate with a one-hundred-fifty-year-old house that had ten bedrooms and way too many bathrooms to make sense. I was somehow the owner of a local farm that bred horses for the Kentucky Derby. Oh, and a whopping two-hundred-million dollars.

I was going to throw up.

What the actual hell just happened to my life?

In just a few minutes, I went from being one of the poorest women in town, to the richest. Though I knew Adeline had no love for me, it still didn't feel right knowing that I gained everything at the cost of her life. I would have much preferred for us to have lived separate lives like she had wanted us to all along. Now, for reasons that were completely unknown to me, I was the owner of everything that had once been hers. And the thought of having to go through the estate and seeing the life she stole from me had my stomach twisting in knots.

I needed air and I needed it fast or I was going to make a giant mess in Mr. Anderson's waiting area.

Stumbling toward my freedom, I yanked the door of his building open. I gulped down giant breaths of air, trying my best to get some oxygen to my brain so I could think straight. And that was when I was hit with the all-too-familiar scent of cedar wood.

Johnny rose from his seat at the bottom of the concrete steps that led up to the building. When he turned to face me, I could see the confusion and frustration he'd felt earlier was still very present. He was never one to let things go easily and I doubted this would be any different.

"What's going on, Lo?"

Just as if he were dressed in his blue jeans and flannel, he tucked his hands into his pockets. Relaxed. Comfortable. And somehow he was also commanding. Intimidating. I knew it when I first laid my eyes on him again after twelve years, but the vision before me confirmed it. Johnny was different. He'd grown into exactly who he was always meant to be, a confident man who knew what he wanted in life and demanded that he receive it.

And right now, he wanted me to tell him the truth.

I clamped my lips together. The desire to show that my will was equal to his rose high.

"Nothing. I just had a few legal questions I wanted to ask Mr. Anderson." I glanced at the door behind me as I tried to cool my nerves. "Sarah recommended him to me." I was shocked at how easily the lie slid from my lips.

I'd never lied to Johnny before and the words felt left a burning trail of regret on my tongue.

Johnny took one step up the stairs and my heart rate immediately kicked up. There wasn't a single hint of golden yellow in his irises as he made another move toward me. The lightness was gone like the final sinking of the sun under the horizon.

I took a small step backward and that only made him hasten his approach. Within a second, he was standing right in front of me. My chest nearly rubbed against his. A muscle ticked in his jaw and I knew he was biting his tongue.

I craned my neck back so I could meet his stormy eyes. Johnny might have changed. But so did I. I wasn't the young, insecure girl who needed his protection from all the people who'd done me wrong. When he left me to pursue his own endeavors, I gave myself the grace to mourn the loss of him, of us. And then I picked myself up, got my ass to work, and made something of myself—without him. As much as I felt my heart open to him last night and as much as the desire to be close to him made it difficult to breathe when we were apart, I didn't owe him anything. If I wanted to tell him what was going on, I would do it because *I* wanted to.

"You're beautiful, smart as hell, witty, and a royal pain in my ass. But you have never been a liar, Lo. Stop playing this stupid game and tell me what the hell is going on. Why did Mr. Anderson call you Ms. Baxley?"

Heat flooded through my veins as my conflicting thoughts bombarded me. His closeness wasn't helping since my stupid body wouldn't stop reacting to him.

I didn't have to tell him about Adeline signing everything to me in her will. Or that I was petrified to walk through that house and see everything I'd missed out on—including time with my mother. But my equally stupid heart kept pulling at me. Quietly nudging me to be honest. That, despite everything that had changed about Johnny, he was still the boy I fell in love with. The one I could trust with my heart, even though he'd been the only one capable of breaking it.

"I really don't want to do this with you, Jonny."

I could feel his hand move before I felt it against the side of my neck and along the edge of my jaw. There was no helping the rush of emotion that assaulted my heart. He would always be my salvation...and my weakness.

"Let me help. Please." His voice was rough, laced with concern that had all my walls crumbling.

I pressed my face into his palm, savoring the way his calloused hands were somehow gentle when he touched me.

I sighed deeply. "This isn't something you can fix."

"Let me try."

Those three little words broke through the last bit of my barrier. "I don't even know where to begin."

He stroked comforting circles along my neck with the pad

of his finger while his other hand snaked around my middle until it rested on the small of my back. It was all I needed to move forward.

"I'm sure that you heard the news that Adeline passed away three months ago."

He nodded, his strong hands continuing to soothe the fire roaring beneath my skin.

"After the news of her passing settled, I received a phone call from Mr. Anderson telling me that Adeline had bequeathed everything to me."

Johnny's eyebrows shot up in surprise, but he remained quiet.

"Yeah." I snorted. "That's exactly how I felt when he called me. It took him over thirty minutes to convince me that it was my name on the will.

"None of it made sense seeing as how the Baxleys had chosen to remove me from the family when they gave me up to the orphanage. Somehow, Adeline decided to put my name on the papers and now everything is being transferred over to me."

Johnny took a deep breath in, his nostrils flaring. "You're sure it's real and not just some final way for her to make you miserable?"

"I'm sure." I reached for the lone silver key in the back pocket of my purse and showed it to him. "I just signed the final papers. The estate, the farm, the money. It's all in my name now."

"Holy shit."

"I know."

The hand he had nestled against my neck slid down over

my shoulder and rested there. "How're you feeling about everything?"

I blew out a breath. "So many things it's hard to sort through all the emotions. Part of me feels really thankful that I'm being paid what I feel like I'm owed. I would have much preferred for them to have accepted me into their family, despite how I was brought into the world." I shook my head in disbelief at everything that had transpired regarding the Baxleys. "Maybe this was Adeline's way of apologizing."

Johnny's face hardened. "I don't think that woman was ever capable of saying she was wrong."

"You're probably right," I sighed.

We stood there for a few moments, a comfortable silence settling in before I said, "Regardless of why she decided to do it, I'm thankful she did. Now I'll have the ability to open my own boutique like I've always wanted. I had a plan to save up for it in the next six to ten years, but now I can make my dream happen a lot sooner."

"Are you opening it downtown?"

"No, in Nash—" I immediately stopped myself, but it was too late.

"Nashville?" Johnny's hand slipped off me. He stayed exactly where he was, but the loss of contact was startling and the look of disappointment on his face had my walls shooting sky high.

"That's where I live now." The words were dusty in my mouth like the simple fact that I lived in Nashville meant that it was the only place I could ever be.

"And this has been your plan all along? To come to get the money and fool around with me just to turn around and leave?" The veins in his neck exposed the rising anger I knew was boiling just beneath the surface.

"I didn't even know you were back in Pebble Brook Falls, Johnny. Seeing you was never part of the plan."

He rolled his eyes which royally pissed me off because I was telling the truth. Johnny was the last person I thought would have come back to our hometown and seeing him had thrown me for such a loop, I almost ran all the way back to Nashville without a penny in my hand.

"But you did see me, Willow. And we started something. Something I thought I'd lost forever and now you're telling me that your plan was always to take the money and leave. You knew, every second that we were together, that you were going to head back to Nashville. You didn't think that was important for me to know before you let me kiss you?" His voice rose slightly and I could sense the pain hiding behind every word he spoke.

But I was hurting too.

"I didn't plan for any of this to happen. I didn't plan for Adeline to write my name into her will. Or to ever come back to Pebble Brook Falls and realize that maybe it wasn't so bad. Or to miss my best friend so much that every time I see her, it makes me second-guess my decision to be so far away. And I definitely didn't plan to run into you. The one person I hoped I would never see again."

His eyes went wide as my chest heaved up and down. A sense of relief and panic shot through me. Relief that I'd said everything on my heart and panic for the exact same reason.

I expected Johnny to say something. To yell at me or turn around and walk away. What I did not expect was for him to thread his fingers through my hair and press his lips against mine with such force, it had my knees buckling from the intensity. I opened for him, letting him take everything he needed because I needed it just as badly.

In that moment, we were two broken souls desperate to be put back together again. Knowing that neither one of us had the answers, but each of us hoped we could discover them together.

And the second our lips parted, anger took hold of us again. Anchoring itself deep, making it nearly impossible to move forward.

"You're breaking my heart, Lo. You've shown me a glimpse of the wish I've hoped for every day for the past twelve years and now you want to take it away."

Tears stung my eyes, making me angrier. "You broke my heart first!" I seether. "The second you walked away from me. You promised! You promised that we would never leave one another and the second you had a taste of freedom you went back on your word."

The small muscle along the back of his jaw ticked wildly. "You think I wanted to leave you? To leave *us*? I phased out of the orphanage, Willow. There was nowhere for me to go. Did you want me to end up like my parents?"

"No!" I sobbed. The tears flowed freely down my face. Tears of anger, frustration, and hurt.

"That's exactly what would have happened if I stayed in Pebble Brook Falls. I joined the Marines to make something of myself. To do better so I could become a man who actually deserved someone like you." His voice cracked and his admission should have disarmed me. But the hurt I'd buried deep was surfacing with a vengeance.

"You could have taken me with you. Or waited until I

phased out too. You could have done anything but leave me, Johnny. *Anything.*"

He raked a hand through his hair as his head hung low. The strong man I knew he'd become was crumbling before my eyes.

But I couldn't stop.

"I loved you, Johnny," I whispered. "I loved you with all my heart and you *left* me."

Chills climbed over my skin as he slowly lifted his head and squared his shoulders.

"Well, I guess I deserve what I'm getting then, huh?"

Like an arrow straight to my heart, my chest squeezed painfully as fresh tears rolled over my damp cheeks. I didn't know how long I stood there, replaying the image of Johnny walking down those three steps and out of my line of sight.

Just like he did all those years ago.

CHAPTER FOURTEEN

Two full days had passed since Johnny and I had our fight outside of Mr. Anderson's office. I'd moped around Sarah's house and ate way too many of her desserts until I finally picked myself up and decided to be productive. Time was dwindling and if I wanted to get back to Nashville in time to meet with some of the shop owners to discuss leases, I needed to make some progress.

"Are you sure you don't want me to go with you?" Sarah asked as both of us stared out of her car door's window at the long paved road that led to the biggest house I'd ever seen. All of it was partially hidden behind a giant iron gate that swirled with decorative patterns around an obscenely large letter B.

I had no idea where my given last name of Mae came from. Ms. Mosely had always called me Willow Mae when I got into trouble so I assumed that was the name my parents had chosen for me before they left me with her. But once it came out that I was in fact a Baxley, I swore off the surname that belonged to Southern royalty. It was a futile attempt to display some sense of control as my world was ripped apart.

As I looked up at the giant first letter of my true last name, strange emotions clouded my thoughts. A sense of belonging was taking hold of me even though I knew with all my heart that I didn't belong in this messed up family who left their own to fend for themselves.

I was slowly learning to accept the conflict within me. The battling thoughts and emotions. This was going to be a waking nightmare and I had to be okay with that.

I turned to look at Sarah. "I'm sure."

She gave me a tight-lipped smile and placed a hand on my shoulder. "I have my phone turned all the way up, so call me if you need anything."

I grabbed her hand and gave it a squeeze. "Thanks, Sarah."

With a deep breath, I climbed out of her car and stood face to face with my harsh reality. For the briefest moment, I wished Johnny was here with me. Holding my hand, providing comfort that only he was capable of giving me. My chest squeezed as the image of him walking away yesterday played out in my mind.

I immediately stomped out the emotion that swelled in my heart.

Today wasn't about Johnny. It was about me.

I opened my purse and took out the gate remote and the small silver key. With the press of a button, the large gates swung inward, the B splitting in half. And for the first time in my life, I stepped onto my family's property. The long straight path to the house was lined with giant oak trees, so huge they must have been over one hundred years old. Tendrils of gray-colored moss hung low from the branches. Not a single leaf littered the immaculate lawn that I imagined took a fortune to maintain. It was the greenest grass I'd ever seen in Pebble Brook Falls and there wasn't a single blade out of place.

My heart flooded with feelings of sorrow for the little girl I wished I could have been. Dressed in a pale blue summer dress, running around the trees playing hide-and-seek with my mother. Spending our summer days sipping on sweet tea while she taught me how to play card games during our daily picnics. It would have been a beautiful life. Or at least that's what I told myself.

Either way, it was a life that I would never have the chance to live.

I blinked against the frustrated tears that started to build and continued my walk along the path, letting go of all that could have been and trying to focus on what was right in front of me.

The house was essentially a small castle. Tall white pillars lined the front porch where a few rocking chairs and double-seated benches sat with small round tables between them. A single chandelier hung low in front of the door that certainly doubled my height of five feet and six inches. Long, rectangular windows sat about every five feet on each level with black shutters on each side. It was a home meant for a Southern Queen and there wasn't a doubt in my mind that Adeline had lived up to that very expectation.

The sheer size of everything was overwhelming and somehow made me feel claustrophobic, like I needed to escape. At the same time, I felt a strong curiosity. It was all so beautiful and perfect and I felt pulled to discover what was hiding behind the closed wooden door.

I tried to will away the shaking in my hand as I fumbled

with the key in the lock, but it was no use. After a few tries, the key finally slid into the lock and I swung the door open.

My eyes went wide as I stepped into the foyer. Deep red panels of wood lined the floor, their shiny lacquer reflecting the natural light coming in from the windows. I gazed upward where the ceiling went as high as the roof, over thirty feet tall at least. Another crystal chandelier hung right in front of the door, with hundreds of pieces of glass circling the lightbulbs.

To my right stood a really long wooden table that had a decorative bowl sitting in between two matching white vases with swirls of blue lining them.

I took another step into the house, shutting the door behind me. The air was cool compared to the sweltering heat outside and I imagined it cost a fortune to have the air conditioner run in a place like this.

I took my time moving through the long hallway that had several doors on each side. There wasn't a speck of dust on the entryway table or along the floor, even though Adeline had passed away months ago. She'd likely set up some sort of cleaning routine for the estate until I'd signed the papers or something.

Eventually, I made my way to the back of the house where a large living room and kitchen sat before three sets of French double doors that led to the back gardens, from what I could see through the glass panels. I explored the living room first where a cream-colored sectional faced an oversized fireplace where a fresh bundle of wood was nestled neatly in the hearth. My gaze trailed upward where a painted portrait of two women hung above the mantel.

They were both blonde with bright blue eyes. The older woman appeared stern-looking with her hardened gaze and sharp cheekbones. Something told me there was a story behind those eyes. One buried so deep, the woman likely forgot the details of it. Adeline's classic beauty was unmatched. She looked like an old Hollywood movie star with her white-blonde ringlets framing her face. The aloofness her features conveyed made her seem mysterious and desirable. It made sense that she carried the Baxley name so well.

My heart skipped a beat as I directed my attention to the woman sitting to the left and a little below her.

Melanie Baxley—my mother.

This must have been painted when she was just a teenager because her face was a little rounder than I'd seen it in the papers following her death. While her smile was still demure, there appeared to be a glint in her eyes of mischievousness. As though, like her mother, she was also hiding a secret, playful in nature. Her features resembled her mother's with her high cheekbones and sharp nose. However, the simple white dress she wore didn't seem to match her personality. It was too pure, too pristine for the chaos she caused that ultimately led to me.

I stared at both of them until I felt my calve muscles strain against the lack of blood flow. Silent questions roamed through my mind about the two women in that painting. But I stowed them away for now. There was a lot of work to be done and I wouldn't get anywhere if I stood around all day.

A tall winding staircase sat off of the living room, the steps matching the hardwood all throughout the house. Each panel creaked beneath my feet as I ascended the steps to the second level where another long halfway extended in both directions.

I'd eventually get through the entire house, but something was leading me to the right.

It appeared this was the bedroom floor because each door I opened hid an immaculate guest bedroom with an adjoining bathroom. Adeline was apparently into themes seeing as how each bedroom was different but still maintained a sense of class. At the very end of the hall was the final door. The moment my hand touched the handle, I felt a whoosh of anxiety course through my veins. Something told me this room would be different and as soon as the door opened, I knew it was true.

The room was huge. It had more space than Sarah's living room and kitchen combined. Placed between two large windows was a white, king-sized canopy bed with black chiffon material draped over the top and down each poster. Across from the bed was a beautiful vanity with a set of pearls hanging off the side of the mirror and a few pictures tucked in along the edges. I swallowed hard, my heartbeat thrumming in my ears as I walked toward the vanity.

Unlike the rest of the house so far, this room appeared to be untouched for a very long time as a thick layer of dust covered the vanity's surface and all the materials on it. An open container of blush lay to the right, the brush a few inches away. Several lipsticks were scattered across the surface as though she had tried on several shades to find the perfect look.

I leaned closer, looking at the photographs. Each of them showed my mother at various events with other people who looked her age. In every single one, her eyes were bright, her head tilted back slightly as she laughed.

She looked so different from Adeline, despite their

features being incredibly similar. The pictures showed how full of life she was and it made me wonder about the portrait downstairs. How she was likely forced to wear something completely out of her true nature to portray that she belonged to the Baxley name.

It made me sad for her and for myself for making so many negative assumptions about her.

Just as I went to explore more of her room, a black leather notebook caught my eye. Peeking out from one of the vanity drawers that hadn't been closed all the way. My fingers burned to reach for it, though I knew it was wrong to invade her privacy, even after death.

Then again, it wasn't like she was here to be upset with me.

Curiosity won out by a mile as I slid open the drawer and pulled out the small book. Her initials were imprinted on the front. With a swipe of my hand, dust flew off the cover, floating toward the floor.

Should I open it? Now that it was in my hands, I questioned myself again. *Do I really want to know what's inside?*

Yes. I think I do.

The notebook may have been empty, or it could have been filled with my mother's heart. Filled with things that I would never know about her unless I read it. It was wrong and terrible but neither of those things prevented me from cracking open the cover to discover her name written in her handwriting on the first page.

I ran my fingers over the swirly letters, noticing how her penmanship looked strangely similar to my own. With a flick of my thumb, I fanned through the pages, noticing how each one was filled to the brim with her words. I sat down on the floor next to the vanity, my back against the wall as I propped the journal up on my knees and started reading.

I hate her. More than anything on God's green earth. I hate her. I don't understand why she has to control every single piece of me. I can't wear the clothes I want to. I can only hang out with people she approves of. Sometimes it feels like I can't breathe when she's around. When she looks at me, I know she's criticizing every little thing I do. Sometimes I wonder why she even had me. It's not like this family hasn't hidden other deadly sins. One day, I hope I'm brave enough to tell her exactly how I feel. Even though I know she'll do whatever it takes to break me, just like she does the wild stallions born on our farm.

Page after page, my mother wrote about her disdain for Adeline. How she felt smothered by her own mother's inability to see her for who she truly was. It made me sick to my stomach thinking about how trapped she must have felt having another person dictate every aspect of her life.

I could see myself in her words, remembering what it was like to walk down the halls of my middle and high school where the other kids only saw me for the clothes I wore on my back and not the person I was. There was no way into the friend groups that controlled the school. Even Sarah had to give up her status to befriend me. A price she told me, again and again, didn't matter. But I always questioned if she truly thought our friendship was worth it after she became a victim of their bullying as well.

I flipped through a few more pages of the same story until I noticed the narrative started to shift from Adeline to a nameless boy.

He's the best thing that's ever happened to me. When I'm with him, I feel free. Like nothing in the world matters except the two of us. I don't care that my mother hates the idea of him. Or how she calls him white trash every time I say his name. He doesn't care either and that's one of the reasons I love him so much. He may have been born without a penny to his name, but he knows how to live. Every day, he teaches me something new about the world. He's opened my eyes to countless possibilities and I want to do everything with him by my side. I just hope she won't destroy us like she destroys everything else in my life.

He was clearly a boy that Adeline didn't approve of, which likely pushed my mother to only fall harder for him.

The next twenty or so pages were a love letter to him. Passion and adoration were written into every single word. It seemed their love grew quickly. So similar and yet different to how Johnny and I grew together.

Damnit.

Just the thought of his name brought a host of emotions that I didn't want to feel—at least not right now. I glanced out the window next to her bed and noticed the sun was starting to fade. I must have been here for a few hours already. My butt bones were aching from sitting on the hard floor and Sarah would be on her way soon to pick me up for dinner. I rose from my spot, leaning to each side to stretch my sore muscles out and as I went to head back downstairs I accidentally dropped her journal, the pages splaying open.

As I bent down to pick it up, I swore my heart stopped beating in my chest when I read the first line on the opened page.

I have to protect her. Well…I'm not completely certain the baby is a 'her' yet, but I can feel it in my bones even if I haven't had the gender reveal appointment yet. I have to admit, it's been difficult. First, I had to end things with him, which nearly destroyed me and now I'll have to say goodbye to my baby girl.

It's for the best though. In a world where there's a judgmental prick behind every corner, she'd suffer for the entirety of her life. Never feeling like she belonged because when the people in my world see someone who looks different, someone who might threaten their sense of security, they strike like a snake in the grass. Their fangs hit deep, while they stay hidden under the cover of wealth and good names. The Baxley name wouldn't be enough to protect her from the venom of propriety. And especially not from my mother. I'm surprised she even let me stay under her roof knowing that I'd damaged my reputation by getting pregnant out of wedlock.

I guess I should thank her for giving me and my baby a roof over our heads. Even if she did hide me away like I have leprosy.

Only six more months and my baby will be free of this world.

Protect me? I slammed the journal shut as disbelief rolled over me in crashing waves. She thought abandoning me, leaving me to the whims of the world would make me better off than keeping me close and protecting me from her world herself? Maybe I was wrong all along if Adeline had been the one to write me into her will while my own mother decided to give me up because of her own delusional beliefs.

I looked at the photos that lined her mirror again. It seemed clear to me that she simply wanted freedom. Not just from the life her mother had her lead, but from me as well. The lies she told herself in her journal did nothing for me but confirm that my mother was always exactly who I thought she was—a selfish woman who only thought about herself.

CHAPTER FIFTEEN

I somehow managed to convince Sarah that I was totally and completely fine when she picked me up. Or maybe she was just giving me more time to process everything that happened in that house before we talked about it. Either way, I was thankful to keep the spotlight on her as she talked about her recent success from the Summer Festival while she stirred the pasta sauce she'd made us for dinner.

"I still can't believe the Jacksons want me to cater little Tommy's birthday party. They usually hire one of the big companies out of Chatanooga or Atlanta to do all of their events, but Mrs. Jackson said she loved my cupcakes so much she couldn't have anyone else make the sweets for her son's birthday."

I envied Sarah's glow and enthusiasm. While I was genuinely ecstatic for my best friend, I couldn't help but hear of her happiness and wish that some of it would rub off on me.

"That's amazing, Sarah," I responded with just enough

mustered joy that was necessary to mask my foul mood. "When is his birthday?"

Keep distracting her, I thought with the hopes that maybe I would become distracted too.

"Not until September, but she promised that she would reach out to me when she started planning. I don't think she would go to all that trouble of saying she wanted me to cater it if she didn't actually want me to, right?"

"Definitely not." I shook my head. "Those kinds of people don't waste their time telling others what they want to hear. Just like she said, when she starts to plan I'm sure she'll reach out to you."

She clapped her hands together and did a little hop. "Yay! She will be my first elite client." Sarah blew out an exasperated whoosh of breath. "I knew it would be tough to get people's buy-in, especially since my parents don't exactly support me doing this. I just can't believe that it's actually happening."

I tried. I really did try to shuttle out my thoughts and focus on Sarah's big accomplishment. But the second she mentioned having her first elite client, I couldn't help but be bombarded with overwhelming emotions about the past three days.

"So, what do you think?" Sarah's voice pummeled through my thoughts.

"Think about what?" I asked.

The corners of her mouth tugged downward and I could see the look of disappointment creep over her face. I was being a shitty friend and we both knew it.

"About the theme...for little Tommy's birthday party. I

asked what you thought about doing Iron Man themed cupcakes with little fondant helmets."

"That sounds like a really cool idea, Sarah. I think any kid would love to have something like that."

The way her forehead wrinkled and her brows drew together told me she didn't buy it.

I dragged my hands over my face and peeked at her over the tops of my fingertips. "I'm sorry," I dragged out the words. "I know I've been terrible and woe is me about everything lately. I can't focus on anything but my own stuff and that's shitty, Sarah." I stuck my bottom lip out. "I promise I'll do better."

When she glared at me I pushed my bottom lip out further and she couldn't help but laugh. "You're right. You have been a terrible friend lately. And it has been all about you." She looked up at the ceiling as her head bobbed side to side. "But...you do have a lot going on so I guess I can forgive you."

I smiled widely at her and she rolled her eyes at me. "Okay," she sighed dramatically. "Tell me what's going on."

I drug my top lip into my mouth with my teeth, then let it go as I sucked in a breath. "Mmm. Which one should we start with? Johnny or my mother?"

Her eyebrows lifted slightly. "I thought everything was going well with you and Johnny?"

I shook my head. "Nope."

"Geez, girl. You need to figure your shit out."

I threw my hands in the air. "Now you know why I've been distracted.

"Okay. Let's start with Johnny."

I started with how he brought me to our place the night of the Summer Festival and we both gushed over the kiss. Then I told her about running into him at Mr. Anderson's office and how it very quickly turned into a mess and Johnny, once again walked away from me.

"Yikes."

"Yeah."

"Why do you both feel the need to put one another through the wringer so much?"

"If I knew the answer to that question, I probably wouldn't be in this situation."

Sarah crossed her arms and mulled over everything I'd just told her. "Can I ask you something?"

"Of course." I had a feeling that I wasn't going to like what she was about to ask, but I also knew she would ask even if I told her no.

"Why didn't you just tell Johnny from the beginning that you were only here for a short period of time? Not that you had to explain the entire story of being here to get the estate sorted out, but you've had several opportunities to let him know you aren't planning on staying in Pebble Brook Falls."

Yup. I was right. I didn't like her question at all. I thought it over for a minute because the truth was that I actually wasn't sure of the answer. I'd been asking myself the same question since we had that argument outside of Mr. Anderson's office.

"I think in the beginning, that very first day when I saw Johnny, I was just in shock. I mean I could hardly get two words out before I just ran away from him. And each time we hung out after that, it just felt so good to be around him and I didn't want to spoil that. Don't get me wrong. There were definitely times when I knew I should have brought it up, but it was so nice to be near him again once the nerves of seeing him settled. And I'd fooled myself into thinking that I could let myself have that time with him without there being any need to complicate things."

It was true. Seeing Johnny made everything feel more complicated and it might have been wrong to keep my short stay a secret, but I just wanted something to feel simple. In a matter of a few months, I'd gone from a single girl trying to make her way in life to an heiress who ran into the love of her life after he abandoned her.

The more Johnny and I hung out, the easier it was to pretend like the past twelve years hadn't happened and we were able to pick up where we left off before everything got messed up.

"Have you talked to him since everything happened?"

A sinking feeling hit low in my stomach. "No. I was hoping he would have texted me by now or something. But he hasn't."

Sarah slowly shrugged her shoulders. "I think this one might be on you, Willow. If he'd kept something like that from you, especially after you both let things go so far, I'd say that it would totally be his responsibility to fix things. But this was a secret that *you* kept from him, so you should probably be the one to make amends."

Her words were like a slap across the face. Not because she was wrong. But because I knew she was right and that pissed me off.

Yes, I probably should have told Johnny that I was here for a very limited time before I let things go too far. At the same time, I'd told him just how devastated I'd been when he left and his only response was that he had no other choice. I'd spent years of my life praying I would one day have the opportunity to tell him how much pain he'd caused me in hopes that he'd be able to take some of that pain away. What transpired at Mr. Anderson's office was the complete opposite of how I wanted that situation to play out and it still stung every time I thought about it.

"I don't even know what the point of making amends would be since I'm leaving soon. Johnny has his store here in Pebble Brook Falls and I already have meetings set up with store owners in Nashville. I can't imagine either one of us wanting to do the long-distance thing."

"That's true. But do you really want to leave here without making things right?"

It was a valid question. And one I didn't have an immediate answer to.

"I don't even know what I would say," I whispered.

"Maybe just start with an apology and then let him know exactly how you feel."

The thought of apologizing to him right now was beyond what I was capable of. But the more I thought about it, Sarah made a good point. I didn't want to leave things the way they were now and go back to Nashville with nothing but regret.

"You're right. I think I do need to at least try to talk to him so I don't leave with anything I might regret. I already spent too long keeping my mouth shut and never saying what was on my heart the first time he left. I don't want another decade to go by feeling the same way."

"That's fair and I think if anything, it will give you a little bit of closure knowing you didn't leave anything unsaid."

I couldn't help but think to myself that closure wasn't what I wanted with Johnny. But the idea of everything working out between us seemed impossible. Fairytales didn't exist in my world. I wasn't some special princess who would get everything she'd ever wanted in the end. Life just didn't work that way, especially for someone like me.

I kept all of that to myself though. Honestly, I was tired of talking about Johnny and me. I felt like a broken record having spent the past week whining about how he left me and how we couldn't be together now because I would be heading back to Nashville soon. I was stronger than that and somehow I'd let my emotions get the best of me lately. That's not how I made a life for myself at eighteen years old. How I was able to pull myself up by my bootstraps time and time again when it seemed like the entire world was out to get me. I was strong and no matter how much it would hurt to leave, it was the only option I had if I wanted to pursue the life I'd worked so hard for.

"You're right. I don't want to leave with a chip on my shoulder. I'll talk to Johnny and clear the air so we can both move on with our lives."

A look passed over Sarah's face like she knew something I didn't. "Good," she said with a mockingly stern tone. "Onward to the next debacle. I knew you thought you could hide it from me, but the second you walked out of that house I could tell something bad happened. I was just waiting for you to sort through it before I pushed too hard. But I think enough time has gone by now," she challenged as she waved the pasta fork in the air. "Out with it."

"It's only been two hours," I chuckled.

Sarah put one hand on her hip and held the other hand with the pasta fork out to her side as she raised a brow at me. "Two hours is *plenty* of time."

"Pshh. Yeah, okay."

She started dishing out the sauce and pasta in two bowls

before lifting one in the air toward me. Just as I went to grab it from her she yanked it back. "Nah uh uh. No homemade pasta for Willow Mae until she fesses up."

"Okay, the fact that you're willing to hold my pasta hostage is an unforgivable offense."

"Do you promise to spill?" she asked, continuing to hold the bowl away from me.

My stomach grumbled loudly. As much as I did *not* want to go there right now, there were very few things...Okay...More like absolutely nothing that would get between me and a bowl of pasta. It was my weakness and Sarah was using it against me like kryptonite against Superman.

"Yes!" I reached for the bowl, wiggling my fingertips and she finally caved, extending the bowl toward me.

"Come to momma," I mused over the bowl of red sauce and noodles. I shoveled a few bites into my mouth as Sarah laughed at me. Once the pains in my stomach started to ease, I set the bowl down on the counter and wiped my mouth.

I looked up at Sarah who had an expectant look on her face.

I rolled my eyes. "Hold on a sec." I left for her guest bedroom and grabbed the leather journal off my nightstand.

When I came back into the kitchen I set it on the island before wrapping my hands around the bowl of pasta again. But before I took another bite I said, "You know how people say never meet your hero?"

"Yeah..." She tilted her head at me.

"Well, I'm pretty sure the saying transfers to mothers who abandoned you at birth as well."

"I'm confused. How could you have met your mom when she's dead?"

I gave her a dumbfounded look and she simply shrugged. "What? It's true!"

"Valid point." We both laughed awkwardly realizing that maybe talking about the dead with such looseness might not be the best idea.

I took another bite and then opened the journal to the page I'd read last, handing it to Sarah. Her gaze darted back and forth as she skimmed over the page before she looked up at me, eyes wide.

"Oh my God," she breathed. "You read through this?"

I didn't have to see my face to know my cheeks were crimson. "I know I probably shouldn't—"

Sarah shook her head vehemently. "No, Willow. I didn't mean it like that. I was just thinking that it must have been hard. If I were in your shoes I would have read it too. At least to get an idea of what she was like."

"That's the only reason I opened it. This entire time I've only wanted one thing from them—to know them. Especially her. And the journal was right there in her untouched room. Almost like it was waiting for me. But after I read that page I realized I was better off not knowing her at all."

Sarah looked back to the journal, rereading the page I'd opened it to.

"Was there something more that you saw than this? It seems like she really wanted to shelter you from her mom."

"Shelter me? I don't know how you get that at all. It seems more like she wanted to get rid of me so she could go on living her prestigious life."

"Willow...I don't think that's right." Sarah's voice was gentle, like she was trying to calm the storm she saw raging beneath the surface.

I crossed my arms, layering my wall brick by brick.

"I mean, she literally wrote *I have to protect her*. And it was her journal. It's not like it was a news clipping or something. I doubt she would lie to herself in her own journal."

"Maybe it was the lie she told herself to make herself feel better for giving me up. And you should have seen the house, Sarah. There were like twenty bedrooms. It's not like keeping me would have even been a bother, especially since they would probably have gotten an in-home nanny. The only reason Melanie wanted to give me up was so that she could go on pretending like she didn't make a huge mistake."

Sarah's mouth popped open, then she clamped it shut, her lips forming a thin line.

I felt frustration bubble up. I was nearing the end of my tolerance for these conversations. First, Johnny, and now this. There was no part of me that could have anticipated this much happening in such a short period of time. All of it was becoming too much.

I should have told Sarah I didn't want to talk about it anymore, but I was in fight mode now. "I know you want to say something, so just say it."

It took her a few moments to decide whether or not she wanted to actually say what was on her mind. And then, "I think you are being a little hard on her and that some of your biases against people with wealth are preventing you from being able to open up and move forward."

I did my best to take a deep breath to calm myself, but my chest barely rose with the shallow inhales. "Bias against wealthy people? Are you kidding me, Sarah?"

Her normally soft features turned to stone. This was the unspoken battle we'd had since we were kids. I was the poor orphan and she was the rich kid who liked to rebel against her parents.

"No. I'm not kidding you. Just because your mother's family had money doesn't mean she didn't struggle with other things." She picked up the journal and let it fall back to the countertop with a smack. "It's clear that *her* mother prevented her from living the life she wanted. And that's something *you* will never understand. To be caged in an ivory castle filled with the finest things. It's no better than struggling because you're poor."

"At least you could afford food and shelter in that gilded cage, Sarah."

"Sometimes the pain of losing your freedom and sense of self is worse than having an empty belly."

"I can't believe you just said that," I seethed.

"And I can't believe that for someone who says they're accepting of people who are different from you, that you can't see the truth of what's right in front of you."

I blinked at her, feeling my blood boil. There was so much more I wanted to say but I knew none of it was good. So, I grabbed my bowl of pasta and stayed in her guest room for the rest of the night.

CHAPTER SIXTEEN

It was the first fight we'd had since we were teenage girls. And this one was worse than any of the ones before because it highlighted just how different we were in our thoughts and that scared me. If we argued about something like this, I worried that it meant we might fight about other things too. Sarah was my best friend and even if it meant agreeing to disagree, I wanted to make things right. I just hoped she did too because a life without Johnny was bad enough. I couldn't even imagine what it would feel like to walk through life without both of them.

With the final words we'd said to one another, I'd taken my bowl of pasta and retreated into her guest bedroom for the rest of the night. By the time I woke up this morning, she was already gone for the day. After about thirty minutes of rolling around in bed, replaying the events over the past few days I decided some sunshine might help...even if it was over ninety degrees out. I'd meandered through the downtown streets, making sure to steer clear of Sarah's Bakery for the time being, and by the end of my walk, I'd found myself in front of The Roasted Bean.

Johnny was nowhere in sight even though he'd told me how much he frequented the small cafe. Part of me hoped I would walk in and find him sipping on a black coffee, while a bigger part of me felt thankful I had the place to myself. I wasn't quite ready to fix that mess and I honestly didn't know if there was a point in fixing it. I was leaving in a matter of days to make the meetings I set with several store owners to find a space for my boutique.

I found a small table in the corner and was working on latte number two while I sketched out some designs for a spring collection. The pencil flowed effortlessly over the thick page as I got lost in the work. It was one of the only things in my life that freed my mind from all its troubles. Sketching had kept me sane during those first few years after Johnny left. A lifeline thrown to me from only God knew who—it was a distraction at the best of times and my salvation at the worst of times. But as I paused to take in the sketch of the floral sundress filled with sunflowers, the only thing I could think of was Johnny's lips as he kissed me for the first time in years. Closing my eyes, I could feel the softness of his lips pressed against mine just before our carnal need took over and we breathlessly devoured one another.

God, I miss him. Miss that. The closeness and the feeling of home every time he was near.

"Wow, that's really beautiful."

Jolted from my thoughts I looked up to see who had paid me the compliment. Anxiety flared as I came face-to-face with Melody Carnelle.

Today is going so well for me, I thought as I tried not to roll my eyes at her.

"Thank you," I murmured through tight lips. I couldn't tell yet if she was being sarcastic or if she genuinely liked my sketch.

"I had no idea how talented you are."

And there it was. The backhanded side of the compliment. Doused in true Southern fashion, Melody had always been an expert of the *Bless Your Heart* wordplay ever since we were young girls.

Images of her and her clique of viper friends walking over to my lunch table just to say something nasty flitted through my mind like a horror film. I tried to stomp out the instinctual feeling to throw my iced latte in her face for all the times she'd made me cry. My hand twitched and my mind reeled with the image of muddy-looking milk draining down her face. The thought brought a small smile to my lips because she deserved that and so much more for the years she tortured me and every other poor soul who didn't fit into her group.

"I knew you were back in town when I saw you here with Johnny Moore last week. But you ran off so quickly I didn't have time to say hello." The saccharine notes of her too-sweet voice were like nails on a chalkboard. It was so strange how she sounded exactly like every other debutante in our class from high school. I wondered if their etiquette teachers had trained them all to sound like the same Stepford wife or if it was just bred into them.

When I was silent she pulled out the chair opposite of mine and asked, "Do you mind if I sit with you?"

Yes.

"No, that's fine."

149

Damn Southern propriety.

With a practiced swipe of her delicate hand, she tossed the long curly locks of her dark brown hair over her shoulder before she set her to-go coffee cup on the table. I tried to get my shoulders to relax, but I was waiting for the blow she always landed with expert precision. After a few seconds of us sitting in silence, taking one another in, my shoulders dropped a fraction of an inch. Maybe she wasn't a total shithead now or maybe she was toying with me as though she were the cat and I were the mouse about to be caught in her claws.

Just before the silence between us turned awkward Melody said, "I'm sorry to hear about your grandmother's passing." It was the last words I thought anyone would say to me since Adeline was only my grandmother by blood. But Melody had been raised with a silver spoon in her mouth and apparently, had the manners to match. Even if there was some flexibility in when she thought someone deserved to be on the receiving end of her politeness.

I shrugged. "She wasn't really a grandmother to me, but I appreciate your condolences."

Her ruby-red lips pulled back slightly, the ends curving upward and my entire body immediately tensed. "You know we were almost cousins right?"

I narrowed my gaze on her. *Where was she going with this?*

"It's true," she said matter-of-factly before taking a quick sip of her coffee. "Before your mother died, she was engaged to my Uncle Henry. Their wedding was only a month away before she died. Such a terrible tragedy for a woman that beautiful and rich to die so young." There was no kindness in Melody's baby-blue irises as she spoke.

Old, tangled memories surfaced in my mind as I thought back to the news coverage of my mother's death. Everything had happened so quickly, it was hard to tease apart the timeline. But somehow my brain had filed away the briefest, and at the time, any insignificant memory of Johnny and I watching the news story unfold whenever Ms. Mosely left her office. The news anchor had talked about the boating accident and how Melanie Baxley's fiance was devastated by what happened.

I never thought to look up who her fiance had been. Probably because I was too shocked to find out that my mother had been alive for my entire life, up until her untimely death.

But the thought of being cousins with Melody Carnelle had my stomach twisting in knots. I could only imagine what would have happened if my mother had married this Henry guy before she died. Adeline would likely have given the estate to him and I'd probably be back in Nashville working double shifts to save up enough money to open my boutique ten years from now.

My throat went dry as that realization settled over me. Then I turned my attention back to the venomous serpent sitting before me.

"Do you have a point in telling me this, Melody?"

That shimmer of fake kindness flickered in her eyes, replaced completely with utter disdain as she leaned forward, her voice lowering, "I just wanted to let you know how relieved I am that your mother died before my uncle had to marry her because then he'd be stuck with *you* and your tainted bloodline. And Lord knows how hard it is to wash away dirt when it seeps into your pores. Your mother and her perilous mistake would have left a stain on my family's name," she sneered as she sat back in her chair.

With a wicked chuckle that sent a chill skating over my arms, she asked, "Do you even know who your father is?"

I gripped the edge of my chair so hard I thought I might splinter the wood and fall right on my bottom. There were so many things I wanted to say and every word kept spinning through my mind as I stared her down, but not a single one of them would come out. It felt like they were all stuck behind an invisible wall of fear that was built years ago when I was just a girl who wanted to be loved and accepted while Melody did everything she could to make sure I never felt that way.

As I sat there, stunned and utterly silent, I couldn't help but realize I was still very much that same girl and Melody had done what she always did—dropped a bomb in my lap while she watched me implode trying to figure out how to disarm it.

"Melody!" Someone called out her name, rocking me from my stupor. When I shifted my gaze to the woman who'd called out her name my stomach dropped.

Valorie Cummings. Melody's best friend and the second person on my most-hated list. While Melody had always sugar-coated her insults, Valorie was just plain mean.

Melody leaned forward one last time and said, "It looks like you need some time alone. I'll leave you to ponder the answer to that question." I watched her rise from the chair with the kind of grace that only money could buy with etiquette classes and just as I thought I was finally rid of her she looked at me over her shoulder and said, "Tell Johnny I said hello." And then she winked at me.

Bitch.

Watching her loop her arm with Valorie's as they snickered at my expense made me want to scream and curl into myself all at once. But I did nothing except sit there until they both left the cafe and I was finally safe to let everything out.

Tears rimmed my eyes and I wasn't even sure what I was crying about. That I let myself be insulted by the same girl who used to make me run home from school crying twelve years after we graduated high school? Or how she pointed out the dirty truth that no one else in the town was willing to say out loud—I was a secret that was so costly, the Baxley family had tried to hide me away, but they didn't do a good enough job. And then there was the fact that I wanted nothing more than to call Johnny and have him fix it all for me, just as he'd done every time I hurt all those years ago. A single smile from him and the wounds I carried didn't ache so badly.

It had been over twelve years since I had him to kiss away the pain, but I remembered those kisses as if they were branded into my soul—a scar of remembrance that would last a lifetime and longer.

But the joy of those memories had been replaced with haunting images of him walking away from me. He'd done it more than once now and it make me sick at the thought of him doing it again. I didn't think I could survive it a third time.

I wiped angrily at the tears spilling over my cheeks. Years had passed since I cried this much and all it took was for me to come back to Pebble Brook Falls to become a blubbering mess.

There were only a few days left of my stay and I felt this sudden urgency to grab my car keys and make the drive back to Nashville right now. I didn't want to face any of it. Fixing things with Sarah. Making amends with Johnny. And I certainly didn't want to deal with the Baxley estate and everything that came with it.

The need to run away grew by the second as I grabbed my sketchbook off the table. Tucking it away in my purse, I dropped off my empty latte mug at the counter and headed for Sarah's house to pack.

Her guest room looked like a bomb went off in it. Clothes were strewn everywhere. Somehow, one of my nightshirts had landed over the lampshade on the bedside table. Blushes, lipsticks, and eyeshadows palettes littered the dresser in front of the large mirror hanging above it. As I took in the mess of cosmetics, it reminded me of Melanie's room at the Baxley estate and how there were countless tubes of lipstick cluttering her dresser.

I'd never been a tidy person and I wondered if that part of me had come from my mother. Exhausted just by the thought of having to clean this mess before I made my silent exit had me slumping onto the edge of the bed. I let my head drop into my hands, the feeling of overwhelm and total defeat crashed over me in relentless waves.

This trip was meant to be simple. Come back. Hang out with Sarah. Sign the paperwork. Rummage through the estate to make some initial decisions. Then head back home.

Home.

I wasn't even sure what the word meant anymore. Nashville was where my apartment was. Where I was trying to start a life for myself. But it had yet to feel like the place I belonged. I had no friends there. No one to call family. It was just me in a tiny loft apartment trying to make a dream work.

And Pebble Brook Falls...well, it wasn't exactly home either. It housed too much pain. Too many memories that I wanted to rid from my mind forever. But there was Sarah. The one person who had never walked away from me even when being my friend meant becoming an outcast from the society she grew up in. She chose to stand by me through the thick of it.

And...*Johnny*. Being in his arms with the smell of cedar floating around me. That had *felt* like home. For years, his embrace was where I found solace through all the trials of my younger years. He was the lighthouse amongst the stormy waters, always guiding me back to the place I belonged.

And then there was the home I never had that was now—somehow—*mine*. Its immaculate walls were filled with secrets that I would never uncover. A constant reminder of how I was a mistake. A problem that never should have been. And a problem that not even hundreds of millions of dollars and a good Southern name could fix. Melody was right. My mother's actions and my birth had been a stain that couldn't be washed away.

As I lifted my head and blinked against the new tears that had welled in my eyes, I realized that while I may have been a mistake, I still belonged to something. I was no longer a child with no true last name. I was a *Baxley* and there had been far worse crimes committed by powerful families and they had been able to bounce back.

I could use this to my advantage. Learn more about who

my mother and grandmother were and how they navigated this society. How they made it their own.

A glimmer of something foreign took hold of me. A quiet desire was blossoming and while it surprised me, I felt a tether pulling me toward it. I needed to learn more about who I was and where I came from. If I didn't, I knew I would never feel truly whole. That any future I had would be empty somehow. Because that's how I'd felt since I was a child—like there were pieces of me scattered all over the place and I didn't have a map to find them all.

My gaze shifted behind me to the bedside table where my mother's journal lay closed.

I have a map now.

The rational side of me was reeling, thinking about how crazy all of this was. None of it made sense, but I guessed feelings didn't have to make sense for them to be true. If I was honest with myself, this is what I'd wanted from the moment I learned Melanie was my mother. Learning about her would finally give me the answers to questions I was too afraid to ask for far too long.

And maybe those answers would help me right the wrongs that happened over the past few days. I could fix things with Sarah and talk with Johnny. To what end, I had no clue. But the haze of the anxiety that had shadowed me since I got the call from Mr. Anderson was starting to lift, giving me some clarity.

And maybe—just maybe—all of this was meant to be.

CHAPTER SEVENTEEN

*M*y eyes strained as I read pages and pages of Melanie's journal. Sarah had been right. My mother loved me. In her own strange way, she thought that giving me over to the orphanage would give me the best shot in life because I wouldn't be forced to carry the weight of the Baxley name and everything that came with it.

She'd documented every week of her pregnancy with me, writing about the severe morning sickness that kept her hidden away from her friends. Not that Adeline would have let her out of the house while she was pregnant. According to my mother, Adeline had her on house arrest, turning away any visitors until they had just stopped coming. They had been told that she was recovering from a riding accident where she injured her spine and any potential stress would only lead to further damage.

I was beginning to understand how calculated my grandmother had been and I could only imagine how stifling Melanie must have felt being pressed under her mother's thumb her entire life.

The tension headache forming between my brows had me wanting to close her journal and be done for the day, but I pressed on, telling myself I'd only read one more page.

I met with Ms. Mosely today and I have to admit that she's not the ideal person I'd like to raise my daughter. Her face was twisted into a permanent scowl and she was much too stern for my liking. But she was the lesser evil when compared to my mother. I've considered looking for orphanages outside of Georgia, but the idea of not being close to her if she needed me was a feeling I couldn't bear. And if—by some miracle—my mother croaked before my daughter phased out of the orphanage, I would take her home and live out our days on the estate. I wish I could just run away with her once she's born, but my witch of a mother rescinded my inheritance and pushed back the date I would receive it, which won't be until my daughter turns eighteen. And there is no way he would take me back after what I said to him and if I'm honest with myself, I have no idea how to live without the comforts of this place. I would only put her in harm's way if I ran.

I still don't understand how I could have been born from such a vile woman. Since I started showing, she looks at me with such contempt it makes my skin crawl. Just another reason why it's best for my daughter to be away from her. I could never live with myself if I let her be looked at that way. I told Ms. Mosely that I wanted my daughter to be raised with class so that one day if the heavens above ever allow it, she will be able to take over the estate and have the tools to do it. My world is cruel in so many ways, but if there's one thing the vultures appreciate, it's a woman with class.

I closed the journal and set it back on the bedside table before I rubbed the palms of my hands against my eyes. My emotions were strung out from reading countless pages that only proved Sarah was right even more.

It wasn't exactly like my mother's logic had been totally sound though. I was sure there were ways she could have made it work by keeping me, but she was so young when she got pregnant and I couldn't fault a scared woman for doing what she thought was best for her child. Even if my chest ached with the pain of not truly knowing her.

My body told me to draw the curtains and curl up in the bed until the next day came, but my mind was still reeling from everything I'd learned and I wasn't ready to stop searching for answers yet. It was the same pull I'd felt at the cafe. Some desire was buried deep within me to learn more about her. To find out more about *myself.* Maybe I was completely wrong in thinking that it would make everything else better, but I had to at least try.

So after a quick refresh in the mirror, I grabbed my purse

and my mother's journal and headed for the *Hope for All* orphanage.

A picture captured in time, the orphanage looked exactly as it did the day I left. The old Victorian-style home had been donated by the county decades ago to house the children who were left behind. It had an eerie vibe with its heavily inclined roof and the white paint was peeling from the siding. The front porch had never been painted during all the years I'd been there and the solid oak steps, railing, and flooring told me Ms. Mosely had utilized the donations she received every year for something else.

The landscaping was the only immaculate thing about the property. With a bright green crisp lawn in the front yard and beautiful blue and violet hydrangeas lining the front porch, it was a shame the house didn't look better because it had a lot of potential. I wondered if Mr. Smith's landscaping company was still the one to take care of it every Friday.

As I approached the white picket gate in front of the side-walk, memories flared to the surface as I paused with my hand on the latch. When Johnny started going to school, I would wait on the steps for hours before he got off the school bus. The smile on his face every time he saw me sitting there made my heart burst. I'd loved him even then. Before I knew what loving a person meant and how easily it could all come crumbling down.

The gate snicked shut behind me as I forged my way toward the house, battling to keep my heart steady as I was bombarded with flickers of more and more memories. When I finally reached the front door, children's laughter sounded through the cracked window to my right.

So many emotions arose that it was hard to sift through them all, so I left them to deal with later. Packing every single one in a tight little box so I would have the courage to open the door and find the answers to all the questions I had beyond it.

With a deep inhale, I grasped the doorknob and twisted it until the door swung open. Just as the outside of the house had remained the same, so had the inside, only it was in much worse condition. Right in front of me was a large staircase that led up to the bedrooms that were probably still jam-packed with twin-size beds to house all the forgotten children of the town. To my right, I found three little girls sitting in a small circle in the center of the den. Each one held a Barbie doll with matted hair and dirt-splotched skin. When I was here, almost all the toys had been hand-me-down donations from children in Pebble Brook Falls who had outgrown them or simply become bored and wanted to trade up for something new and shiny.

Not that it mattered to any of us because we hadn't known any different. Every time someone dropped off a trash bag full of toys, it felt like Christmas had come early. On the actual day, we were each allowed to pick out one brand-new toy. Mine had always been some version of a fashion item. Either plastic necklaces and bracelets or a small bundle of threads and needles so I could sew patterns into my jeans. While

Johnny had always opted for something more practical like a gardening shovel and carrot seeds.

I giggled to myself as I thought back to all his attempts of making a vegetable garden. One spring he'd finally gotten a sprout from some tomato seeds he'd planted only for it to be dug up by some animal that had rooted in the backyard the night after he discovered the green little twig. He was so angry he stubbed his toe kicking the metal watering jug he'd picked out the Christmas prior.

"Who are you?" A squeaky little voice broke through my thoughts. All three of the little girls had turned their attention to me, their eyes wide with curiosity.

I smiled at them. "I'm—"

"Willow Mae."

Looking past the staircase into the dimly lit hallway, Ms. Mosely was waddling toward me. She stopped at the edge of the staircase and leaned on the railing as though she might very well topple over from the exertion of walking down the hall. It was always her stern voice that had kept all of us kids in line because there was no way she could chase us down given her bad hips. She told me once about the accident that led to a double hip surgery when she was only twenty-two years old. Prior to this gig, Ms. Mosely had been a champion barrel racer but had a stint of back luck when she fell during a competition and her horse landed on top of her.

"Hi, Ms. Mosely. It's good to see you."

She huffed a breath, seeing straight through the lie. "If there is one thing you've never been and never will be, it's a good liar. What can I do for you?"

Stealing a glance at the little girls in the den, I saw that every one of them had their attention directed at me and Ms. Mosely.

"Do you mind if we talk in your office?" I asked, tilting my head to the left where the door to her office was wide open.

"Sure." She gestured a hand outward for me to head in.

I never thought to be curious about her story, but as I sat in the dusty wooden chair in front of her desk, I eyed the shelves behind her chair that were lined with barrel racing trophies. Most of them were a few feet tall and even though I was too far away to read the inscriptions, I guessed they were likely for first place given how tall and detailed they were.

How did her road lead her here? Where her days were filled with breaking up fights over toys and making sure all the kids came home after school. Did she want this life for herself or was it forced upon her by some wicked twist of luck?

When she finally made her way to her side of the desk, I looked into her deep brown eyes and felt too afraid to ask. My mother was right when she described Ms. Mosely's face as being twisted into a permanent scowl.

Profound lines marked the sides of her mouth where the edges of her lips were turned downward even as she spoke, "What would you like to talk about?"

I swallowed against the dryness in my throat. The only other times I was in this office were when I was in trouble for sneaking out with Johnny or when Johnny and I had snuck in to watch the television that was still nestled in the far corner behind her desk. Although, it appeared she updated it to a small flatscreen.

With a quick inhale, I let my shoulders drop. I was a twenty-eight-year-old woman now. Not a child who was under her authority. And I had questions that I wanted answered.

"You've probably heard by now that Adeline Baxley left me her estate after she passed." Ms. Mosely gave a subtle nod so I continued, "I recently visited the estate and found some... papers that my biological mother had left behind." I didn't want her to know that I had invaded Melanie's privacy by reading her journal so I kept that detail to myself.

"And what did those papers say?" Her gaze narrowed on me and I fought the urge to curl inward as I'd done when I was a little girl and she'd caught me doing something naughty.

"There was some information about her decision to place me in the orphanage instead of raising me herself." I swallowed and tried to steady my shaky voice. "And there was some information about how she met with you and I was wondering if you could tell me more about those meetings."

Phew. I said what I wanted to say and didn't pass out. That was a win in my book.

Ms. Mosely just stared at me and I started to worry that coming here was a mistake. Then her gaze softened and she leaned back in her seat with an exasperated sigh.

"I was wondering if you'd ever come around here asking questions about your mother. You weren't like that Johnny boy who knew exactly where he'd come from. But even after the beans were spilled about who your mother was after her death, I was a little surprised you hadn't asked me anything then."

I shrugged. "I think it was so overwhelming to have the entire town find out who she was to me at the same time I did. The kids at school were awful about it too and I just wanted it to go away so I could go back to being invisible."

Ms. Mosely's lips pursed as she shook her head. "The

people of this town can be cruel and they raise their children to be just the same."

I raised my brows at that because I'd never once heard Ms. Mosely speak ill of the people of Pebble Brook Falls. She'd done her best to teach us to have understanding, even for those who did us wrong.

"To answer your question, Melanie Baxley did come and see me several times throughout her pregnancy with you."

My heart kicked up and I felt myself leaning forward. "Really?"

Ms. Mosely adjusted herself in her chair as she nodded. "She was a pistol, that one. The first time she came here, I thought she was going to burn the entire place down with her gaze alone. She had a knack for attention to detail, asking a ton of questions about the safety of the house and if there was a way I could ensure you never snuck out once you were older." Her laugh sounded like a strangled cough, probably because she didn't do it very often.

"She was a little shocked when I told her that not even a high-security prison would be able to keep a teenager inside if they really wanted to get out. But I did my best to assure her that you would be safe and she seemed satisfied enough with that."

Safe. My mother had wanted me to be safe. A flood of emotions threatened to sweep me away, but I held them at bay. There were more questions I had to ask and if I turned into a blubbering mess now, I wouldn't be able to get them answered.

"Did she...um..." I cleared my throat and continued, "Did she talk with you about how she wanted me to be raised?"

Somehow, the lines etched into Ms. Mosely's face seemed

to deepen as she steepled her fingers in front of her. Her eyes grew distant as though she was lost in time, trying to figure out how much she wanted to tell me. Or maybe she was thinking back to the details of the conversations she had with my mother.

The clock on the wall to the right ticked loudly in the silence between us until she finally answered, "I guess you have a right to know everything since you're an adult now. Sometimes it's hard for me to get past the children you all were when some of you come back looking for answers." Ms. Mosely lifted herself up a few inches and settled back into her chair, likely moving around to manage the pain in her hips.

"Melanie asked me to raise you in preparation to take over the Baxley estate. She wanted you to know the social graces that her society would expect to see from someone with that sort of...pedigree. And she asked me to keep you out of trouble. To keep you away from anything that could lead you down the wrong path."

The world shifted slightly as though I was seeing it with new eyes. There were so many things running through my mind, but the first thought was how Sarah had been right and Ms. Mosely's confession was further proof of how I'd messed up. I was too afraid to face the idea that my mother really did love me even though she gave me up and now my relationship with Sarah was suffering for it.

It was so difficult to reconcile. How could the words on my mother's journal page and the words coming from Ms. Mosely's mouth be true? My mother loved me.

She loved *me*.

And yet, she still gave me away. And now I would never know her.

A pit formed in my stomach as Ms. Mosely's words ran through my mind again and again.

…keep you out of trouble.

…lead you down the wrong path.

Johnny.

"Oh my God," I breathed as I brought trembling fingers to cover my gaping mouth. "The letters…The letters that Johnny wrote to me. He said he wrote to me every single week when he was allowed to. But I never got them. The whole two years I was here after he left, I never got a single one."

Something flickered in Ms. Mosely's eyes as I raised my voice in a frantic panic. "You said she asked you to keep me out of trouble. To not lead me down the wrong path. And you always hated Johnny. You disciplined him more than the other k—"

"I did that for his own good," she cut me off curtly.

I snorted. "How could treating him differently from all the other kids do him good?"

Ms. Mosely's voice was stern as she said, "That boy had trouble running through his veins from the moment he was born. He needed direction and stability and that's exactly what I provided him."

Shaking my head, I glared at her. "You had no right to keep those letters from me. No right!" Tears burned my eyes as I traced back the last twelve years of feeling like he had abandoned me. While the entire time he was feeling the exact same way because he'd written to me and Ms. Mosely stole what was meant to be between us.

Her finger was steady as she leaned forward and pointed right at my face. "I had the *only* right. That boy was going to drag you down a path that wasn't meant for you to take."

I was seething and her words were only fuel for the fire running through me. I hated her. I hated her and I hated that my mother's intentions had gotten me twisted into this mess. While she asked Ms. Mosely to protect me, she was simultaneously keeping me away from the one person who had always put his needs...his *life* below my own.

"Do you still have them?"

I didn't care about this battle with her anymore. She was no longer my keeper and I no longer felt afraid of her.

Her hand dropped back to the armrest of her chair and she was silent for several moments, telling me exactly what I needed to know.

"I want them."

"I don't think that's a good idea, Willow." Her voice had softened a fraction.

"That's not your decision to make anymore. I'm a twenty-eight-year-old woman and I want what's mine."

Ms. Mosely sighed deeply and I was ready to fight whatever excuse she was going to come up with to not give me the letters. But she surprised me as she rose from her chair and slowly ambled behind me where a large oak wood cabinet stood.

I rose from my own seat to meet her as she snicked the cabinet door shut and turned back toward me with a bundle of envelopes tied neatly together with burlap string. A strangled sob burst through my mouth and I raised a hand to cover my trembling lips. There they were. The love letters Johnny had written to me every week while he was away for those first two years. So many of them that Ms. Mosely had to use both hands, one holding the bottom and the other securing the top of the stack.

"I only kept them from you because I thought it was the right thing."

Looking into Ms. Mosely's silver-lined eyes I could see how my reaction was impacting her. Now that the letters were in my sight, the hatred I felt toward her only moments ago started to fade away.

"I guess I can't blame you for that," I said with a shaky breath. "Thank you for keeping them for me."

As she extended them toward me she said, "I honestly don't know why I kept them all this time. But they're yours to do with what you wish. Just promise me you'll be careful."

My brows furrowed as I tilted my head.

"I know I could have done a better job at giving you support when that boy left. I saw how devastating it was for you to be left behind a second time by someone you loved. Just don't let that happen to you again, okay? Promise me."

As I took in the woman who had bathed me, fed me, and given me a warm bed and a roof over my head, I realized that she had never been the one to blame. She'd made a promise to my mother and Ms. Mosely was a woman of her word. Something she'd engrained in all of us orphans from the moment we came through her front door. In a way, we were all her children and I knew that without her, I wouldn't be half the woman I was today.

So, I took the bundle of letters and wrapped my other arm tightly around her. For the first time in my entire life, I gave Ms. Mosely a hug and whispered, "Thank you...for everything."

CHAPTER EIGHTEEN

Chocolate ice cream dripped onto my left hand as I licked on the mint chocolate chip ice cream in my right hand. I probably should have thought of a better plan... like asking Sarah if she was even willing to talk to me before I went and bought her favorite ice cream that was beginning to melt down my forearm.

Great.

Her cousin, Stephanie, was working with her today and I'd asked her to go grab Sarah from the kitchen, but that was five minutes ago per the giant pink clock hanging behind the cash register. As the clock ticked just past six minutes, Sarah appeared through the kitchen door with a frown on her face.

Pinning her anger-filled eyes on me, I gulped. Two confrontations in one day wasn't exactly how I wanted to spend my Tuesday, but the ball was rolling and all I could do was keep rolling with it.

Sarah crossed her arms in front of her chest as she stopped before me. I jutted my left hand out and offered her the half-melted cone of her favorite flavor.

"I got you ice cream," I said cheerily with a broad smile tugged at the corners of my lips.

Her gaze flicked to the ice cream cone and back up to me. "It looks more like soup than ice cream."

I sighed heavily. "The plan was to see you before it melted, but you took longer than I expected to come out."

She narrowed her eyes on me for several seconds which had my heart racing against my ribcage. I had no idea what I would do if she didn't accept my apology. Sarah was all I had in this world right now and I couldn't stand the thought of us not being okay.

Finally, she took the ice cream cone from me and bit into the melted mess. "It's still pretty tasty," she said around her bite.

My shoulders dropped immediately as I took a big breath in to calm my raging heart. "Walk with me?" I asked.

"Okay. But let me grab you a napkin first. Your left arm looks like you were just in a mud pit wrestling match and we all know what kind of rumors the biddies would start up if they saw you like this."

I laughed a full belly laugh, mostly because it was true. The older women of Pebble Brook Falls had a tendency to create stories of their fellow townsfolk as they sat around and sipped on sweet tea. It was honestly impressive how little inspiration they needed to turn a totally benign thing into a full-blown scandal.

After I wiped the remnants of Sarah's ice cream off my hand and arm, we stepped out and followed the sidewalk down to the park.

I stopped right before we passed the part of the sidewalk that turned into a gravel path that wound through the small grassy area. Sarah stopped as well and shifted her body until she was facing me.

"I'm sorry, Sarah. I'm sorry for letting my emotions get the best of me and ruining our pasta night." I bit my lower lip to keep it from trembling as my eyes darted back and forth between hers.

The moment I saw her lower lip tremble too I lost it. Tears spilled over, making my vision go hazy as Sarah stepped forward and wrapped her arms around me.

"I'm sorry too, Willow. I've hated the past twenty-four hours so much that I burnt an entire batch of cookies because my mind was preoccupied with our argument. And I *never* burn *anything*."

I couldn't help but chuckle at her self-proclaimed awesomeness as I squeezed her tighter. When we pulled apart I said, "Let's never argue ever again, okay?"

"I think that's a promise I can make," she sniffed.

We fell back into a synchronous stride, both of us wiping the tears from our faces. "Well, I'm glad that didn't last long because twenty-four hours of feeling like I couldn't talk to you was torture."

She bumped me with her hip. "It was torture for me too! I'm honestly really thankful you came to the bakery. Otherwise, we would have had to wait another four hours," she dragged out the words in a complaining tone that made me giggle.

"So, what have you been up to all day?" she asked before taking another bite into her ice cream cone.

"Honestly, that's a pretty loaded question with how much I've been up to." She raised her brows at me, waiting for me to continue on. "I guess I could start with how I ran into Melody Carnelle this morning at The Roasted Bean."

"Ick." Sarah's face twisted into a grimace. "Did she say anything to you?"

"Only that my mother was engaged to her uncle and that we would have been cousins if my mother wouldn't have died. Oh! Also that she was glad that we weren't cousins because my mother and I would have tainted her family's name."

Sarah gasped, her mouth popping open in shock. "You're kidding me."

"Nope. I just can't believe I let myself fall for her antics again." I took a bite of my ice cream and swallowed the chocolate minty goodness down. "You remember when we were in high school and she would start off talking to us by giving us a compliment or asking us a question like she was genuinely interested in our lives, all to set us up for the sneak attack?"

Sarah nodded, her brown eyes wide.

"Well, she used that same exact method on me this morning and I fell for it, just like I did every time it happened in high school. I was trying to give her the benefit of the doubt thinking she had to have grown up over the past twelve years, but I was so wrong to assume that a tiger could change its stripes."

"You know she's only like that because she's miserable with herself, right? I mean, her family sucks from what I've heard through the grapevine."

"Really?"

"Mmhmm." Sarah plopped the final bite of her cone into her mouth. "Apparently her mom is deep in the cup by midmorning most days and her dad is always traveling for horse shows and rodeos. Melody went off to college once we all graduated, but she doesn't work or have any prospects for marriage. Not that I blame the men around here. I wouldn't want to get in bed with that snake either."

I snorted. "She might have crappy parents, but that's no excuse for her to be such a villain. Especially now that she's almost thirty years old."

"You're right," Sarah replied. "I still can't believe what she said about your mother."

"I know. I'd actually forgotten that she was engaged to Henry Carnelle. After her death and everything came out about me being her daughter, it was such a whirlwind that her engagement was the last thing on my mind. But I have to admit that I agree with Melody. I'm really glad we didn't end up being cousins either. I feel like she would have had even more ammunition to make my life a living hell."

"You have a good point there."

We walked in silence for a few minutes until we found ourselves at one of the picnic tables underneath the giant oak tree in the center of the park. My gaze followed the length of the tree, from its gnarled roots poking out of the ground up to its full branches where the leaves caught the slight breeze flowing around us. This side of the trunk was bare, but I knew the other side held my initials, etched deep into the wood right next to Johnny's.

I looked back at Sarah and said, "I went back to the orphanage today."

Her dark brown eyes shone with surprise. "Why?" she whispered.

"You were right. About my mother." My throat felt strained as emotion welled in my chest. "I read more of her journal. She wrote about me every single week during her pregnancy. She wrote about how much she loved me and how she wanted to protect me from her Adeline. Apparently, Adeline had put her on house arrest and didn't let a single person visit her for the whole nine months she was pregnant. When people asked why they couldn't visit, Adeline told them Melanie had suffered from a fall and broke her back and that stress would only make it worse."

"Damn." Sarah's gaze shifted to where her hands were placed on top of the picnic table and I could see the wheels turning in her mind as a distant look shadowed her face. "That's a lot to take in. How're you managing it all?" She looked back up at me.

Blowing out a harsh breath, I shrugged. "I think my knee-jerk reaction yesterday was to bury all my feelings and I think that's why I lashed out. It almost feels like it would have been less painful to not know who my mother was, you know? There would probably always be this question of who she was, but finding out who she was and how she was within reach for so long was...difficult. Now, it's even worse because I not only knew how close she was but that she loved me and she wanted me to be safe. And the only way she thought that could happen was if I was away from Adeline and their world.

"After I read those journal entries, I still felt like none of it was real. Like there was no possible way she could love me— the little girl she opted to leave behind. That's why I went to the orphanage. I wanted to talk with Ms. Mosely about it."

"How would Ms. Mosely know?" Sarah asked.

"My mother wrote about her in her journal. How she told Ms. Mosely to raise me to understand the workings of my mother's society. And to keep me from going down a wrong path."

"What did Ms. Mosely say?" Sarah reached across the table and took my hands in hers.

I laughed out a sob as all the emotions from the past two days came over me in a rush. "She basically told me it was all true. That my mother *did* love me and she genuinely thought the orphanage was the best place for me. And how my mother had asked her to raise me with the intention of one day taking over the estate and entering into her world on my terms. I think my mother thought she was going to outlive Adeline when she was coming up with this master plan and that we would eventually be reunited when the time came. But that didn't work out."

"Oh, Willow. I'm so sorry." Sarah let go of my hands as she rose from her side of the table and came over to sit next to me. I shifted toward her and leaned into her embrace as she ran her hands up and down my back.

"I just wish I could have known her. I wish I could have at least met her one time."

"Me too, Willow. Me too."

I rested my cheek on my friend's shoulder and let everything out. All the years of feeling like I never truly belonged anywhere. The heartbreaking moment of finding out that my mother had been fifteen minutes away from me for most of my life. Endless questions that would go unanswered. Never having the opportunity to hug my mother or to hear her voice.

It all came rushing out like a dam bursting loose. When I finally pulled back and took in Sarah's face, I realized she'd been crying too.

"Why're you crying?" I asked.

"Because this is really freaking sad and I hate that you've

had to go through all of this. It's not fair," she sniffed as she wiped her nose.

"Well, thank you for shedding some tears for me." I laughed and she laughed too.

"Please tell me that's all the sad stuff that happened to you today."

I bit hard on my lower lip as my gaze darted to the side.

"There's more?!" Sarah whisper-shouted.

"Remember how I told you the other night that Johnny had written me letters while he was in the military but I never got them?"

"Yeah." Sarah dragged out the word.

"Ms. Mosely kept them for me and I have them back at your house."

"Oh my God," she whispered. "How many are there?"

"Too many to count. He was writing to me for two years before he stopped."

"Have you read any of them yet?"

I shook my head.

"Are you going to?"

"Yes. I just...haven't exactly figured out when I'm going to. I'm supposed to be leaving to head back to Nashville in six days, Sarah. How am I supposed to read the love letters Johnny wrote to me that I never got the chance to read because my foster mom hid them from me at the request of my real mother to make sure I didn't get into any trouble? And apparently, everyone thought that Johnny was trouble. Which, he kind of was because he walked away from me and even though he wrote me all those stupid love letters, it still feels like it's not enough for me to fully trust that he wouldn't walk away from me again in the future. Not that a future with us is even something he wants."

"Whoa." Sarah threw her hands up to stop me from rambling on any further and I took in a deep breath. "You're getting a little nutty on me, so let's just calm down and take another deep breath."

Sarah's shoulders rose and fell as she guided me through a few deep breaths and I had to admit that it kind of made me feel better.

"Obviously, it's your decision to do whatever you want with the letters. But I have to tell you, Willow...I think fate is trying to tell you something here."

"What do you mean?"

She grabbed ahold of my shoulders and gently shook me. "I mean I don't think it's simply a coincidence that you and Johnny happen to be in Pebble Brook Falls at the same time after twelve years. And how all these signs are basically screaming at you to make things right with him." Her hands dropped from their hold on my shoulders. "Listen. I'm not saying that you should run off and marry the guy tomorrow, but I think you should at least read the letters and then talk to him. No harm ever came from talking, right?"

"Mmm. I'm pretty sure some wars have been started because someone did too much talking."

"Valid point," Sarah chuckled. "But I don't think a war will start from you talking to Johnny."

"Ugh," I groaned. "This is why I've stayed away from here, you know."

"Because you hate to face the fact that I'm always right?"
"Yes!"

We both laughed and the lightness I felt in my chest was a

warm welcome. Today may have started out terribly, but it was definitely ending on a good note. Sarah and I were back to our normal selves and with all the unknowns ahead of me, I was thankful to have her as my anchor.

She stole a peek at her phone from the back pocket of her jeans. "Need to head back?" I asked.

"Yup. I don't want to leave Stephanie alone for too long. She's still learning the ropes and some of the customers can get cranky."

"We definitely wouldn't want her to experience that. Come on,"—I rose from my seat—" I'll walk you back."

CHAPTER NINETEEN

I was drunk. Very, very drunk. And that was because I took one look at the pile of letters Johnny had written me when I got back to Sarah's place and knew there was no way I would be able to read them without some liquid courage.

Somehow, those few glasses of wine I stole from Sarah's bottle of Cabernet led me to a small dive bar named, *Joanne's Tavern*, in the middle of downtown Pebble Brook Falls. It was a Tuesday night, so the only people in the place were me, the bartender, and a few locals who were quietly nursing their drinks down the bar from me.

I took another swig of my rum and coke before I finally had the nerve to untie the burlap string and open the first envelope at the top of the stack.

I can do this, I said to myself. Or at least I thought I said it to myself until I realized the bartender had shifted his gaze to me and a quizzical brow raised. Ignoring him, I slipped the piece of paper from the envelope and gently opened it with shaky hands.

Tears immediately welled in my eyes as I saw Johnny's chicken scratch handwriting sprawled across the page.

Dear Willow,

I don't even know where to begin, but I guess the best place to start is by saying I'm so sorry. I'm sorry I left you and I'm even more sorry that I didn't fully explain why. The truth is that joining the military felt like the only path I had to keep myself from turning into my parents. There was no money for me to go to college and if I tried to get a low-level job in Pebble Brook Falls, I would have hated it. Working in the grocery store or the ice cream parlor just isn't me and you know that. I want to make something of myself and I think the military will help me do that. Although, my sergeant is already busting my balls. I've never been good at making my bed, but here they force me to do it every single morning. It's good for me though. The structure keeps me in line and I've already opened a savings account so I can pay for you to come visit me in Washington soon. I think you'd love the west coast. There's no fields like our special place back home, but the trees here are huge! Anyways, I hope you can forgive me, Willow. I miss you. The softness of your skin and the bright blue of your eyes. I miss everything about you and I can't wait to see you again.

Love,

Johnny

Teardrops speckled the paper and some of the ink started to run. "Oh no!" I sniffed loudly as I grabbed the napkin from under my glass tumbler to lightly dab at the wet spots on the page before I used it to dry the streams cascading over my cheeks.

"Are you alright, miss?" I looked up to see the bartender

leaning over the bartop with another napkin extended toward me. He was really tall and had a weathered look to him as though he spent every day for the last several decades in the sun. Deeply set wrinkles crinkled the edges of his kind-looking eyes.

I took the napkin from him and said, "Thank you. And yes. I'm okay." Taking a deep breath in I closed my eyes and pinched the bridge of my nose. "Actually, no. I'm definitely not okay. Because I have this entire stack of letters written to me from the love of my life. The only problem is that I was supposed to get these letters over twelve years ago, but I didn't and now that I'm reading them I'm realizing just how badly I *need* to be with him." I finally opened my eyes and let my hand drop onto the sticky bartop.

"But I don't know if he wants to be with me," I whispered. The pain of that harsh realization squeezed my heart. I rubbed the center of my chest with the palm of my hand to ward off the ache, but there was nothing I could do against the anguish of my heart splintering.

As I looked up at the man standing in front of me, I watched his deep blue eyes shift to the open letter I laid next to the stack. When he looked back at me he gave me a gentle smile, his white teeth peeked through his lips and the unruly mustache hairs that branched over them.

"It sounds like you have a pretty big question on your hands," he said and I nodded.

He swung a dirty dish rag over his shoulder that he'd been using to wipe down the bartop before he leaned on his elbows and interlaced his fingers. "I'll tell you something I learned a long time ago that saved my marriage too many times to count. Assumptions will get you into trouble and if you want to know what the other person is thinking, all you need to do is ask."

I blinked at him. This perfect stranger who didn't know me and had no reason to spend his time giving me advice other than it was the kind thing to do. That's how it had always been during my childhood. Whether it was a teacher intervening when they saw a child being bullied. Or when Mrs. Sheehan gave me an extra scoop of ice cream because Ms. Mosely could only afford for us all to have one. Small moments of generosity and compassion that left lasting imprints on the people around them.

Pebble Brook Falls may have people—like my grandmother—who were consumed with the need for power and got off on causing other people pain. But there were also those who gave from their hearts, even if it cost them something to do so.

"I've also learned the hard way that alcohol doesn't make the pain go away. It only makes it worse." The bartender looked toward my half-empty rum and coke and I sighed.

"You're probably right about that."

"Would you like me to get you some water?" he asked.

I mustered up a smile and nodded. "That would be great."

He turned around to fetch another glass. "And thank you."

With a quick look over his shoulder at me, he smiled before he went back to pouring me a glass of water.

What am I doing? I asked myself silently, raking my fingers through my hair. My mind was still swimming from the alcohol and I could hardly make sense of my emotions. Through the mess of it all, one thing was clear to me. The bartender was right. If I wanted the answer to my question, I was going to have to ask it.

I had the choice of staying here and reading through all these letters or...I could go to him.

Urgency took over as I scrambled off the barstool and gathered the letters and shoved them into my bag. The bartender placed the tall glass of water in front of me and I reached for it, taking a moment to gulp it down with the hopes it would dilute some of the alcohol that was starting to make me dizzy from the sudden movements I made.

He watched me with laughter in his eyes as I swallowed down the final sip and accidentally slammed the glass back onto the counter.

"Whoops!" I giggled, wiping my wet lips with the back of my hand.

"It's not a problem," he chuckled. "Be safe out there, okay?"

"I will. And thank you again..." I paused, waiting for him to fill in his name.

"Michael."

"Thank you, Michael."

With a final wave to him over my shoulder, I stumbled my way out of his bar and into the sticky summer night air.

That last drink was doing a number on me as I tried not to trip over my feet while I walked along the sidewalk on Johnny's street. Or at least I thought it was his street. Everything looked different under the cover of darkness with the only light coming from the high moon.

I narrowed my gaze at the house on my right trying to see through the haze of my drunkenness. My normal limit was two glasses of wine, but tonight I had lost track of how many drinks I had before I decided that going to Johnny's house in the middle of the night was a good idea.

White house. Black shutters. Wrap around porch.

I kept saying it over and over to myself so I wouldn't forget what I was looking for. As I passed a few more houses, I finally came to the one I was looking for on my left and my heart immediately started to race.

"Johnny!" I yelled in excitement before a fit of giggles burst through my lips. "Johnny!" I hollered again and this time I was met with the sound of a dog barking.

Asher! Images of the giant yellow lab flooded my mind as I started walking up the path to their front porch. When I was halfway there, a light flicked on and I stopped moving, suddenly feeling like I'd been caught doing something naughty. Nerves raked through me as the front door of Johnny's house creaked open, but they went away the moment Asher barrelled through the opening and ran straight for me.

He nearly knocked me over as he wound through my legs leaning hard against them as I leaned down to give him pets. "Hey there, boy! Awe," I cooed. "You missed me, huh?"

Asher licked my hands and arms as I scratched him just above his tail.

"Lo?"

I stood straight up at the sound of Johnny's tired voice, but I moved too quickly that dizziness struck me hard and I started to wobble on my feet.

"Whoa," I murmured, grasping my head with both hands as I squeezed my eyes shut, but that only made the dizziness worse. So, I leaned forward, placing both hands on my knees until the wooziness subsided enough for me to slowly straighten again. When I did, Johnny was right in front of me. Shirtless. With gray sweatpants that hung so low on his hips, I could see the deep cut of his V that had my eyes trailing further down where his manhood was pressing against the soft fabric.

I licked my lips as heat struck the apex of my thighs. Damn, he looked good.

"What're you doing here, Lo?" His voice was gravelly as I flicked my gaze toward his face. There was no humor in his eyes as he assessed me with an unwavering stare.

I suddenly felt like I was the target in the enemies' camp. We hadn't exactly ended things on a good note the last time we talked and now I was showing up to his house in the middle of the night. Drunk. With his love letters burning a hole in my bag.

"Are you drunk?" His words came out on a growl and I swallowed the lump in my throat as he took another step forward.

"Um…" I didn't want to say yes, but I also didn't want to lie to him so I opted to zip my lips and not say anything at all.

Another step and he was standing toe-to-toe with me, his height forcing me to tilt my head back to look at him.

"You think getting drunk and walking the streets alone in the middle of the night is a *smart* idea, Willow?"

He never used my full name and the shock of it had me reeling, but there was no time for me to think about what it meant because his hand was on me. Palm splayed against my bare chest where my V-neck t-shirt opened, my chest rose and fell as I sucked in quick breaths of air that matched the wild pulse of my heart.

"You could have been hurt," he husked as his hand trailed up the center of my neck, pausing just a moment before his fingers met the edge of my jaw and his thumb pressed against my bottom lip, dragging it downward.

"I'm fine," I managed to say, even though I was anything but fine. My skin felt like it was on fire from the heat he pulled from me. My body ached for his touch and where his hand held my face wasn't near enough contact.

His smoldering gaze dipped to my lips. "I want to kiss those lips. Every fucking day that we've been apart I've dreamt of those sweet full lips pressed against mine."

"They're yours, Johnny. They've always been yours to kiss," I whispered into the space between us and I could see the conflict in his eyes. He leaned closer and my eyes fluttered shut, waiting for him to take me. To give me what we both wanted.

But then I felt his hand drop from my face and a deep rumbly sigh from him had my eyes shooting open.

"Not like this."

My heart cracked at his words and I went to step toward him as he moved away from me, but the world started to spin. The mixture of wine and hard liquor betraying me as my stomach roiled.

"Oh no," I whispered and Johnny's eyes flared with concern. "Oh no!" I said again just before I hurled onto his perfectly manicured lawn. I heaved and heaved until there was nothing left of my stomach contents or my dignity.

Once the dry heaves finally stopped, I realized that Johnny

was right next to me with one hand rubbing my back and the other hand at the nape of my neck holding my hair back. Embarrassment flooded my cheeks even though there were so many times when he'd done the same thing for me—rubbing circles along my back when I had a cold or making sure my hair didn't wind up in the toilet when I had the stomach bug. Taking care of one another was what we'd always done.

But a lot of time had passed since then and I was on my own for so long that it felt strange to have someone take care of me.

The sickness had me feeling pretty sober as I slowly hinged up from my hips. Johnny's hand lingered around the base of my neck, but I stepped away from him, afraid of what my breath must smell like.

"Feeling any better?" he asked, his dark eyes scanning me for any more signs of impending illness.

"Mmhmm," was all I could manage to say because the truth was that my stomach was already feeling queasy again.

"Why don't we get you cleaned up inside?"

I moaned and shook my head because the last thing I wanted to do was bring my mess into his home.

"Come on." He nudged his chin toward the front of his house. "There's no way in hell I'm giving you back to Sarah in this condition."

Johnny started off toward his front door while Asher sat right in front of me staring expectantly with the cutest smile on his face, his tongue lolling to the side. I rolled my eyes at him. I may have been able to turn down Johnny out of sheer stubbornness, but there was no way I could turn my back on those big puppy-dog eyes.

"Fine," I whispered and Asher gave a happy whimper as I started toward Johnny's front door.

He was waiting for me with the door wide open as I slowly made my way to the top of his porch steps. Under the porch light, I noticed how tired he looked. As if he'd already been awake when I stumbled into his yard screaming his name. I wondered if it had to do with the traumas he experienced overseas, but decided we had a long way to go before I even had a right to ask those kinds of questions.

The inside of his home smelled just like him—cedar wood and fresh linen. The warm, fresh scent calmed my stomach a little as I followed him through the foyer and into his living room where a large cream sofa sat in front of a fireplace with two rust-colored velvet accent chairs framing the left side of the area rug. The fireplace was lit, flames dancing along the large slivers of oak wood. It looked like my hypothesis had been right, Johnny was already awake before I got here.

"Wow. This is really nice, Johnny."

His only reply was a tired grunt as I watched Asher hop onto the long sofa and do three circles before plopping down, landing his head on his paws.

"Make yourself comfortable. I'll get us some tea." He didn't look at me before he crossed in front of me to where the kitchen was.

"Okay," I whispered to myself, dragging the word out because now I felt like an imposter in his home. Which, to be completely honest, I was. But this was a different version of the Johnny I'd seen over the past week and a half. He was cold and distant and yet...when we were outside and he almost kissed me, I could feel the need from him like it was a tangible thing.

Part of me wanted to leave. I was sober enough now to make my way back to my car at the bar or at least call an Uber. But the weight of today was starting to feel heavy, my eyelids drooped and every muscle in my body felt like it had been run over by a semi-truck.

As I sat down on the sofa next to Asher, I told myself I'd only stay for a little while. I'd have some tea to ease my stomach and then I'd call an Uber to take me back to Sarah's. Leaning my head back, I let myself settle into the deep cushions of the couch as I thread my fingers through Asher's long coat, giving him little pats and scratches as I made my way from the top of his head to the middle of his back. His body shook in gratitude as I rubbed my nails along his spine.

"I'm glad you want me here at least." Asher lifted his head and gave my wrist a little kiss with his tongue before he settled back down.

The faint sound of water boiling came from the kitchen behind me. He was probably going to be a few more minutes, so I took the opportunity to look around. From what I could see, there wasn't a TV anywhere. There weren't any pictures either. The walls were mostly barren with the exception of the American flag in a clear case that was standing on the wood beam mounted above the fireplace with a pair of dog tags draped over it. The silver metal of the tags shone in the firelight and I wondered if they were his or a friend he lost in the war.

I was about to get up and see whose name was printed in the embossed letters, but Johnny appeared next to the couch with two steaming mugs in his hands.

"Thank you," I said, standing to grab one from him before sitting back down again.

I scooted closer to Asher, but Johnny surprised me by sitting in the chair closest to the fireplace. The physical distance felt like a direct reflection of our relationship. Close, but never close enough to make something happen. Not for the long-term anyway.

That thought sent a sharp pang to my chest. Was Johnny *that* guy in my life? The one that almost every woman had. Where no matter how much you loved them, there was always something that would never let you fully have them.

I blinked against the stinging in my eyes and brought the mug to my lips, letting the hot liquid be a welcome distraction. Cooling peppermint with a hint of honey was like a balm to my hollow stomach.

Shadows flickered across Johnny's face from the movement of the flames in the fireplace. I hated this distance between us. I hated that every time I tried to say something, the words lodged in my throat like a cotton ball. But as the silence continued, I couldn't stand it anymore.

This man—the one I loved since I was a little girl—was hurting. I could see it in the way his eyes were fixed on the fire, unblinking. How his shoulders were stiff and drawn up toward his ears. The way he avoided looking in my direction even though I knew he was tracking my every movement as I rose from the couch, set my mug on the coffee table, and made my way in front of him.

Crouching down, I rested my hands on his knees and tilted my head until he finally looked at me.

"Talk to me," I whispered.

His jaw tensed and then he set down his mug on the side table next to him. "Why're you here, Lo?" he asked for the second time. He was clearly still upset.

"I got your letters...from Ms. Mosely. She kept them for me and I picked them up today."

Johnny shifted in his seat, but he stayed silent.

Tears welled in my eyes as I continued on, "I read the first one. And I couldn't stand knowing that you thought I didn't write back to you after you spilled your heart to me on those pages. I didn't want to read any more of them because it didn't matter. It didn't matter that you left and I couldn't go with you. It didn't matter that I was stuck there for two more years and still didn't have a way to find you. And it didn't matter that I spent the last twelve years thinking you abandoned me because now I know that you didn't.

"You were trying to make something of yourself and I could never fault you for that, no matter how much it hurt to watch you walk away."

Johnny leaned forward, his eyes softer, the coldness gone and he tucked a strand of hair behind my ear before wiping the tears off my cheeks with the pad of his thumb.

"It doesn't matter," I cried. "Because I'm still in love with you. After all these years, after all this time, *you* are still the one I want and nothing could ever change that."

My eyes darted back and forth between his, frantically hoping he felt the same way. I was so aware of how his thumb grazed down my cheek until he captured my chin between it and his forefinger.

A single tear slid out of the corner of his eye as he said, "You have no idea how much I've hoped for you to say that. Because the truth is darlin', there was never a moment that's passed by when my entire heart wasn't yours."

I choked out a laughing sob as I threw my arms around his

neck. His arms wrapped around my waist and he lifted me into his lap, holding me close to his chest.

He's mine, was the last thought I had before I drifted to sleep in the arms of the man I loved. The one who always had my heart. And the one I could never let go of ever again.

CHAPTER TWENTY

*M*y entire body ached with regret as I stretched my arms far over my head which was still covered with the sheet I was twisted up in. As I peeked my face over the edge of the white linen, my head immediately throbbed when the sunlight streaming in from the window next to me hit my eyes.

"Ooph," I murmured to myself, squeezing my eyes shut and running my thumbs in circles along my temples.

As I lay there, flickers of memories from last night swam through my mind. Bringing Johnny's letters to a bar. Getting really, really drunk. Reading one of his letters. Walking to his house. Yelling his name until…"Oh God," I breathed.

Throwing the covers off me, I winced against the harsh pang in my head as I looked around the room. This was *not* Sarah's guest room. Nope. I was pretty sure this was Johnny's room as the smell of cedar wood floated around me as though he were standing right in front of me.

I brought my hand to my lips as another memory soared

across my mind. He'd brought me into this room after I'd fallen asleep in his arms in front of the fireplace. With a gentle kiss to my lips, he'd tucked me into bed—gaining the first full night's rest since I'd been back to Pebble Brook Falls.

I looked at the door that was cracked open, likely leading out to the hallway. There was no sign of Johnny or Asher in here and I wondered if he'd slept somewhere else because the pillows on the other side of the bed weren't disturbed. Rising slowly from the bed, I took in my surroundings. Curious to see what his space was like...how he'd grown and shifted into a man who owned a house. It was still so strange to reconcile the wild boy I fell for with the responsible man he'd become.

He'd written in his first letter that it was all for me. That he wanted to become a better version of himself and I could tell that he'd achieved that. Where his childhood bedroom was laden with broken hand-me-down toys and his bed was never made, the military certainly left its mark because his current bedroom was pristine. With a large king-sized canopy bed made of light oakwood, a sheer draping of white chiffon hung over each post. The walls were a light mauve and just like his living room, there wasn't art or pictures hanging on display. But there was a large dresser that matched his bed and heavy white curtains hung over the windows, both panels pulled to the side.

To most people, the space would probably come across as cold or bare, but to me, it felt comforting. Like there was space to breathe without all the clutter that normally filled up a bedroom.

A loud clang sounded from outside the room and it instantly made my head throb. I was in desperate need of coffee to alleviate the headache from my drunken antics last night. But my neck grew hot at the thought of seeing Johnny again. So much was said last night and yet, it still felt like there was a lot we needed to talk about.

Before heading out to face him, I found his en suite bathroom and thankfully discovered mouthwash and an extra toothbrush under his sink. There was no way I was going out there with dragon breath after puking all over his lawn. I moaned to myself at the embarrassment I caused myself last night and made a silent vow to never drink that much alcohol ever again.

After a quick washing up, I strolled out of his room with my head held high. I may have lost all my dignity last night, but there was still time to retrieve some of it...I hoped.

A sizzling sounded and the smell of fried bacon hit my nose before I rounded the hallway corner and found myself in his large kitchen that rivaled Sarah's in both size and beauty. Marbled white countertops sat flush over deep navy blue cabinets and I truly wondered how the version of Johnny I knew when we were children had turned into such a well-traveled and...*domesticated* man.

But all questions emptied from my mind as my eyes shifted to where he stood at the stove. Shirtless. Gray sweatpants hanging so low on his hips that I could see the divets of his lower back where they met the curvature of his perfectly sculpted ass.

Yes. I was staring at Johnny's ass because...well...because it was damn perfect and there wasn't a woman on this planet who wouldn't be doing the exact same thing given my current position.

Asher gave me a warm greeting as he nuzzled his wet nose

against my hand. Johnny turned toward me as I took another step into the room and when my gaze met his, I knew I'd been caught by the smirk on his face.

"Like the view?" he husked, that stupid dimple making its appearance and once again sending a pang straight to my heart.

My mouth bobbed open, but when nothing came out I snapped it shut. Since when did I become this groveling woman who couldn't even think straight in the presence of him?

Since the first time he held your hand at the orphanage, I answered my own stupid question.

It was true. As far as crushes went, mine had been as bad as they came. Growing from pure infatuation to insatiable lust and then to...*love*. And I guessed that was why I was here, standing in Johnny's kitchen after twelve years of not knowing him. There would always be a part of me that wanted to fulfill the 'what if' fantasy that had stuck with me all this time. The wondering of what our life might have been like if he hadn't left me. Or if he'd at least asked me to go with him.

When Johnny shifted back toward the stovetop I squeezed my eyes shut against the growing headache that these thoughts certainly weren't helping. Opening them again, I slowly made my way to a stool at his island and plopped into it.

I watched intently as Johnny placed the tongs on the counter, grabbed a coffee mug, and placed it right in front of me. "Here. This should help with that headache." He winked at me and I nearly fell off the stool.

Yup. I'm a goner.

Wrapping my hands around the porcelain mug, I took in the golden skin of his abdomen, remembering what it felt like to run my hands over the ridges and valleys the first time we made love under a blanket of stars on a warm summer night. But there was something different about him now. Narrowing my gaze, I realized there were scars peppering his center from right below his chest, all the way down to his navel. And on his right side, there were two large scars, circular in nature.

My mouth went dry and my heartbeat kicked up as he turned his back to me, focusing on the food at the stove.

Those scars...

My eyes immediately welled with tears at the thought of him being injured. I understood the reality of war. Had heard the horror stories on the news over the past twelve years while our troops were in the Middle East. But to see the consequences etched into Johnny's flesh was indescribable. The emotions pulsing through me were wild and raging like a bull bucking against the metal stall before the gate swung open.

I swiped at my eyes when Johnny started dishing out the eggs and bacon onto two plates. The last thing I wanted was for him to see me crying.

"Breakfast is served," he said as he set down the plate in front of me. "I hope you still like breakfast food."

"I do. Thank you." I lobbed a smile his way making sure I avoided looking at his abdomen.

Several bites in and with half my coffee drained, the headache was finally starting to fade away. As if Johnny could read my thoughts he asked, "How's your head feeling?"

"A lot better. Thank you."

His dark brown eyes grew serious as he sat a little

straighter. "I don't like that you drank so much last night. Or how you thought it was a good idea to walk from a bar to my house all alone in the middle of the night."

I snorted. "I wasn't doing a lot of thinking last night. It all sort of just...happened."

There was no kindness in his voice, no hint of the boy I once knew as he retorted, "There are people in this world who would have taken pleasure in hurting you if they'd found you walking the streets alone last night, Lo."

"Like the people who hurt you?" I asked the question before the thought of whether or not it was a good idea even crossed my mind.

Johnny's face was set hard as stone, those beautiful eyes growing distant for the briefest moment before he angled his head to look at me. "Yes," he whispered.

I had no right to ask the question that came out of my mouth next, but the pull to learn about the man he'd become...to know everything he'd gone through during all the time we were apart was palpable. So I crossed the line drawn between us, hoping to open the door that would lead us down the path I hoped both of us wanted to take.

"Will you tell me how you got those scars?"

He took a deep breath in and let it out on a long sigh. "You really want to know?"

I nodded. "I do."

Leaning both elbows on the island, he centered his coffee mug between his hands before he started, "It was during my second deployment to Afghanistan. Our squad was working through a small village after we received some intel that one of our targets was likely there. We didn't have a lot of time to move through because our target kept moving locations and we'd been after him for a while. So we didn't get the chance to do a proper sweep before we went in for a night raid. The entire village was rigged with IEDs and I triggered one that went off across the street from where I was standing."

Johnny leaned back and tugged at his skin where several small scars were slashed against his lower abdomen. "My vest saved me from a worse blast, but the damn thing still got me pretty good."

"What about these?" I gingerly stroked the area of his side where the two larger scars were and I noticed his skin rose with goosebumps, his stomach retracting slightly. "I'm sorry," I whispered pulling my hand away and searching his eyes for any sign of distress. The edges of them crinkled as he smiled and grasped my hand with his own.

"Don't be sorry." His brown eyes were molten as he rose my hand to his mouth and pressed his lips against the pads of my fingers. "I love it when you touch me."

I wondered if he could hear my heart racing, feel the quickened thud of my pulse against my wrist as he lowered our joined hands to his knee.

"I was shot that night too."

"You were shot?" I blurted out and he chuckled at me with a mocking smile, that dimple doing strange things to my insides.

"It hurt like a bitch, but thankfully our medic patched me up pretty good."

I knew my mouth was wide open as I stared at him, but I couldn't help it. He was so nonchalant about the fact that he'd been shot. Meanwhile, the thought of that had me wanting to crawl out of my skin. Mostly because I had missed it. I had missed being there for him when he was severely wounded and I hated that.

"What's going through that pretty head of yours, darlin'?" The twang of his accent shone through his affectionate words, sending a shockwave of desire through me. I did my best to hide it though. There was so much we needed to talk about and letting myself get swept away by his charm would only lead us down one road.

"I…" I trailed off feeling overwhelmed by all the emotions swarming through me.

With a gentleness that I knew he only reserved for me, Johnny swept the loose strands of hair behind my right ear, trailing his fingers along the sensitive cuff. "It's just me, Lo. You can tell me anything."

Losing myself in his eyes, in his encouraging words, I let myself speak from my heart. Something I hadn't truly done since the day he walked away from me in that field. "I hate that I wasn't there for you during that. And it terrifies me to think that you could have been taken away from me. That if those bullets had struck you in a different place, I wouldn't be sitting next to you right now. That I would never have the chance to tell you that these past twelve years have been misery. No matter how hard I tried to move on with my life, there was always a piece of me that was missing. A piece I never thought I would get back until I saw you kneeling down with Asher. And…" I sniffled through the tears streaming down my cheeks.

"And what?" he asked quietly.

"And now it feels like fate is playing a cruel game. It put you right in front of me when I finally thought I had my life figured out after you left. Now I feel more lost than ever—

stuck between a life I made for myself and the one I felt like I was always meant to have."

"You make it sound so complicated, Lo."

"It is complicated!" Johnny flinched at my raised and frantic voice. There was no more I could do to hold back the swirl of conflicting emotions that were starting to boil over. I was a mess and the weight was starting to wear on me.

Recovering, he gripped my chin between his thumb and forefinger, boring his gaze deep into mine until I saw every hint of his own emotions reflected back at me. "This life is simple. Do what makes you happy. *Be* with who makes you happy. Don't give a shit about what other people think of you or all the what-if scenarios I know are running through your mind. It's too damn short to waste away on frivolous worries, darlin'. Just do what your heart wants you to."

He was so earnest in his proclamation of what life was supposed to be like. Johnny had always been that way. Holding such conviction in his words that it almost made them tangible. I felt it now. The whispers of what he was trying to say but couldn't fully let himself say it because I was leaving and we both knew what that would mean for us.

My entire body screamed at me to close the distance between us. To grasp his hand that held my face and press my lips to his. For all this mess to fade away and to let myself have what I knew my heart wanted.

But the past twelve years of his absence stopped me. I wasn't ready yet. To fully let go and trust that he wouldn't leave me stranded again.

I knew he thought that leaving for the military was the best decision for us. But he made that decision alone and I needed more time to find out if he was capable of being the partner I needed him to be. More time to heal the wound that had never fully scarred over.

The only thing I thought could move us in the right direction was to share my truth—no matter how much it scared me.

"I need to show you something," I whispered.

CHAPTER TWENTY-ONE

*J*ohnny was silent as I pressed the button on the fob that made the giant iron rod gates swing open. I eyed him sidelong, hoping he would say something…anything. But he remained quiet, eyes fixed on the long driveway ahead of us that led up to the extravagant house that could have fit four orphanages inside of it easily.

He parked the truck in the semi-circle drive and I hopped out of the passenger side before he had a chance to come around and open the door for me. I let Asher out of the back seat and he took off, bounding toward the line of oak trees hunting for some squirrels.

At least he's happy.

Wringing my hands together, I took a few steps onto the front porch. Although, *front porch* didn't quite fit the grandeur of the estate with its insanely high pillars and marble foundation.

Johnny let out a long whistle as he raked his gaze over the front of my new house. "I never thought I'd set foot on an estate like this."

"Me either," I huffed.

"Why're we here, Lo?" Johnny shifted his body toward me. He was a vision in his Levi's jeans that hugged him in places that some would consider improper. I fought the urge to kneel in front of him and unzip those pants.

Stepping into his space I tilted my head back to look at him. "When you left and I didn't hear from you, I nearly lost my mind, Johnny. I almost failed out of school and if it weren't for Sarah making sure I did my homework, I probably wouldn't have graduated. After two years went by and I finally phased out, I had to get away from Pebble Brook Falls. There were...too many haunting memories for me to stay and survive.

"So, I moved to Nashville. Got a job as a waitress during the night and worked in retail during the day. It took a while, but I finally started to dream of a new life. The possibility of me opening my own boutique where I could house some of my own designs. I obviously didn't have any money to start out so I worked two jobs for the past ten years to save up to open my own place. I was still several years away from making that happen when I got a phone call from Mr. Anderson telling me that Adeline Baxley bequeathed me the entire estate and the Baxley fortune."

I laughed thinking back to that phone call and how I hung up on Mr. Anderson thinking it was some kind of cruel prank.

"I honestly thought it was a joke until he sent me a copy of her will." I darted my eyes passed Johnny, feeling nervous. I wasn't quite sure what I was nervous about. Maybe that he would judge me for all the wealth I had at my disposal now. Or maybe I was judging myself.

I looked back at him, keeping my hands behind me to hide the nervous tick of wringing and tugging at them. "Once the news settled and I finally came to terms with it being real, I realized I had a way to make my dream come true much sooner than I could have done on my own." I tossed my hands in the air and let them fall back down to my sides with a light slap. "And maybe that makes me a sellout. And maybe you'd judge me for that, but I finally feel like something is going my way, Johnny."

Those brown eyes narrowed on me as he stalked forward, stopping just as our toes nearly met. "You honestly think I would *judge* you for taking what was rightfully owed to you? What that serpent of a woman stole from you?" His laugh was harsh as his Adam's apple bobbed. When he met my gaze again, I went utterly still from the look in his eyes as he spoke, "I have spent my entire life trying to prove to myself that I am worthy of your love, Willow. I went into the military to become a man with honor, to make a living to support us, to support *you* and whatever dreams you wanted to come true. There isn't a bone in my body that could judge you for taking the money or this house from Adeline. You deserve to have the entire world laid at your feet." His lips were only an inch from mine, our breaths heaving as one. "My only wish was that I could have been the one to give it to you."

And then he kissed me. He kissed me like he was trying to make up for the past twelve years in one single moment. Like I was the very oxygen he needed to survive. And I kissed him just the same. Our arms were a tangled mess as we found one another. Roaming. Discovering. Remembering. When his tongue swept fervently against mine, my knees nearly buckled from the swarm of butterflies that flitted through my middle.

I opened for him, letting him claim what had always been his. I'd been a fool...an utter fool to think he had abandoned me without a thought. That he hadn't spent all our time apart loving me as I did him. I'd let my own doubt eat away at the only pure thing in my life—the love we shared. But Johnny kissed away any remnants of that doubt. Leaving nothing but searing desire in the wake of his lips as he trailed them along my jaw and down my neck, holding me close against him with the palms of his hands splayed wide over the small of my back.

Bark! Bark!

We broke away, the moment stolen by a furry little brat who wanted all the attention for himself. Johnny moaned, his eyes closed, forehead pressed against mine. I couldn't help but laugh as I looked down and saw Asher sitting right next to where we stood, his golden eyes bright with joy and his tongue lolling to the side as he panted.

"You're a little stinker," I whispered, glaring at him.

"Oh, he'll get what's coming to him. No treats for an entire week."

I gasped. "That's a bit harsh, Johnny." Kneeling down to love on Asher I couldn't feel frustrated by him for a second more because he whimpered at me and started licking my forearms as I scratched his chest. "Don't worry, boy. I'll make sure you still get your treats."

Johnny chuckled. "It's barely been a week and you two are already conspiring against me."

"Can you blame us?" I batted my lashes and stuck out my bottom lip and Johnny laughed, his broad shoulders shifting up and down.

"Yeah"—he rolled his eyes—"you are pretty darn cute. But

that won't take away from the mischief I know you'll both cause."

I didn't miss how he spoke about the future. Of me being in his life longer than the next few days when I was set to leave for Nashville on Monday. Not wanting to ruin the moment, I kept that to myself. Mostly because the thought of leaving him made my stomach twist into knots. And if I was honest with myself, the dream of opening a boutique in Nashville was feeling more and more distant the more I spent time with Johnny, feeling an old dream—one that had been buried beneath the mistakes of others for so long—come back to life.

But I kept that to myself too as Johnny reached for my hand, intertwining his fingers with mine and we walked through the door of the Baxley estate.

"You know, I never understood why someone would get such a huge house when there were only two people to live in it." Johnny's voice echoed off the marble floor of the grand foyer.

"It does seem like a waste, doesn't it?"

My hand felt small in his as I guided him through the foyer and into the formal living space next to the kitchen. He stopped just behind the cream sofa and shifted his attention to the large painted portrait of my grandmother and mother.

"It's so strange," I whispered. "Seeing how much I look like them. I'm honestly surprised no one noticed the similarities before her death."

"People see what they want to see," Johnny said, turning to

me. "Adeline always seemed like the kind of person to hide away things she didn't want seen. Even if that meant destroying someone else's life."

Seconds of silence ticked by until I couldn't stand to look at Adeline's face any longer—I felt the heat of her haunting eyes as though the painting had captured her soul and she found joy in watching me question everything. Johnny followed as I opened the middle pair of French doors and stepped onto the back porch overlooking the immaculate garden.

"I don't think my mom was like that," I said quietly, keeping my gaze fixed on the view in front of me.

When I finally had the nerve to look his way, Johnny's face was neutral. No hint of judgment or questioning. He was simply present. Giving me the space and support I needed to continue just as he'd always done. "The first time I came here a few days ago, I found my mother's old room. It's the only part of the house that hasn't been touched. I think in her own twisted way, Adeline loved my mother, and keeping her room preserved was a way for her to keep the memory of her daughter alive. When I looked through it, I found Melanie's journal. I..."

Swallowing against the lump in my throat, I braced myself for the revelation that still brought me shame. "I read it," I blurted out. "And maybe that makes me a terrible person who has no boundaries, even for her dead mother. But I couldn't help myself. Ever since I found out who she was and how close we'd been, I always questioned why she gave me up. I knew I'd never get the truth from Adeline, even if I ever got the nerve to ask her. So, for years I walked around thinking that I was the mistake Melanie wanted to bury in her closet. I knew it wasn't the money"—I spread my arms wide, gesturing around us—"because they had more than enough to provide for me. The only other option was that she didn't love me."

"Willow," Johnny hummed my name like a prayer as his face softened and he made his way to stand behind me, draping his arms over my shoulders so I could lean against him. His body acted as a pillar of strength—a symbol of what he'd always been in my life.

"It's okay, Johnny." I pressed my back tighter against his front and grasped his hands that were lingering at my midsection. "It's okay because I found out that she really did love me. Some people might think it's messed up for me to have read her journal, but I think I was meant to find it. Because she wrote about being pregnant with me and how badly she wanted to protect me."

"Protect you from what?" he asked, nuzzling my cheek with his nose as he leaned down.

I fought against the urge to just close my eyes and let myself get lost in the feeling of having him so close because I needed to talk about this. I needed to tell him everything that was on my heart if there was going to be a chance of us having any sort of future. I didn't want there to be any more chances for things to go wrong between us…even if I was supposed to be leaving in a few days.

I shoved that thought away. A problem for future me to deal with.

"Melanie wrote in her journal that she wanted to protect me from the people in her world, specifically Adeline. I guess she felt like Adeline had done her best to control her own life and she didn't want that for me. That's why I went to Ms. Mosely. I wanted to hear it from her because Melanie had written about their conversations. How she wanted Ms. Mosely to raise me in a way that I would be prepared to take everything over once Adeline died and it was just me and my mother left. But Melanie didn't outlive Adeline like she thought she would."

I turned in Johnny's embrace, needing to see his face.

"What did Ms. Mosely say when you went to see her?" he asked, his face growing stoic again. He'd never been fond of Ms. Mosely.

"She said everything was true. That Melanie had come to her when she first found out she was pregnant and that she had strict stipulations for how she wanted me to be raised." I swallowed as a chill ran over my arms despite the heat. "Melanie told Ms. Mosely she wanted to keep me out of trouble. That she didn't want me to get caught up in anything that would be bad for me. And…"

"And that's why Ms. Mosely kept my letters from you." Johnny's voice was gravelly as he took a step backward, just out of my reach. The movement felt like a slap in the face, the sting of it reverberating in my heart.

"I told her she was wrong." I moved toward him, taking his hand in mind, but he wouldn't look at me. This wound ran deep—the pain of it was etched all over his face, burned into the chestnut brown of his irises.

I knew now. I knew that Johnny had carried the weight of his parents' troubles for his entire life. To the point that he decided to leave the only sure thing he had so that he could become the man he needed to be to never slip over the dangerous ledge that led to his parents' demise. He had a wild streak, a rebellious nature that coursed through his veins that not even a decade in the military would change.

So, I understood his fear of turning into his parents, letting addiction rule his life. But that didn't take away from the agony I knew he felt from being judged by everyone around him—everyone except for me.

"Look at me, Johnny." When he continued staring right over the top of my head I told him again, "Look at me, please!" His brown eyes shifted to mine and my heart cracked at the vulnerability shining in them.

"You are *not* your parents. Even in all the years apart, I never thought once that you would become them. You are too good. Too driven to be the opposite of what they were. So, please don't let Ms. Mosely, of all people, dictate how you feel about yourself right now."

The edges of his mouth tilted up in a sad smile as he brought his hand up to cup my cheek. I grabbed his wrist and leaned into his touch. "You've always seen the best in me, darlin'. Even when I couldn't see it myself."

"And you've done the same for me, Johnny," I whispered, bringing his hand down to the top of his knuckles. "You've loved me even when I thought no one else in the world could."

He grazed his lips over mine with such gentle affection I nearly wept. "But now you know that she loved you too. That you had a parent who was willing to sacrifice getting to raise you as her own so that you would be protected from the evil of her society. It's pretty powerful—the love your mother had for you. I'm really glad you were able to discover that and I think you were right. Finding her journal was meant to happen."

I nodded slowly as his words sunk in. Wondering how he must be feeling after learning that we were different. Throughout our childhood, we were kindred spirits. Two souls who'd been cast away...unwanted. But now. Now, he knew, just as well as I did, that my mother had wanted the best for me. And that made us different because his parents had always been too concerned with their next fix to show him any kind of love or remorse for their actions.

I wanted to tell him that I loved him. That I had remorse for so many things, especially for blaming him for leaving me. For pitting all my anger toward him when it had been misdirected all along.

But my phone rang loudly from my back pocket and we both started. "I'm sorry," I murmured, fishing my phone out from my jean shorts.

Sarah's name flashed across the screen and I showed it to him.

"Answer it," he said, shoving his hands into his pockets.

"Hey, Sarah." I kept my gaze fixed on Johnny.

"Willow? Are you able to come to the bakery, I really need you right now." Her voice was frantic and my stomach immediately plummeted. Sarah never asked me for anything, but I could hear the desperation in her voice.

"Of course! What's going on?" Johnny's brows furrowed with concern.

"I...I don't want to talk about it over the phone. Can you just come here?" Her voice cracked and I could tell she was holding back tears.

"Yes, I'm at the Baxley estate so it'll be about fifteen minutes but I'm leaving right now."

"Thank you," she whispered before hanging up the phone.

"What's going on?" Johnny asked, rubbing my back up and down with his large palm as we strode back through the house and out front where his truck was. Asher followed closely on our heels.

"I don't know. She said she didn't want to talk about it over the phone, but whatever it is she's really upset and wants me to meet her at the bakery."

"Okay. I'll drop you off and stick around downtown in case you need me."

"Thank you," I told him before he opened the passenger side door and I climbed into his truck.

CHAPTER TWENTY-TWO

*S*arah was a mushy pile of tears in the corner of her bakery's kitchen when I walked in. Stephanie was working the front and had a look of disdain on her face when I first arrived. I knew better than to ask her what happened since there were prying eyes peering at us from all the tables, waiting to get their fill of the gossip. I would do everything I could to make sure Sarah didn't fall victim to their pettiness.

"Oh, Sarah," I soothed as she looked up at me with swollen, bloodshot eyes and I knelt down to take her in my arms.

Her tears soaked through my cotton t-shirt as she sobbed into my shoulder. I rubbed her back in large sweeping circles until the sound of her crying slowly came to a stop and she finally leaned back, running her hands over her sodden face.

"What happened?" I sank lower onto the floor and crossed my legs. She drew her knees upward and rested the side of her face on them, a sad distant look clouded her eyes as she sniffled.

"My mom came by the bakery today."

I swallowed the sigh that threatened to pass through my lips. That statement alone was enough for me to understand why Sarah was in such a tizzy. Mary Lynne Williams—Sarah's mother—was similar to Adeline in a lot of ways. Consumed with the desire to be well-liked by her elite peers and that meant she had to keep a tight leash on her children to prevent them from doing anything that might cause the Williams' name shame. Unfortunately, Sarah had already done that in Mary Lynne's eyes when she had forgone the route of becoming a doctor, or at the very least finding a suitable husband and raising a perfect brood of children.

"What did she say?" I took Sarah's hand in mine and she sat up a little straighter, eyes fixed on mine.

"Apparently Theo finally decided he wanted to quit law school and pursue the rodeo. He called me last night and told me how he had a big falling out with our parents when he told them he was leaving Virginia and coming back here in a few months. He never wanted to be a lawyer. He only pursued law school to keep the peace with our parents after I opened the bakery. I told him not to worry about it. To not let them rule his life, but you know him. He wants everyone to be happy."

It was true. Theo had always been the kind-hearted one. The kid who couldn't stand to see other people hurting, including his sister, so he would often sacrifice his own well-being to ensure the happiness of others. But sacrifice often caught up to those who did it too often, leaving them drained and burnt out. Even though it ultimately led to Sarah having conflict with her mom, I was glad to see Theo standing up for himself. Going after what made him happy.

"So, your mom came here?" I gently urged Sarah to continue.

She nodded and fresh tears spilled over the rims of her eyes. "She started yelling at me in front of everyone. I've never seen her that mad before, Willow. To lose her cool in public...everyone was staring. Some of my regulars even left in the middle of it and they'll probably never come back again."

"Of course they'll come back," I tried pacifying her rising anxiety. "You make the best sweet treats in all of Georgia. They won't be able to resist."

That got a small smile from her. The tears had her eyelashes sticking together as her bright brown eyes flicked up to meet mine. "Thanks," she muttered.

"I only speak the truth."

Sarah's shoulders slumped downward again. "I haven't even told you the worst part."

"What's that?" I asked, rubbing her hand back and forth with mine.

"You know how I told you Mrs. Jackson wanted me to provide little Tommy's cake for his birthday?"

I didn't like where this was going, but I replied, "Mmhmm."

"Well, right after my mom left the bakery I got a call from Mrs. Jackson saying that she found someone else for Tommy's birthday and she wouldn't be needing my services." Sarah buried her face in her hands. "That was the biggest account I've gotten since opening the bakery and I know she took that away from me. She probably called Mrs. Jackson on her way over here and conspired against me before I even had a fighting chance."

"I am so so sorry, Sarah."

"Why would she do that, Willow?" Sarah's eyes grew wide.

"She's my mother! Isn't she supposed to want what's best for me?"

I didn't know how to answer that question because my only experience with mothers was reading the journal of mine who was taken from me before I had the chance to know her. The only thing I did know was that becoming a parent wasn't an immediate pass to becoming a better person. I imagined Mary Lynne was always this way. Worried about what other people might think of her if she did the slightest thing wrong in the eyes of Georgia's finest. It seemed like that trait carried over into motherhood and now she was trying to shape her daughter to fit those same expectations.

It worried me. Because as much as Sarah claimed to be a rebellious child and even though she had done the damn thing and opened a bakery despite her parents' wishes, she was a gentle soul. The anguish this single argument had caused her was written all over her face. My best friend preferred for all to be well. To avoid conflict at all costs. She was a baker for Christ's sake.

"Stand up," I said, rising to my feet.

"What?" she blubbered.

"Stand up," I said again with a little more oomph, extending my hands toward her. "I'm not going to let you sit around sulking all day because that's exactly what your mom wants. She's trying to get inside your head and find any way she can to have you second guess your choices and I won't have that. This is what you *love* and even if Mrs. Jackson decided to go with another bakery for little Tommy's birthday, you will find another large account, Sarah. I know you will." I wiggled my fingers at her and she took my hands. I leaned back a little as I helped lift her from the cold tile floor of her kitchen.

"I know just the thing to make you feel better." I smiled at her and she rolled her eyes at me with a groan.

"I doubt that, but thank you for saying all that. I...I've missed you, Willow. And I really hate that you won't be staying longer."

Her words pulled at my heart, tugging it in a direction that felt terrifying and...*right* all at the same time. It was a path I stared down, wondering what kind of future might await me if I chose to forego my original plans and shift course. But this moment wasn't about me, it was about my best friend.

So I brought my attention back to her and gently said, "Me too, Sarah." *Me too.*

"I don't see how shooting a bow and arrow is going to make me feel better," Sarah huffed.

Thankfully, Stephanie had planned on helping Sarah with the bakery all day and she'd graciously taken over when I told her Sarah needed to take the rest of the day off. Johnny drove us to his archery store and set up the practice area behind his shop for us to shoot.

"Johnny told me that archery is very peaceful and if it helped him, it might help calm you down too."

Johnny came out the back door of his store with three longbows and a tall sleeve of arrows. My heart raced as he looked my way and shot me a wink with a one-sided grin that had his dimple on full display.

Asshole. He knew exactly what he was doing when he looked at me like that. I cleared my throat and turned back to Sarah.

"Everything alright?" Johnny asked. "You don't look too pleased, Sarah."

When she opened her mouth to complain, I cut in, "She's just throwing a pity party. She'll get over it soon." Sarah glared at me and I nudged her with my hip.

Johnny handed Sarah and me a bow and sat his on the picnic table next to where we all stood. "Have either of you shot with a bow before?"

Sarah and I shook our heads.

"Okay, I'll run through the basics and fire a few shots so you can see my stance and how I pull back before you try. Sound good?"

"Yup," I said and Sarah nodded.

Picking his bow up he showed us how to grip it. I adjusted my hand so the space between my thumb and forefinger was aligned with the smooth grip in the middle of the bow.

"Each bow has a different draw weight depending on the strength of the archer, as well as the expertise. Mine is sixty pounds, but I brought out forty pounds for both of you to try out. You can test it by bringing the bow up"—Johnny raised his bow and pulled the string back until his hand aligned right next to where his dimple normally appeared—"and pulling the string back like this."

Sarah and I took a step back and did as Johnny suggested. The string cut into the index and middle finger of my right hand as I drew it back toward my face. The pull wasn't too hard as I kept the string taut.

"Good," Johnny praised. "If your draw fingers start to get sore let me know and I can get you a leather finger tab to protect them."

"I think I might need one of those already," Sarah giggled letting the string fall back and shaking her hand out. Only a few minutes in and she was already laughing. I was thankful for it, though I kept the observation to myself to prevent another glare from her.

Johnny's brown eyes shone golden in the afternoon sun as he smiled at Sarah. "No problem. I'll grab you one in just a minute."

He loves this, I thought to myself as I took him in. The way his broad shoulders were relaxed and how easy it was for him to smile as he continued talking about the best way to draw back and how to take the wind into consideration for increasing accuracy. Archery was clearly his passion and I couldn't help but feel warmth spread through my chest seeing how settled he was. How joyful his face looked. Especially after our difficult conversation this morning, it nearly brought tears to my eyes knowing that he had something that made him feel *good*.

I hope I make him feel good too.

The thought surprised me as I once again found myself staring down that alternate path. The one I had once hoped I could walk down, but had let go of after Johnny left for the military. It was starting to take shape, becoming clearer than it had ever been before. A path that seemed to lead to truth and happiness and...love. A concept that had become so foreign to me over the years as I threw myself into working and saving and trying to conjure another dream.

"Willow," Sarah hissed, jabbing me with the end of her longbow.

"Ow!" I swatted at her bow and she cackled.

"You're the one who dragged me out here. Pay attention." She cocked her head toward Johnny who had moved a few feet away from me amidst my daydream and was now aiming an arrow at the target that seemed way too far away.

His back was a tangle of muscles under his white t-shirt. I bit my lower lip as I took in the way his broad shoulders held steady, despite the strain I knew it took to hold a bowstring for that long. Those shoulders tapered down to his thin waist and I couldn't help but recall the small divets that sat right above his ass when I gawked at him this morning. My mouth watered as my eyes continued to trek lower, over his butt that fit perfectly in those Levi's. It wasn't fair. It wasn't fair how good he looked. How his forearms were thick, corded with veins that showed just how in shape he was.

That isn't the only thick part of him. Dirty, raunchy thoughts flooded my mind as I realized I was nearly panting like a bitch in heat.

Cut it out, Willow. A few kisses and you're a drooling fool over the man.

But damn those kisses were amazing. And it wasn't like I'd spent the last twelve years satisfying the itch with someone else. I was trying to find my way in the world and spent most of my time pining over a man who I thought didn't love me. Sure, I had a few dates, but they were all frogs. Not a single one of them gave me the barrage of butterflies soaring through my stomach with a single look. Nor did they make me weak in the knees by simply brushing their lips against mine. Or leave me completely dumbfounded, unable to pay attention to anything else except the way he looked in Levi's jeans.

None of them were *him*. The one who always had my heart, even when I didn't want him to.

Johnny released the arrow and within a split second, it found its mark. Landing in the middle of the bullseye.

"Holy shit," Sarah whispered and I echoed her sentiments. "I didn't realize he was that good of a shot."

Johnny looked at me over his shoulder and winked. *Bastard*. I rolled my eyes and turned to Sarah who had a mocking grin on her face. "What?" I asked, sliding a hand to my hip.

"I think I've discovered my secret weapon to get you to stay in Pebble Brook Falls."

I simply raised my eyebrows at her and she laughed.

"There's no way you can tell me that you are going to leave when you have all that"—she ran her hand up and down in the air, gesturing toward Johnny as he walked to the target— "waiting for you to devour. Honestly, I don't know if I could still be friends with you if you left all that manly goodness behind for some other hussy to claim. I mean he is *ho*—"

"Okay!" I nearly shouted, cutting her off. "I get it. Johnny is amazing. He's hot and sexy and sweet and I'd be a fool to walk away from him. To leave a chance at love behind to go back to Nashville where I will be all alone. Are you enjoying yourself? Pointing out all the reasons why I should stay."

Sarah's smile turned absolutely feral like I was a mouse that had just been caught in her expertly crafted trap. "I think I'm going to grab a drink from inside," she mused, leaving her bow on the table and heading for the back door of Johnny's store.

I seared a hole into the back of my best friend's head with my scowl, not realizing that Johnny was standing right behind me as he asked, "So, you think I'm hot and sexy?" I nearly jumped out of my skin at the sound of his gravelly voice.

I'm going to go to jail, I thought. *Because as soon as Sarah comes back out here, I'm going to kill her.*

"You heard that?" I groaned.

His lips curved upward, melting me where I stood. "How could I not hear it, darlin'? You basically yelled it for all the world to hear. Not that I'm complaining." Johnny took another step toward me and knelt down to whisper into my ear, "I want everyone on this fucking planet to know how you feel about me so that it won't be a surprise when they hear you screaming my name from the pleasure I fully intend on bringing you."

A shiver ran down my spine from the intimate promise laced in his words.

"Are you willing to let me give that to you, Lo?"

I swallowed as he leaned back, a challenge dancing in his eyes. This was a far cry from the boy I fell in love with—the one I gave everything to in that field. We were both a mess of tangled gangly limbs, hungry for a taste of that first release, but neither one of us had a clue as to what we were doing. We were just teenagers, madly in love, and now... Now things were different as my body hummed with the need to be touched by him.

Heat flushed my neck and cheeks as I said, "I think I would like that very much."

"That's my girl." His lips caressed my own. A tease that had my stomach coiling tightly just as I heard the door of his shop open again.

Johnny left me with a smirk and I blew out a long breath. *He's going to be the end of me.* But not a single fiber of my being was upset about that fact.

CHAPTER TWENTY-THREE

"*L*ook who I found!" Sarah called out to us.

A tall man with rugged features was standing next to Sarah, almost looking pained that he had to be around other people. But that didn't stop Sarah from gesturing for him to come over to the picnic table and meet us. She was clearly feeling better from the tumultuous morning with her mom given the sunny disposition she now had as she sauntered over to us, her man-friend in tow.

He was a few inches taller than Johnny and shared the same chestnut brown hair peeking out from a baseball hat that had a bass with a hook hanging out of its mouth stitched onto the front of it. But his eyes...they were the most vivid green I'd ever seen and they carried a haunted look that reminded me of the way Johnny's eyes would glaze over when he talked about his parents or the war. Jeans covered his strong legs and he wore a black t-shirt that had a fishing company logo written over the chest pocket.

I felt Johnny step next to me and I looked up at him. He returned my glance with a knowing look—his right eyebrow lifted as humor danced along his sensuous lips. He'd caught me gawking at the stranger. Not that Johnny had anything to worry about. Looking was one thing, but there was no part of me that wanted to touch anything other than Johnny's body and he knew it.

So, I shrugged and winked at him and he tilted his head back, letting out a full laugh that was like music to my ears. It was the best sound I ever heard and reminded me of countless happy memories we shared despite the lot we were given as kids.

"Lo, I haven't had a chance to introduce you to the co-owner of *Far Away Archery*. This is Deacon Calhoun. Deacon, this is Willow Mae."

"It's nice to meet you, Willow" Deacon extended his hand toward me and I shook it, feeling the calluses of his palms scrape against my skin. While the guarded look in his eyes didn't waver, the harsh contours of his face softened with the slightest tilt of his lips. It was a strained smile at best, almost like the gesture was so foreign to him that his facial muscles had a difficult time lifting.

"It's nice to meet you too, Deacon. How do you and Sarah know each other?"

I eyed her suspiciously wondering if he was a secret she'd kept from me. But the look she gave him was platonically kind as she replied for him, "We met at the Summer Festival last year and have worked some of the farmer's markets together. He fries the fish he catches and the entire town gobbles it up within an hour. Honestly, it's kind of annoying seeing how successful he's been when it's taken me years to sell out before the markets end."

"Well, that's not the case anymore," Johnny butted in and I

knew he did it on Sarah's behalf after she told him what happened with her mom this morning when he drove us here. "You're booth always sells out now."

"Yeah, I know." She grinned. "I just like giving this big guy a hard time." Sarah elbowed Deacon in the ribs and he looked down at her with fondness.

"Sounds about right," Johnny chuckled and I realized at that moment that I had missed out on so much since Johnny moved back here and I had been in Nashville. Sarah and him jested so easily and I was reminded of all the years we shared together as friends. I hadn't realized how much I missed that until this moment and maybe that was because I spent so much time running away that I never stopped to consider exactly what I was running from.

"How about you boys finally teach us how to shoot?" Sarah asked as she retrieved her longbow from the picnic table and handed it to Deacon.

"I think we can manage that," Johnny replied with a glint in his eyes as he set his longbow on the table, grabbed an arrow from the sleeve, and moved until he stood right behind me. I could feel the warmth of his body radiating into my back as he gestured for me to raise my bow.

When his hands landed on my hips, I sucked in a sharp breath at the contact. "Shift this way, with your left leg shining forward and your right leg a step back. Good, darlin'," he purred against my neck and I nearly fumbled the bow right out of my hands.

"Steady," he chuckled. "We don't need your shot spraying to the side."

"Maybe my shot wouldn't *spray to the side* if someone weren't trying so damn hard to distract me."

The five o'clock shadow on his chin scraped against the sensitive skin over the nape of my neck as he whispered into my ear, "Oh, I plan on doing a lot more than just distracting you, Willow Mae. But no harm ever came from having a little fun during foreplay." He gave my ass a little smack and I yipped, turning to face him with my mouth gaping open in shock.

Johnny just stood there with a wicked smile on his face. *Bastard.* I glanced over at Sarah who was enthralled with whatever Deacon was telling her. Thankfully, neither one of them had noticed that Johnny was taunting me—or maybe they just chose to stay out of our little game.

"While you are being *very* naughty, *I* am actually trying to learn how to shoot. So, would you mind helping me?" I gave him the best neutral staredown I could manage, despite the roaring in my veins to throw the longbow to the side and tackle Johnny to the ground so I could lick every delicious inch of him. But if he wanted to play the teasing game, I'd make sure to best him.

Turning my back toward the target, I raised the longbow up again waiting to feel him at my back again. His presence was palpable as I felt him near, sliding the arrow alongside the bow until it was slotted against the side and the part he called the nock sat tightly against the string.

His left arm fell across me, guiding my own arm upward. "You want to make sure that your line of sight is directly behind the arrow point. Where you look is where the arrow should fly."

I angled the bow slightly upward so I could see the arrow point better. "Good girl," Johnny husked in my ear, sending a cascade of goosebumps over my arms. His large frame enveloped me from behind, so close that I could feel the ridge of his fly rubbing over my backside. Leaning back so he was flush against me, I ground my ass into his crotch.

Johnny's chest rumbled with a low growl right before his teeth grazed my earlobe. "Keep that up and I'll bend you over that table right now, darlin' and give you exactly what you're asking for."

I felt my lips tilt upward in a feline smile. "Maybe that's exactly what I want."

He snorted, checking my bluff. "When I take you, this entire town will hear you screaming my name."

White hot need had my sex throbbing and I knew my pink lace thong was soaking wet from his words alone. "But we will have to wait for that," he crooned. "You said you wanted me to teach you how to shoot, so let's shoot."

I groaned and he chuckled, his breath hot against my neck. I was too wild for him, too affected by his touch. And he was far too in control of himself that there was no way I would ever win this game. "Fine," I pouted. "How do I do this damn thing?"

With another soft laugh, he gripped my right elbow and raised it until it was jutting outward, my fingertips gripped around the string with the arrow snuggly between them. "Pull the string back slowly until the arrow nock is next to the crease of your mouth."

The arrow wobbled a little as I did what he told me to, but once I had the string pulled back the arrow righted itself. "Good. Now focus on the bull's eye and line up the arrow point where you want it to go."

I was surprised by the strength I had keeping the string pulled back and the arrow nocked steadily. Keeping my eyes trained on the bullseye, I shifted my elbow down slightly so the arrow point was aimed right at the middle of the target.

"Now take a deep breath and on your exhale, release the string." Balmy summer air filled my lungs as I drew a long inhale and at the top of my breath, I rolled my fingers off the string and let the arrow fly. Time almost seemed to slow as I watched the arrow soar through the open space and land just to the right of the bull's eye.

"Holy shit!" I yelped. "I did it!"

Sarah started clapping next to me and Johnny took hold of my shoulders, giving them a gentle squeeze. "Nice shot." He pressed a kiss to my cheek as I beamed at my success.

Sarah was next up and Deacon helped her align her stance and her drawback, standing not nearly as close as Johnny had to me. When the arrow sprung from the string, it landed a little further right than mine had, but she still hit the target.

"Yes!" she shouted, raising a fist into the air.

"Nice job, Sarah!" I high-fived her noticing that all remnants of her earlier strife were gone.

The three of us took a few more shots as Deacon took a seat at the picnic table, watching us in silence. All four of Johnny's arrows hit the bullseye while two of mine sprayed wide and two landed within the inner ring. Every shot Sarah made landed in the grass next to the target, giving me the perfect opportunity to poke fun at her.

Deacon even chimed in after her final shot with, "It's okay, Sarah. Sometimes all you get is a one-hit-wonder."

Johnny and I shook with laughter and I was genuinely surprised the quiet giant had it in him.

"So, how did you and Johnny meet?" I asked Deacon after we all joined him at the table.

"We served together in Afghanistan during his first deployment."

"Oh, wow. You were in the Marines too?"

"Nope. Army. We were stationed at the same base during our deployment. I served in the 75th Rangers Regiment and we did a lot of work with the Marines when we were overseas."

"I wouldn't say you did *a lot* of work, Deacon. You Army guys are known to leave a lot of the real work to us."

It was the first time I saw a flicker of a smile on Deacon's lips.

"Well, I think Air Force guys are hotter than any of you fools," Sarah said with a cunning look on her face.

"What?" Johnny snorted at the same time Deacon said, "No fucking way."

Sarah looked my way and a crack formed in her deceitful facade as she blew a raspberry and burst out laughing.

"So are you planning on being at the bonfire tomorrow night, Johnny? I was hoping to drag Willow along with me before she leaves for Nashville on Monday."

My happy balloon deflated the moment she said Nashville and judging by the way Johnny's jaw worked as his teeth ground together, he was feeling the same way. Everything was happening so quickly and all of it was completely unexpected. There was no time for me to take a moment and figure out what the heck I was doing now that so much had changed. I came to Pebble Brook Falls with one goal in mind—get the money and get out. I didn't even plan on figuring out the estate until my next trip back because I had three meetings scheduled over the next few weeks with store owners to finally start leasing a space for my boutique.

But now... I peeked at Johnny and saw the same torment in his face that was raging in my heart. To be parted from him again would be...unbearable.

"What do you think, Willow?" Sarah interrupted my thoughts and I shifted my attention away from Johnny to look at her.

"Yeah." I cleared my throat. "I think that'd be fun. Where is it?"

Deacon answered, "It's on my property. I have a few acres on the north side of town. Badger Creek runs right through it."

"It's actually pretty romantic," Sarah mused looking straight at me. She either didn't notice the tension she created between Johnny and me with her comment about me going back to Nashville or she was choosing to act oblivious. It was probably the latter.

"I'm in." Johnny bumped fists with Deacon, his face unreadable now—even to me.

Sarah lifted a brow at me. "Sure. Sounds like fun," were my famous last words.

CHAPTER TWENTY-FOUR

"*I* can't believe you've never hooked up with Deacon," I said to Sarah after we made it back to her place. We were on a pasta kick this week and she was layering a dish of lasagna.

With a shrug, she replied, "I never saw him in that light before. He's a little too reserved for me I think. I need someone more…wild."

"Wild?" I peered at her over the rim of my wine glass. I'd forsaken the vow I made to swear off alcohol forever when she taunted me with a very expensive bottle of Cabernet

"Yeah. I was raised to be such a good girl that I feel like I missed out on those wild teenage years, you know? Maybe part of me wants to try it on for size."

While Johnny and I had dragged Sarah out for some good fun, we never let her stay out past her curfew after one incident when she and I were fourteen. We were out at the river bank, and some of the older kids got a hold of some beer, and being stupid kids we didn't know our own limits. When we brought Sarah back four hours past her curfew...I'd never heard Mr. Williams yell so loud before. And Mrs. Williams had given Sarah the silent treatment for three straight weeks, making Sarah feel like an outcast in her own family.

It made sense she had a delayed urge to sow her wild oats.

"So, um, are there any *wild men* around here you might have your eye on?"

Sarah nearly choked on the sip of wine she just took. "No." Her eyes went wide as she wiped her mouth and took another long swig from the glass.

"Mmhmm. Right," I laughed.

"Enough about me." She waved a hand through the air. "You have three days left in Pebble Brook Falls. Things have progressed between you and Johnny. It kind of seems like a dumpster fire from where I'm standing."

"You're not wrong there," I sighed.

"Have you at least talked about it?"

"By talking about it do you mean telling him that I'm still in love with him?"

Sarah went still, the long noodle in her hands sagging between them. "Oh, Willow. What did he say?"

A heavy weight settled deep in my chest. "He told me that his heart has always been mine. That there's never been a day when that wasn't true."

"What are you going to do?"

Burying my face in my hands, I murmured, "I don't know."

"And what does Johnny think about that?"

Recalling how his face looked earlier today when Sarah brought up the fact that I was leaving in a few days, I doubted he was happy about my indecisiveness.

"I don't know for sure, but I imagine he's pretty upset. This isn't an easy decision for me, Sarah. I've built a life for myself in Nashville. I had plans to make it work out there. I'm supposed to be meeting with shop owners next week to talk about leasing in some of the most well-known shopping districts. I still want to open my boutique. Letting go of that dream doesn't feel...fair."

Sarah cleared her throat, finally letting the noodle drop over the layer of meat sauce. "Um, Willow. I don't know if you have realized this yet, but you could literally buy out an entire shopping center with the money you have now. So meeting with these people kind of seems like a moot point. I mean shit, you could buy out every storefront in Pebble Brook Falls and make the entire downtown area one big boutique."

We both laughed at her ridiculousness, but she was right. Buying a store outright wasn't something that had even crossed my mind. Probably because I'd spent my entire life salvaging people's hand-me-downs and working multiple jobs to make ends meet. I knew the inheritance would help me in some capacity, but I never thought once about the magnitude of just how much money I now had.

"It seems that Captain Obvious has evaded me because no. That honestly never crossed my mind."

She smiled widely at me. "You can do whatever the hell you want now, Willow. There are no limits with the kind of money you have."

I wrung my hands under the counter, the insanity of her statement taking hold. There was over two hundred million dollars in my bank account now and as uncomfortable as that fact made me feel, Sarah was right. The world was my oyster and maybe it was time that I finally let that be okay.

As I watched Sarah complete the decadent lasagna dish, my mind wandered to a corner storefront with white shiplap walls.

My heart fluttered from the text message on my screen.

Good morning, beautiful.

I read it five times before I replied.

Good morning to you, handsome.

It was Friday morning, the day of Deacon's infamous bonfire gathering. Sarah informed me that his parties always got a little crazy. Apparently, he made his own moonshine and soaked some grapes in it last year. By the end of the night, Sarah had stumbled on Deacon beating up a guy behind some bushes who'd come from a few towns over. And most of the crowd had crashed in the grass of Deacon's field. I didn't really take Deacon as the fighting type, but Sarah said the moonshine had a tendency to make people go against their true nature, so I made a mental note to stay away from any fruit tonight.

Excitement and nerves battled within me because while I had a sense of peace about changing my plans to head back to Nashville, Johnny and I haven't talked about it yet. Since he left for the military, I'd grown cautious with my heart. Never giving anyone the ability to come into my life. I even grew distant from Sarah for fear that she would find some reason to leave me too.

But I wanted this chance. If I was honest with myself, I'd wanted it from the moment I saw Asher running up to Johnny. Hope had become a fragile thing in my life—a beacon of disappointment that had a history of shattering me completely. Now, it was the only thing I had to hold onto if I wanted to walk that path that seemed to beckon me in the same way that birds flew south for the winter. It was instinct that drove them and mine told me that wherever Johnny was is where I was meant to be.

I reached for my mother's journal on the nightstand, thinking of how her decision to place me in the *Hope for All* orphanage had brought me to Johnny. If I had grown up in her world I probably wouldn't have looked twice at him when we finally met at school. Although, it seemed like dating the rebels ran in our blood. My dad was out there somewhere, but I hadn't read anything that might point me in the right direction to find him. If finding him was even something I wanted to do—I wasn't quite sure yet. The little I read about him made it seem like they really loved each other, but that didn't necessarily mean that he would love *me* or want me in his life.

But maybe…

I opened to the page I had last left off on. It was one of the entries she made about a year after I was born and she'd given me over to Ms. Mosely. It was difficult to read about her love for me and how she suffered from depression after my birth. My heart ached to know the woman who had been so selfless in her love for me. Selfless enough to give up her own chance at being a mother so that I could have a life unbounded by the pressures of her society.

I would have given it up though. The freedom that came with my upbringing if it meant having the chance to know her.

At least I have this. I ran my hand over the page, feeling the impression of the ink on the paper. Her handwriting was so similar to mine. The slanted curve of each *s* and how she alternated between regular and cursive script. More and more, I was discovering how similar we were and even though I had no love for Adeline, I was thankful she'd kept my mother's room untouched after her death so that I could have her words to know her by.

I've done everything she's asked of me and it still wasn't good enough. I wear the clothes she tells me to wear. I dye my hair the perfect shade of platinum blonde. I even wear the red lipstick she says looks best on me, even though I prefer pink. It's my punishment for falling out of line and getting pregnant out of wedlock. Even though she was able to hide it well from everyone by locking me up in my room for nine months, I know she wants revenge. And her revenge comes in the form of Henry Carnelle. The most infamous bachelor of the Southeast. Not that anyone would dare say a word about his indiscretions because he carries one of Southern royalty's most prominent names. It's all such a joke. I should have just taken Willow and ran with her father

when I had the chance. But it's too late now. She's
tied up all my money and gives me a measly
allowance. Not even enough to get more than two
states from her. And I know she'd find me.

There it was. Etched in ink. My mother was afraid of
Adeline and what she was capable of. When I first learned that
Melanie was my mom after she died, I remembered having a
ton of emotions. Anger in knowing how close she was and
thinking that she simply didn't want to deal with the burden
of having me. Sorrow for the life I never got to have with her.
And…something else that, at the time, didn't add up but now I
was starting to wonder if my intuition of thinking her death
wasn't just an accident could have been right all along.

I spent countless nights thinking about the news story.
How they said she fell overboard and drowned. But my
mother had written in her journal about her days at the lake
with her friends. How she loved the water and that it was one
of the few places in town that brought her a sense of peace.

I flipped to the next page and kept reading.

I never understood the saying 'You have to kiss
a bunch of frogs until you find your prince' until now.
Henry was most definitely a frog and his darting
tongue proved it. Ugh. I thought that Georiga's
favorite bachelor would at least have skills in the sex
department, but he was just like most other men. Too
keen on getting their rocks off that they don't pay

much attention to the lady beneath them. At least I kept him satisfied so he could run back to Daddy and report that I was giving him what he wanted. It probably wouldn't be long now until I had an obscenely large diamond on my hand, but at least I'll make my mother happy and get back access to my inheritance. It's not the best plan because I don't know how long I'll be able to keep up this act with Mr. Dartfrog Tongue, but it's the only plan I have right now.

What was this? I thought to myself. The way she wrote made it sound like both Adeline and Henry's dad were scheming to get them to get married and that she had little choice in the matter. I guessed it wasn't totally unheard of in the South. Wealthy families liked to keep their circle small, so it made sense Adeline and the Carnelles wouldn't want their children to marry outside of the elite society.

Something wasn't quite adding up though and I could feel it in my bones as I read and read and read. It felt like my mother was nudging me toward something, as though her spirit wanted me to find the missing link and she had buried it within these pages.

But all I found was the same thing over and over again. She went on dates with Henry and her disdain for him kept growing, despite their impending engagement. Her friends were shallow and only cared about themselves. She hated her mother. It was all the same.

Feeling a tension headache beginning to form, I leaned my head back on the headboard with a sigh. Maybe I was looking into something that wasn't really there. Trying to find a deeper connection to my mother by chasing after these wild suspicions.

One more page, a voice seemed to whisper in my mind. Yup. It was official. I was starting to lose my marbles over this.

I should have just set the journal back on the bedside table and started on some sketches instead of going down this endless rabbit hole. Instead, I found myself flipping the page and fueling my own dumpster fire.

Now I knew why Evaline had warned me to stay away from Henry. No amount of makeup would hide the bruise along my jaw from where his fist had slammed into it. Adeline didn't say a word when she saw me walk in the door tonight. Not that I expected her to come running to my rescue after what she endured with my father. Alcohol and a temper never mixed well. I can still hear the sounds of breaking glass against our walls as he dragged her by her hair down the hall that night. I guess she didn't expect my fate to be any different. My only job was to marry into another wealthy family to keep our generational wealth rolling. I never understood why they cared so much about what would happen to the money when they died. It wasn't like any of our parents actually care about us or their grandchildren. None of it *matters anymore. This will only be my future for a little while longer. I can push for a short engagement and once we're married I'll get my money settled and divorce his abusive ass. Then maybe I can finally see her again. My sweet baby girl.*

I wiped the tears from my cheeks as I closed my mother's journal. Rage and sadness pulsed through me like a wildfire burned through trees.

He hit her.

That asshole had punched my mother and left a mark on her and instead of fighting back or leaving him, she felt like that type of behavior was normal in a relationship.

I remembered the news saying that her fiance of six months had been on the boat with her when she died. So for at least six months, she had endured his abuse and it was all because her own mother had some kind of vendetta against her for getting pregnant with me.

This world was so twisted and I was starting to regret listening to that voice that told me to keep reading. I didn't want this. I didn't want to know how my mother suffered in the hopes of one day bringing us back together. Guilt racked my body. Some part of me knew it was misplaced. A reminder that I was a baby when all of this was happening and there was no way I could have controlled any of it. But it was still there. Nagging at me—showing me that her death was on my hands because if she wouldn't have tried so hard to gain access to her inheritance to build a future for us, then maybe she wouldn't have been on that boat with that terrible man who probably…

"Oh my God," I breathed, raising a shaky hand over my mouth. "Oh my God."

The truth was painted before me as clear as the summer sky hanging above the Blue Ridge Mountains.

CHAPTER TWENTY-FIVE

"Willow, slow down," Sarah said through the phone. "What do you mean you think your mom was murdered?"

"I mean"—I dragged out the words—"that my mother wrote about Henry Carnelle in her journal, Sarah. She wrote about how he punched her and left bruises on her face and when Adeline saw, she did nothing." I was nearly screaming into the phone, the adrenaline pumping through my veins making it difficult to remain calm.

"Wait, are you serious?" she asked, and then her voice dropped to a whisper, "He actually *hit* her?"

I pinched the bridge of my nose as I tried to control my breathing. "Yes," I hissed. "She was only with Henry to please Adeline. Apparently, if she went through with marrying him Adeline promised she would get access to her inheritance again. She..." I paused, swallowing down the tears that threatened to spill from my eyes. "She wanted to build a life for herself so that she could take me back from the orphanage and we could be together again."

"Oh my God," Sarah whispered. Then a crash sounded through the phone line. "Hold on a second." There were muffled voices for a few moments before Sarah came back on, "Okay. I told Stephanie to watch the front while I stepped out back. It's a madhouse today with all the weekend special orders coming in."

"I'm sorry, Sarah. I shouldn't be bothering you with this while you're at work. I just—"

"Uh-uh. Don't start with that BS. It's not like you're calling me with some trivial matter, Willow. You found out that, at the very least, your mother was abused by a *Carnelle*. And at the worst, someone may have killed her. I'd be pissed if you waited until I got home to tell me about this."

Panic rose in my throat hearing the insanity of what I was proposing to Sarah. "Surely the police would have figured this out, right? I'm just losing my mind." I started pacing around the guest room, my thoughts streaming in a million miles a minute.

"Are you still at my place?" Sarah asked.

"Yup."

"Why don't you head over to Johnny's so you're not sitting alone with this information? I'll talk to Stephanie and see if she can cover me again and meet you there as soon as I can."

I sucked in a heaping lungful of air. "Okay."

"Willow?"

"Yeah?"

"It's going to be okay."

"Thank you."

"I'll meet you in a bit."

We hung up and I texted Johnny asking if he was home or

at his store. He texted me back right away and I grabbed my purse and my mother's journal before heading out the door.

I wasn't sure if it was the fresh summer air blowing gently in the trees that made me feel more at peace since finding out that Henry Carnelle had abused my mother, or that I was standing outside of Johnny's house. Either way, I was thankful for the small respite from my tangled emotions as I knocked on his door and heard Asher's welcoming bark.

Johnny answered the door, Asher darted out and started whimpering for me to pet him. So, I stooped down and gave him a few quick scratches behind his ears before I stepped into Johnny's embrace. He gave me a kiss on the cheek before leaning back to look at me.

"What's going on, Lo?"

"I...I think my mom might have been murdered." The words came out in a rush.

A deep river formed between his brows. "What do you mean?"

I reached down into my oversized purse and grabbed her journal. "It's all in here."

He made us both a glass of sweet tea before I read him all the entries she'd made about Henry Carnelle. I closed the journal and set it on my lap. Johnny reached under my knees and swung my legs into his lap, resting his hands on my shins.

"It's certainly hard to deny that there was likely foul play involved if it was just the two of them on that boat the day she died."

I absently ran my hand over the top of Asher's head as he lay in front of the porch swing. "She knew how to swim, Johnny. She wrote about going to the lake all the time and swimming in it with her girlfriends. There's no way she would have just drowned from falling overboard. Not unless something else happened."

Johnny took a long swig of his sweet tea, gazing out over the front yard before he swept his eyes over to meet mine. With a gentle stroke of his hand over my bare skin, I saw the worry etched into his irises.

"What're you thinking?" I asked quietly.

His nostrils flared. "This isn't like accusing some crack addict off the street. If you bring this to the police, you'll be opening Pandora's box with some of the wealthiest families in the country. And if Henry Carnelle was actually involved in her death somehow...that's a powerful family to pit yourself against, Lo."

I sighed, letting his words sink in. It was a harsh truth I hadn't let myself face until now. Just because I had a smoking gun didn't mean that I should use it. But the thought of this hunch being true, that my mother had spent months suffering at *his* hands only to die by them and for everyone to know of her death as an accident when all that time she was just trying to find a way to get back to me was too much. It wasn't enough to sit here with this evidence and not do something.

"I know." I scooted forward until my bottom met the side of his thigh and I could lean my shoulder into his chest. "But I don't think I can let this go, Johnny. At least not until I at least bring her journal to the police."

"And what if the police have already been bought by the Carnelles?" he countered.

"Well, I can put my hundreds of millions of dollars to good use then."

Johnny chuckled against my ear as he pulled me closer to him. "My obstinate, headstrong woman. If this is what you really want, then I'll fight by your side with everything I have."

His brown eyes glittered like freshly poured honey under a sunlit sky and when he pressed his lips against mine, I tangled my fists in the lapels of his open flannel. Warmth flooded my senses as he deepened the kiss, exploring, playing, nipping. Driving me so damn wild, I started to fumble with the button of his jeans. Needing, desperately, to claim him as my own. To feel his body pressing into mine.

That was until a car honked and I almost jumped out of my skin and I felt Johnny flinch beneath my touch.

I looked over my shoulder to see what asshole had ruined the quiet to find Sarah's car rolling into Johnny's driveway. I groaned. At this rate, there was no way I was going to have my way with Johnny. Every opportunity we had seemed to get interrupted by either my own stupidity or someone else's.

"I'm going to kill her," I seethed under my breath.

"Not if I get to her first." Johnny adjusted himself so that his raging hard-on wasn't as prominent in his Levi's before we both rose and met Sarah at the porch steps.

"I totally interrupted something, didn't I?" Sarah looked back and forth between Johnny and me with a mischievous grin on her face.

When neither one of us answered she continued, "Fill me in on what the hell is going on."

We moved into his living room and Johnny brought her a

glass of sweet tea. Asher laid his head in my lap and I was stroking the space between his eyes as I caught Sarah up to speed.

"Holy shit," she said before taking a sip from her glass. "You're really going to let her go through with this?" she directed the question at Johnny.

"If I had my way, no. I think it's way too risky and if these people really did kill her mother and covered it up then their influence goes deeper than I think any of us could imagine. But it's not my call to make. Lo wants to do this and that means I'll be standing by her side the entire time."

I let out a breath, thankful he didn't try to use Sarah's hesitance to shut me down. Though, the way his shoulders were set, I knew he was struggling to see things my way.

Protector. It's what he'd always been and there were a lot of things in this situation he couldn't protect me from and that kind of terrified me.

Sarah rose from her seat and started pacing the living room. "One of my brother's best friends just started at the police station." She whirled around to face me. "Maybe we could take it to him. He's new to the department and if the cops on your mom's case were dirty, they probably haven't sunk their claws into him yet. It could be a good place to start."

Flicking my gaze to Johnny, he gave me a subtle nod. "That would be great. Do you think Theo could get us in contact with him?"

"I don't think that will be a problem."

"Okay. So, I think it's a fairly solid plan to start. Sarah, can you call Theo today to give him a heads-up?"

"Sure thing."

"Johnny, would it be okay if you asked Deacon to cover the shop this weekend? I...don't know if I can do this without you."

"I already asked him and he's got it covered."

If he'd already asked Deacon to cover the shop I wondered if that was in anticipation of this being my last weekend in Pebble Brook Falls or if his training had taught him to plan ahead for when shit hit the fan.

As though Sarah could read my thoughts, she said, "I guess this means you'll be staying a while longer."

It was Johnny who I looked at when I replied, "Yeah. I guess it does." There'd been no time to talk about it. No time to tell him that I had already decided to stay before I knew any of this about my mother. I just hoped he would believe me when I finally found the right moment to tell him that *he* was the reason I wanted to pack up my life in Nashville and build a home in Pebble Brook Falls.

It was crazy and I was quickly discovering how much of a whirlwind this life could be. But seeing him here, in our hometown, was a reminder of the life I truly wanted. Second chances didn't come around often, but this was mine and there was nothing I would allow to get in my way of having him.

"Well, at least we get to go to an epic party before we all get sniped off for digging up some skeletons."

"Sarah!" I screeched at her blunt, ominous words. I didn't think she was aware of just how much Johnny had endured overseas and the ghosts that still haunted him, but it didn't take a rocket scientist to understand that talking about getting *sniped* probably wasn't the best choice of words in front of a veteran.

But as she shrugged nonchalantly, Johnny's laughter filled the room—warm and raspy. Asher lifted his head from my lap, tilting it back and forth while his big golden eyes looked at Johnny as though the sound were foreign and he needed to inspect what was going on.

I sighed, shaking my head. If Johnny was okay with Sarah's morbidity, then I guess I could be too.

"I need to get back to the bakery to work on some of the special orders for the weekend before we close for the night. Willow, do you want to come back with me so you can make some calls to cancel your Nashville plans?"

"Um, yeah. That's probably a good idea. I'll just meet you at Deacon's tonight?" I asked Johnny.

"Yeah, I'll meet you there."

Johnny and Asher walked Sarah and me to the front porch. When Sarah got into her car, I turned to face Johnny. "There's something I want to talk to you about later tonight."

"Sure you don't want to talk about it now?"

I glanced over my shoulder at Sarah waiting in her car. "There's not enough time right now."

"Okay." A shadow passed over his face and I wanted nothing more than to tell him everything on my heart, but Sarah needed to get back to work and I had a long list of people to call. "We'll talk tonight, darlin'."

Butterflies swarmed my stomach as he palmed the back of my neck and brought me in for a swift sweet kiss.

More. I wanted more of this. More of *him*.

His release of me came too quickly, but I promised myself that I would find a way to get more time with him before the craziness ensued and we lit the Southern world on fire.

Deacon's land was on sprawling hills covered in tall shoots of wheatgrass that waved in the breeze of the early night. The sun had just sunk below the horizon, casting an orange-pink glow across the sky that reminded me of the Flinstone push-up pops Ms. Mosely always got us during the summertime.

Cars lined up in three rows at the edge of his property. It looked as though the entire town had caught wind of the party and decided to spend their Friday night surrounding the bonfire. Sarah parked the car just as a text from Johnny came through letting me know he and Deacon were at the smoke pit.

"The crowd is even bigger than last year," Sarah said as we crested the small hill in front of the car line to find the entire field filled with people.

My fingers twisted into knots as I wrung them together, feeling heightened from the day's revelations. For the first time in a long while I felt vulnerable. Like the moment I walked into the crowd, people would stare at me as though I had a giant stamp on my forehead that read: MY MOTHER MIGHT HAVE BEEN MURDERED.

It was ridiculous of course because the only two people who knew outside of myself were Sarah and Johnny and there wasn't a doubt in my mind that they wouldn't keep this between us until it was time.

The closer we got to the crowd, the more people I recognized from high school.

Old wounds started to ache—fear of rejection, fear that no

one would see my worth. Or even worse, that they would and would still refuse to be kind.

"Hey, you okay?" I hadn't realized I'd stopped moving until Sarah turned around to face me.

Clearing my throat, I brought my hands behind my back, tugging and pulling on my fingers. "It's just been a while since I've seen these people and I'm…"

"Nervous?" she answered for me.

"Yeah," I said with a laugh. "That's probably stupid, right?"

She stepped toward me, grabbing my forearms until I finally let go of my own hands letting her replace them with hers.

"There are two kinds of people in this world, Willow. Those who stay stuck in the same version of themselves forever, never growing, never knowing what it is to change. And then there are those who evolve, who actively choose to work on their flaws. That crowd behind me is filled with both kinds and it'll be up to you to seek out the ones who chose to change."

I let her words sink in—let them give me the strength to slowly stitch that wound close until I finally rolled my shoulders back and let out a long exhale.

"You're right. If I don't want to be judged, then I shouldn't judge them for things that happened over a decade ago."

"Exactly," she smiled, giving my hands a squeeze. "Ready?"

"Yup."

Sarah kept hold of my hand as we walked together into the crowd.

CHAPTER TWENTY-SIX

*P*lumes of smoke billowed into the crisp night air while Sarah and I weaved through the crowd toward the large black smoker, the savory smell of roasting meat becoming stronger and stronger. My heart raced as I felt the eyes of those we passed scanning over me—assessing, questioning.

They're just curious, I kept telling myself. Over a decade had passed since they'd seen me and were probably wondering why I left and if I was planning on staying. Simple, non-judgmental questions.

Adopting Sarah's perspective helped, I started to realize as the tightness in my throat eased and I eventually found myself smiling at them.

"Sarah!" A woman's voice sounded from somewhere to our right. Sarah stopped and I watched as she looked for the person who'd called her name. Her lips shifted into a bright smile as the crowd parted and Katherine McKale nearly tackled her with a hug.

"Kat!" Sarah giggled as they swayed side to side in a tight

embrace. Katherine McKale had been in our graduating class. Her petite frame and classic beauty with long curly black hair, high cheekbones, a slim straight nose, and striking blue eyes made her the perfect cheerleader type. She was the first junior to be named captain of the varsity team and had won the team two back-to-back championships.

Time hadn't changed her appearance one bit, other than her sense of fashion. Where she used to only wear Sofie shorts and t-shirts to school, she was now dressed in a white cotton summer dress that had gorgeous flower detailing along the skirt and bodice. Her feet were clad in deep maroon cowgirl boots with black rhinestones edging the sole lip. It reminded me of my own style and what I hoped to bring into my shop... whenever it would be opening. At this rate, there was no telling what else might get in the way of that.

When they pulled away, Sarah gestured to me and said, "Kat, you remember Willow, right?"

"Willow Mae! Yes! I heard you were back in town, but I've been so busy coaching the girls I haven't been around much to say hi. How've you been?"

An easy smile graced my face. *This isn't so bad.*

"I've been good. I left for Nashville after high school and have been saving to open a fashion boutique. I love your dress by the way."

"Thank you!" she grabbed the hem and swayed her hips back and forth. "I've come a long way from wearing cheerleader attire twenty-four-seven. I remember you always had the coolest designs in your jeans. Did you sew them yourself?"

I felt my eyes widen from the shock of her remembering that. I'd always felt like a forgotten wallflower in school as people either didn't notice me at all or I was the target of their attacks. It was...*nice* to hear that someone had actually taken notice of my efforts.

"Yeah, I did. There wasn't much for me to work with, but I did my best with what was given to me."

"That's all we can do, right?" Her blue eyes glimmered with authenticity.

I nodded. "You mentioned coaching, are you working at the high school?"

"Oh, no! I'm working at the Georgia All-stars gym."

Sarah chimed in, "Kat here has three Worlds Championship titles under her belt as their head coach and from what I hear, she'll be adding another trophy to the shelf this year."

"Damn. That's pretty impressive."

Kat's shoulders rolled inward slightly as though the compliments made her feel uncomfortable. "It's really the girls who do all the heavy lifting. I just guide them in the right direction and then they kick ass."

"There you are." I shifted my attention toward the husky voice belonging to a tall blonde man with frost-blue eyes that were slightly covered by the rim of a cowboy hat standing behind Kat. He wrapped her up in a big bear hug from behind. Her laughter was infectious as she leaned into him.

She turned around and kissed him in a way that made my cheeks flame from the intimacy they displayed. I looked at Sarah and noticed she was observing them longingly and it occurred to me that in all the years we've been friends, she's never really had a boyfriend. Sure, she had crushes on boys when we were in school, but she never truly dated anyone. She told me once that whoever she brought into her life would need to be strong enough to go to war with her parents because neither of them would make it easy, especially because the boys she always gravitated toward fit well into the 'bad boy' category.

Out of everyone I knew, Sarah deserved to be loved with everything the person had because that's what she did. And she'd proven that again this past week by taking days away from her bakery to support me in these wild revelations.

"Ladies," Kat interrupted my thoughts," this is Bryantt. He's a rancher from Canton. Bryantt, this is Sarah and Willow. We all went to high school together."

He tipped his hat towards Sarah and me as the right corner of his lips tilted upward in a lopsided grin. "It's a pleasure to meet you, ladies." His Southern accent was thick as honey. "It's been a long week on the ranch and I've been missing my woman. Would you ladies mind if I stole her away for a little while?"

"Not at all," I said at the same time Sarah crooned, "Steal away."

"It was really good to see you girls! And I'm so glad you're back in town, Willow. We'll have to go for coffee sometime."

"I'd really like that. And it was great to see you too!"

Kat's laughter fluttered through the air as Bryantt steered her toward the edge of the crowd and I had the feeling they'd probably find themselves busy in his truck or somewhere in the brush along the edge of the river.

Sarah nudged me with her elbow. "That went well."

"Yeah." I nodded. "It actually did."

"See? Some of us really do evolve." She shot me a wink and I laughed before she locked her arm with mine and we bounded toward the smoke pit.

Johnny's back was turned to me as he worked the meat on the rack. It wasn't just the savory notes hanging in the air that had my mouth watering. I raked my gaze over every inch of his strong body from his broad shoulders that flexed with each movement, down to his narrow waist that had me wanting to run my tongue over every pink scar that etched his abdomen. And further down to his tight ass that I imagined grabbing as he rolled his hips into me while my legs were wrapped tightly around his thick thighs.

"I think you have some drool running down your chin," Sarah whispered to me with a serpentine smile on her bright red lips.

Indeed, my mouth was hanging open, but thankfully there was no drool to be found as I discreetly wiped around my lips with the back of my hand. "You're awful." I glared at her and she just tilted her head back and laughed which caught Johnny's attention.

Great, now he's going to think I'm some sex-crazed lunatic who only wants him for his manhood.

It took everything I had not to peek at his crotch where I knew his sizeable bulge was likely on full display in those tight Levi's. Honestly, those jeans should be banned. There were probably countless women who fell victim to the lure of sexy Southern men in their tight-ass jeans giving them lopsided grins just as Johnny was doing to me now.

It's not fair.

But that didn't stop me from smiling back, feeling the dimple at the edge of his lips do strange things to my stomach. And it certainly didn't stop me from walking into his widespread arms, allowing him to dip me dramatically as he pressed those sensuous lips to mine for the entire world to see.

I wrapped my arms around his neck as he righted us,

feeling heat creep along my spine, settling deep in my core. I clung to him, not wanting the moment to end. That sweet smell of cedar wood was a blanket of comfort around us.

"I've missed you, darlin'." Johnny nuzzled his face into the crook of my neck. Sparks of fireworks shot through me from the way his stubble scraped against my sensitive skin.

"I've missed you too." Somehow, the words we spoke to one another carried a heavier weight to them. Like we weren't just talking about the last few hours we spent apart, but the last twelve years. All the time that was stolen from us by others who placed unfair judgments on a boy who turned out to be better than any of them. Sacrificing himself for his country, his brethren, and *me*.

Running my hands over the thin fabric of his t-shirt, I felt the raised bumps of his scars and suddenly felt unworthy of the love this man had for me. I should have known better—should have tried harder to find out why I never heard from him instead of assuming the worst like everyone else in his life.

"Hey." He ran his fingers through the strands of my hair over the top of my ear. "What's going on in that beautiful head of yours?"

Those brown eyes shone with concern and if he'd asked me that question a week ago, I would have made up some sort of excuse. But my heart was tired of harboring secrets, especially from him. But I didn't want to talk about it now. This conversation was better suited when it was just the two of us.

"I'll tell you later." I pressed a kiss to his cheek. "Promise."

"I'll hold you to that." His eyes softened before his lips met my forehead and he shifted us around until we were facing Deacon, Sarah, and a few others who looked vaguely familiar.

A short guy with freckles splattered across his face was nearly sloshing his beer all over Deacon as he told an animated story about chasing piglets at the county fair last summer. The redheaded woman next to him was enthralled with the story, never taking her eyes off him as he continued on making everyone chuckle along the way.

"I feel like I know him." I leaned back, whispering into Johnny's ear.

"That's J.J. Coleman. He was in the class behind yours I think. His dad owns the blueberry farm on the south side of town."

"Yes! That's right. Wasn't he the one who let that wild boar hog into the school gym?"

Johnny's throaty laugh sent a cascade of goosebumps over my arms. "Oh yeah. Him and a few of his buddies."

I shook my head remembering how pissed Mr. DelRay, the old P.E. Teacher, was. He didn't stop talking about it for almost three months. Probably because the hog chased him around while all the kids laughed at him.

Curiosity struck me as I took notice of the tall man standing close to Sarah. He was about six inches behind her and her brown eyes kept darting to the side as though she wanted to turn and look at him but didn't want anyone to notice. Similar to most of the men's style around here, he wore a white V-neck t-shirt under a flannel with crisscrossing lines of blue, black, and gray. The sleeves were rolled up just below his elbows, showing off intricate details of various tattoos that reached all the way down to his hands.

He looked so familiar...

"Ranger Adams," Johnny whispered in my ear as his hands trailed over my ribcage, landing snuggly on my hips where he swirled his thumbs over my exposed skin peeking out between the hem of my shirt and my jean shorts.

He must have caught me staring, trying to piece together where I knew him from. "I thought Sarah told me he was in prison for assault."

"He was released six months ago. Served almost ten years."

"Should I be worried that he is standing that close to Sarah?"

I could feel Johnny shake his head behind me. "Nah. He's a good guy. Though, I doubt many people around here would say that since the guy he beat up was LeRoy Cummings. That's why Ranger went away for so long. LeRoy's lawyers twisted the case up and tried to make Ranger out to be a danger to society."

"LeRoy...Valorie's brother?"

"Mmhmm."

"Do you know why he did it?"

Johnny dropped his chin to rest on my shoulder. I closed my eyes, soaking up the feeling of his body wrapped around mine.

"Apparently he didn't say a word during the entire process. But I've seen a lot of bad men in my life. The kind who takes pleasure in bringing pain to others. Like they get off on it or something. When I look at Ranger, I don't see that demon hiding behind his eyes. So, whatever LeRoy did must have been bad enough for Ranger to risk going to prison for."

When I opened my eyes again, I looked toward Ranger. His eyes flicked up to meet mine and he held my gaze with quiet assessment and I wondered what he must have been thinking. There was a hardness to him—the same kind that I saw in Johnny. Quiet and hidden beneath the surface, but I didn't miss the way he seemed to take in everyone around us as though there might be some kind of threat and he wanted to be ready for it.

I wished I could have learned some of that myself as I heard Valorie Cumming's voice break through our small group like a bulldozer knocking over a beloved tree. "It looks like we've stumbled onto some riffraff, Melody." The sound of her shrill voice was like nails on a chalkboard; it sent a cascade of terrible shivers down my body. Johnny's hands slid around my front, pulling me further into him. Protecting. Shielding. As he'd always done, but now it seemed even more significant somehow.

Valorie Cummings was a severe looking woman. Her nose was ramrod straight and very narrow, which matched her slim face with jutting cheekbones and hollowed cheeks. Her eyes were lined in black with a knifelike wing that made her look even more dangerous than I knew she was despite her silver tongue that had dished out enough lashings to last me a lifetime. She knew exactly what to say to spill a pound of salt into her victims' wounds.

Even though her presence made my skin crawl, it was Melody Carnelle's wicked smile that had my heart banging against my ribcage.

"Hi, Johnny," Melody said in what I was sure was her sweetest voice. "You're looking good."

I felt Johnny go still behind me, not saying a word. It seemed like their little interaction at The Roasted Bean was simply Johnny trying to be cordial toward her just as he'd said. Now, I could feel the heat of his animosity.

When he didn't respond, Melody raked her gaze over me from head to toe ending with a snicker bubbling from her perfectly painted lips. Those hazel eyes finally met mine, piercing through me and that's when something in me snapped. Maybe it was the realization that I finally knew her family wasn't perfect and that whatever mean-girl front she tried to portray, there was nothing but a miserable shell of a human behind it.

"Your juvenile intimidation tactics don't work anymore, Melody. So you can stare at me all you want." I took a step out of Johnny's embrace, toward Melody and continued, "But just know one thing. While you're hiding behind Mommy and Daddy's empire, I have one of my own now. And given this is the first time I've ever had more than a few hundred dollars to my name, one might even say I'd be reckless enough to use every single penny to destroy those who try to tear me down."

A muscle feathered in her jaw and that's when I knew I'd spoken her language. Melody always had more than me our entire lives. More money. More friends. More resources and boys and clothes and hell...just *everything*. But the one thing her kind respected was money because money meant power. Everyone in this town knew my grandmother was the richest woman south of the Mason-Dixon Line and now all that wealth belonged to me.

Her stony gaze faltered for the briefest moment before she gathered her composure again. I stood my ground as she took a step toward me even though those old habits of cowering were creeping up on me.

"You may have the money in your bank account now, Willow Mae, but you were born an orphan and that's what you'll always be." She cackled, Valorie joining in with her. "Your mother didn't want you and even if she'd decided to keep you, you'd still be the daughter of a whore who got off on chasing guys from the wrong side of the tracks."

Those ice-like eyes shifted to Johnny for a moment before looking back at me. "You'll never be one of us, so stop pretending."

Flames of hatred licked at my entire body and it took every ounce of willpower to not slap her right across the face. I wanted to feel the sting of my palm as it met her cheek so badly my hand itched. But that would only prove her point— that I was a wild orphan-born scoundrel with no class. Instead of giving her what she wanted, I curled my fingers tightly, feeling my nails bite into my flesh.

What Melody didn't know was that while she had words like daggers, cutting, and painful, *I* had something far more dangerous. The truth. And I would burn her entire family to the ground with it.

As though someone other than myself had stepped into my body with the confidence of a bull rider in his eighth second, I puffed up my chest and said, "Melody Carnelle, you are the last person I would ever want to be. You're self-serving, you tear people down just for the enjoyment of it, and instead of using that giant head of yours to do some good in the world, you seek nothing but to destroy. Only miserable people do shit like that, so you're right. I won't ever be anything like you. Karma always has a way of coming back around and all the shit you've dished out over the years might be heading your way a lot sooner than you think."

Not giving her the chance to make some snide retort, I turned my back on her and slid my arm around Johnny's waist, and looked at our circle of friends. "Come on, y'all. Let's get the hell out of here."

CHAPTER TWENTY-SEVEN

"*D*amn, girl! I knew you had that in you somewhere, but I sure wasn't expecting to see it come out tonight," Sarah said with a wolfish grin.

"I guess all those years of her harassing me finally boiled over," I chuckled, trying to mask the reeling of my mind.

I just told off Melody Carnelle in front of a crowd of people. Who the hell am I?

Sarah raised her red Solo cup to cheers. "I have to say, as your best friend, I really like this side of you." She took a swig of whatever concoction was in her cup and then said, "Mind if I leave you two alone? I'm going to get a refill."

"You just got that one."

"True. But it's been a rough few days and your girl's on a mission to forget."

"Noted," I said, watching her saunter off through the crowd.

"Are you okay?" Johnny shifted toward me, reaching up to hold my face between his hands, the light from the fire reflecting in his eyes as they darted back and forth between mine.

It took me a moment to realize I was trembling. I'd never stood up to Melody before...hell, I'd never stood up to *anyone* before. Johnny was always the one to fight those battles for me while I cowered in the corner, taking each proverbial blow to the chin like a human punching bag. But this time...this time had been different and it felt good to stand up for myself. To let my lifelong bully know that I was no longer her plaything to torture in pursuit of some twisted vendetta she had against people who were different from her.

"Yeah," I breathed, feeling my body relax more and more. "I'm actually really okay."

He pressed a firm kiss to my forehead before tucking me under his shoulder. I knew he would have jumped in to defend me if I hadn't stepped up to the plate. I could feel his need to tell her off the moment his body tensed behind me and I loved that about him. How there was never a moment when we were together when I didn't feel safe. And it wasn't just me he protected. He was always the first to sacrifice himself for the betterment of others.

Johnny was quite literally the exact opposite of Melody Carnelle and when I looked up at his handsome face, the shadows from the dancing flames flickering across his rugged features, my entire body stilled at his beauty. Not just the honey color of his eyes, the way his sensuous lips tugged upward revealing that dimple, or how his sculpted-by-the-Almighty-himself ass looked in Levi's. No. It was his soul—gentle, kind, compassionate, giving, selfless. *Those* were the things that kept my heart wanting him after all these years.

And I was damn tired of not having *all* of him.

"Wanna get out of here?" I whispered.

Those full lips smiled wide and my stomach did a tight somersault as he said, "I know just the place."

Watery silver shone from the full moon hanging high above us as Johnny laid the quilted blanket amongst the tall grass.

Our spot. Where so many memories had been forged, imprinted deep within my soul that I knew I would carry with me for the rest of my life. It was a quiet safe haven from the rest of the world. A wild retreat that was left untouched by the progress of the world.

Long muscular legs stretched out as Johnny leaned back on his hands. "Come sit with me, darlin'."

With a serene smile pulling at my lips, I knelt down between his legs, letting my bare thighs rub against his jeans.

For a moment, he just looked at me. His steely gaze softened as his eyes brushed over my face, traveling down to my collarbone and sweeping across my breasts that were now rising and falling with the quick pace of my breaths. Hunger flashed in his eyes, the edge of his jaw moving from the way he clenched his teeth together as though he was using all his strength to restrain himself.

I wanted to tell him to stop. To unleash himself upon me so that I could finally feel what I'd been missing these twelve years. Just as my mouth popped open to tell him as much, he said, "I'm really proud of you." His words hit me like a ton of bricks. Not because he'd never said them before, but because of the weight they held.

Nervous laughter bubbled from my chest. Now that we were away from the crowd, the reality of what I said to Melody was sinking in. "I honestly don't know what came over me. It felt like an out-of-body experience." I huffed out a long breath. "I just didn't want her thinking that she had control over how I feel anymore. When we were kids, I let her get to me so many times and I regret not standing up to her sooner."

"Well, I'm sure the town will be buzzing about that exchange for a good long while. I don't imagine Melody, or anyone else in her family, encounters that kind of backlash often." Johnny's legs squeezed tighter against my thighs. I placed a hand a few inches above his right knee and I swore his breath hitched. *Good*, I thought. I wasn't the only one of us who was so primally affected. Apparently, a simple touch from me brought him the same kind of delicious torment I felt when his skin brushed mine.

"If anything comes of my mother's journal entries, the town will have a lot more to talk about than just that brief tiff between Melody and me."

"And you're sure you want to do this, Lo?" A question, not to make me second-guess my decision, but to make sure I wanted to risk myself. "The case has been closed for a really long time now, I'm not sure that your mother's journal entries would even be enough for them to open it back up."

I tilted my head back, staring at the cratered surface of the moon. Noticing that after all the hits it had taken over the countless years, it still looked beautiful. When I looked back at Johnny's handsome face, I said, "There's not a lot of reason behind it, Johnny. You're probably right. But on the off chance that someone—anyone—might listen, I want to do it for her. Maybe that's stupid. Trying to bring Henry Carnelle to justice, especially since doing so won't bring her back. But I feel it in my gut, that I need to see this through."

"Okay. You can't blame me though for trying to prevent you from getting twisted up in something like this."

"I don't." I looked up at him through my lashes.

He smirked as he leaned forward, gripping my chin between his thumb and forefinger. "I may not like it, but at least it keeps you in town for a while longer. It's been nice having you around again."

My core quivered with an ache for him that ran so deep it rattled my bones. It was more than just how my body reacted to him with such unhinged desire. Since we were kids, my soul called to his like a butterfly drawn to sweet nectar. It was innate. A love that transcended time and heartbreak and the meddling of others and some part of me knew that the moment I saw him after those twelve years apart. I was a fool to believe that my plans of moving back to Nashville would stick. Seeing him again felt like taking a breath of fresh air after I'd been held underwater for far too long. He was my life force and I didn't want him thinking anything different for another second.

"I need to apologize, Johnny."

His head tilted to the side. "For what?"

"For spending the last twelve years being angry with you. For thinking that you left me without a word and for...for not trying harder to find you. I hate myself for—" With a single finger pressed against my lips, he silenced me.

"I'm not going to allow you to talk to yourself like that, Lo.

We were so young when that happened and I don't blame you for questioning me when you didn't get my letters. Hell, there were certainly moments when I questioned you for not writing back to me. That time was taken from us, but not because we didn't share love for one another."

"I know." My voice cracked. "And I wish more than anything that we could have those years back. It was such a long time and I tried...I tried so damn hard to move forward. To start a life for myself, but there was always something missing. I was just too stubborn to acknowledge that it was *you* I needed, who I wanted to call when I could finally afford a decent apartment. Or when I was having a bad day and felt like there was no way in hell I was going to save up enough money to open my boutique."

I sat up, moving to straddle his hips so I could feel him beneath me. His large hands gripped my hips, holding me firmly against him.

"And most of all, I've had to live with the regret of wondering..." Tears welled in my eyes, blurring the image of him. I blinked them away. "I've had to live with the regret of wondering what would have happened if I'd asked you to stay."

"Lo," he whispered my name into the night like a prayer as his strong arms enveloped me, the comforting smell of cedar wood mixing with the warmth of the night was a welcomed cacoon. I laid my head against his chest, listening to the steady hum of his heart as I let my hands roam up and down his muscular back.

Johnny's hand cradled the back of my head as he brought his mouth to my ear. "Every moment we've been apart, there hasn't been a single second when my thoughts weren't of you.

271

How your blonde strands feel like silk against my fingers. The way your blue eyes remind me of sweet summer days filled with your laughter. And how your cute button nose crinkles when you're frustrated or thinking too hard about something. But most of all"—his thumb grazed the bottom edge of my lip, tugging it down slightly and I swore an entire field of butterflies flew came to life in my stomach—"I missed these pretty pink lips and how they taste like honey pulled straight from the hive."

I closed my eyes as his hand slid up to cup the side of my cheek and a quiet moan escaped from my lips.

When I opened my eyes again, I said, "Coming back to our home made me realize that there is no place I'd rather be because this is where *you* are, Johnny. I'm not staying for a few more weeks just to see what might come of this thing with my mother's journal. I'm staying *forever* to see if I might have a chance of you loving me again."

A raspy chuckle and then, "Darlin', haven't you been listening to a word I've said? Since the first time I held your hand in the garden behind the orphanage, and probably even before then, every breath in my lungs, every beat in my heart has been for you. I love you, Willow Mae. Nothing has and nothing ever will change that."

And then he kissed me. Slow. Tender. With such agonizing gentleness, it brought tears to my eyes because this was what I had held onto for twelve long years of his absence. The song his heart sang to mine when he was near—and even when he was far, far away.

A rolling sweep of his tongue along the seam of my lips had me opening for him. When his tongue met mine, I couldn't help but grind my hips against him—needing desperately to be closer, to make up for lost time.

Frantically, I grabbed the sides of his flannel shirt, rolling the sleeves down his large biceps until he finished the rest by pulling them over his hands. His t-shirt was my next priority, but I took my time as I lifted the hem and trailed the pads of my fingers over the ridges of his six-pack. He shivered beneath my touch as I gently caressed his side where the splattering of scars revealed a roadmap of the years we'd been apart.

He still loves me, I thought as I raised his shirt higher until he finally pulled it over his head revealing his bare chest.

"My turn," he husked, gripping the bottom of my tank top and pulling it up. Chills ran over my chest as his rough hands covered my breasts. I felt the calluses on his thumb as he ran it along the edge of my white lacy bra. Teasing. Taunting. And when he finally pulled the fabric down, I let my head fall back as he claimed my sensitive peak with his mouth.

"Mmm," I purred, grabbing the back of his head and pressing my breast further into his mouth feeling the swirl of his tongue lashing against my nipple.

My entire body was fevered with a need for him that was so feral I was starting to lose my mind. Breaths ragged, my core tightened...*more. I need more.*

A suckling pop sounded as he leaned back from my chest, his deft fingers making quick work of unclasping my bra. I giggled as he tossed it far away from us, that wicked mouth of his twisting upward into a heavenly smile.

In a swift movement that had my mind reeling, Johnny grabbed my waist and shifted me over until I was laying on the blanket and he was on top of me, straddling my hips and pinning me to the ground.

Surprise crackled through me as I lay there, the entire top of my body exposed under the heat of his gaze. The last time I was this naked in front of a man was the last time we'd made love in this very field under a different moon many summers ago—right before he left. I thought I would have been nervous, but the only thing I could think of was needing more of him. To feel the weight of his body as he ground his hips into me.

"You're so beautiful," he breathed, bending down to trail a line of kisses from my collarbone, across the top of each of my breasts, and down along the center of my stomach. "I think these are getting in the way." He tugged at the rim of my jean shorts.

"I agree," was all I could manage to say as my heart thundered in my chest.

My legs shuddered, not from anxiety but from the anticipation as he undid the button and pulled the zipper down. Lifting my hips, I watched the look on his face as he slid my shorts down my thighs. His eyes never left where my sex was covered in a matching white lace thong. The shorts around my knees, Johnny paused, his brown eyes flicking up to mine.

His dimple slowly carved out next to his lips as they tilted upward. "I fucking love you in white, darlin'."

A crimson blush spread across my cheeks, matching the heat flaring in my core. "Well, I love you when you're out of those jeans."

His smile widened as he cocked a brow at me. "Is that so?"

"Mmhmm," I nodded, biting my lip.

As Johnny rose to stand, I propped myself on my elbows to

watch him in all his beautiful glory. The veins in his forearms popped more as he undid his jeans at the same time he kicked his boots off. With the moonlight at his back, a wild dance of shadow and light played along his tan skin as he shed his jeans and socks. My mouth watered as I took notice of his large member tenting his boxers.

He was ready for me and I was tired of waiting to have him. "Those need to go too," I crooned.

"Yes ma'am," was all he said before he slid them off, my breath catching in my chest as I stared at the sheer manliness of him.

Time had sculpted him from a gangly country boy into a force of nature and he was *mine*. And as he knelt before me, the moon shining high over his head, I'd never felt more like a woman. More powerful or loved.

With an open palm, he pressed against the center of my chest. A silent plea for me to lay back down, and so I did. That fire he started was licking its way up my legs as he nestled himself between them and started kissing along my inner thigh. Starting slow, making his way up until I could feel the heat of his breath along the edge of my soaked panties.

"Stop teasing me," I ground out and he laughed. Pouting, I said, "Haven't I waited long enough?"

I felt his smile against my skin right before he reached under my butt, lifting me upward. His teeth grazed along my stomach sending a thrill of butterflies through me. And then he tugged on the edge of my panties with his teeth, taking his time sliding them all the way down to my ankles where they stayed as he found himself between my legs again. I was pinned beneath him, my nipples erect as he went back and forth between each one, tugging and rolling the sensitive peak between his fingers.

I arched my back into his touch just as his mouth clamped around me, his tongue rolling over and over my pulsing sex.

"Yes," I breathed. "Oh my God, yes!" He sucked at my sensitive nub sending me into a spiral of euphoric sensations that had the blanket twisting under my grip. I lifted my head to watch him work, those dark sensuous eyes trained on me as he stroked my pussy with three long laps of his tongue.

"You're so fucking wet for me, baby girl," he growled.

"I need you closer," I whimpered. "I need more of you." I stretched my arms out to him and he lifted himself forward until his hips were hovering above mine, the head of his cock slick against my entrance.

"Is this what you want, darlin'?" With a small thrust of his hips, I felt the tip of him teasing me. That dimple playing at the edge of his smirk.

Twelve years had been far too long and now this bastard thought he could torture me with the tip of his cock? If he wouldn't give me what I wanted, I'd take it.

Reaching down, I grabbed his ass cheeks, lifted my hips, and pushed him into me.

"Holy fuck, Lo," he ground out as his length pulsed inside of me, stretching me wide.

"Yes, honey," I answered his question. "Your cock is exactly what I want, so stop trying to keep it from me."

Johnny's laugh was hot against my neck and I would have laughed with him at my attempt to talk dirty if he didn't feel so fucking good grinding in and out so slow that I could feel every ridged vein of him against me.

His pace quickened and I saw the raw, unharnessed need

reflecting in his eyes as he thrust into me harder this time, my hips moving up to meet his. He kissed me breathlessly, never slowing his pace and I could no longer tell where my body ended and his began. We were one and I held him tight against me, terrified that a single wrong move would make him disappear again.

My friend.

My protector.

My lover.

My first.

My *last*.

"I love you, Johnny." My words were a mere whisper on the night air that surrounded us. "I love you."

His hands came to frame my face as I hooked my legs around his waist, not able to give an inch of our closeness.

"Say it again," he murmured as he pulled out slowly until I felt the head of his length rim the edge of my entrance.

"I love you," I smiled at him, my heart clenching as I noticed the tears that rimmed his eyes.

So so slowly, he pushed himself into me once again until I felt his hilt pressed against my clit. Never once did he take his eyes off mine as he stroked that spot deep within me—the place only *he* was capable of reaching.

"I love you, too." He pressed a kiss to the tip of my nose as he rolled his hips again. "More than words could ever convey." Another kiss to the right edge of my mouth. "But I will try"—and another to the other side of my mouth—"every day"—and one more at the base of my neck—"for the rest of our lives."

A promise woven with words and sealed with the oneness of our bodies, but this time I could feel it. As though every moment over the last decade was leading up to this second chance. Another shot at the love we both shared.

"Forever," I cried as he thrust into me again and his lips covered mine, drowning out my moans as he pounded faster—faster, chasing the release we both needed.

And when I screamed his name into the night, he roared his love for me one more time.

CHAPTER TWENTY-EIGHT

A long wet tongue licked the side of my face, stirring me from a dream of tall waving grass, passionate breaths, and a glittering moon watching over Johnny and me.

"Yuck!" I groaned, wiping Asher's slobber from my cheek. "That's no way to wake a lady, Asher."

He let out a whimper as he moved on to my hand dangling off the side of the bed, nudging it relentlessly with his nose.

"Nah-uh, boy. She's all mine." I squealed as Johnny grabbed my waist and tugged me into him. Asher just placed his head on the side of the bed and looked over at me with those big golden eyes.

"I have to tell you, Johnny, if he keeps looking at me like that with those puppy-dog eyes he will win against you every time."

"Mmm. Somehow I doubt that." His hand dipped under the sheet landing against my stomach. My back arched on instinct, pushing my butt against his hard morning wood. Teasing lips caressed the cuff of my ear as his fingers explored lazily, as though he had all the time in the world.

But life taught me that time could be stolen and the more he roamed my lower stomach, the more I needed his touch *elsewhere*. I scooted away from him until I was laying flat on my back, my legs spread open.

Johnny's eyes turned molten, the same desire I felt reflecting back at me as his hand slid between my legs, his palm resting firmly above my clit as his middle finger slid along my wet lips.

"You're already so fucking wet for me, darlin'." His finger stopped moving and I sighed.

"Are you really going to tease me again, Johnny?"

He growled, "Not a chance, baby girl. I'm just trying to decide if I want to eat your pussy for breakfast or if I want to fuck you until you can't move out of this bed."

Oh.

My core clenched and I rasped, "I think I'll take the latter."

Not a second later and the sheets were ripped away, exposing our naked bodies. Those rough hands scraped against my hips as he picked me up until I was straddling his hips, my wet sex pressing against his hard ridge. But I wasn't facing him, I was facing his wide open window and somehow that was super arousing? *Who am I?*

With one hand holding me up, Johnny reached between us and guided me onto him. "Holy fuck," were the only words I could say as he filled me slowly, making sure I adjusted to the angle. But once I was sitting firmly on his cock, he released my hips and placed both hands gently at the small of my back.

"Lean back," he coaxed. My hands found his chest and I felt him flex inside of me, touching that sensitive spot that had my entire body flushing with heat.

"Good girl," he praised. "Now ride me."

Something in that command turned a switch in me as I tilted my head back, my hair sweeping against his torso as I slowly rose and sank back down.

"Fuck, yes," he ground out, encouraging me to keep going.

Again, I raised and lowered my hips until I no longer felt the slight twinge of pain from our escapades last night, but pleasure. Only pure, blissful pleasure built deep in my core as I slammed down onto him, fueled by his moans and whispers of my name.

Our bodies shifted slightly as he leaned forward, his hand reaching over my leg, finding my sensitive clit. He rubbed me in slow circles as my movements became wild, my body craving that euphoric release.

When he found a rhythm with his fingers swirling to the pace of my hips, my arms started to shake from my rising climax, but he didn't miss a beat. With one hand still on me, he helped take the pressure off my hands as he pressed me up and started thrusting into me so fucking hard I saw stars.

"Yes!" I shouted, no longer able to restrain my need for release. "Don't. Fucking. Stop."

"Not a chance, darlin'," he husked, picking up the pace and finally sending me toppling over the edge. I clamped around him, my entire body pulsing from the release and the only thing holding me up was his strength.

One. Two. Three more thrusts and he pulled out, spilling his seed onto the sheets as I collapsed next to him. With the little strength I had left, I wrapped my arm around his waist and kissed his neck as a haggard groan escaped his lips with the final release of his orgasm.

When he finished, he rolled over to face me and pressed a gentle kiss to my lips. I felt a wide smile grace his face, right before he said, "All those years in Georgia and now you can finally call yourself a cowgirl."

I slapped his arm with a laugh before he pulled me into him. We lay there for a long while before my stomach growled loudly and he said, "Well, that's my cue to get cooking."

I snuck a piece of bacon to Asher under the table, but when I looked over to Johnny his raised brows told me I'd been caught.

"What?" I shrugged. "I told you. I can't resist those puppy-dog eyes." Asher rested his head on my lap while I finished the rest of my plate and went to sip on the third cup of coffee Johnny poured me.

I have a feeling I'll be regretting this dosage of caffeine later. But that thought didn't stop me from keeping my hands curled around the ceramic mug.

"So, have you thought about your next steps now that you've decided you'll be moving back here instead of going back to Nashville?" Johnny's face was unreadable. A mask of calm even though I knew the question was loaded.

So much of my life had been altered in the last two weeks and my mind was still playing catch up. My finger tapped on the mug as I said, "Well, I'm going to need to cancel my apartment lease. I already called the store owners for the leases I was planning on checking out, so at least that's taken care of. And honestly, I didn't have much in my apartment. I really only used it to sleep and eat dinner because I was working two, sometimes three jobs. But now...I guess I'll have a lot more time on my hands."

"More time to get some ideas about a new boutique location."

I beamed at him. "Exactly. Which is so wild to think about. Finally having the opportunity to fulfill a dream I've been chasing a really long time. It feels strange."

Johnny stretched his arms out wide before clasping his hands behind his head, giving me a full view of his beautifully sculpted biceps.

"It was strange for me too—opening *Far Away Archery*. I'd saved up almost every penny from my years in the Marines and it took a lot of that money for me to invest in the shop. I was really fucking scared that I was taking a chance on something that wouldn't work out. And I think for people like us, who grew up with nothing, we have a decision to make."

"What's that?" I asked.

"Well, we can either stay scared and play it safe, or we can leave the cards on the table and invest in ourselves. I chose to do the latter and it worked out. And I think your boutique will work out as well."

"Yeah." I nodded, looking down at my thumbs that had tiny faint scars the size of pinpoints from all the years I spent sewing with a thread and needle. It was hard work and perseverance and sheer grit and determination that had me believing in his words. That, and the stubborn streak that ran a mile wide in me. I wanted this boutique and even if I lost every dime of my inheritance tomorrow, I knew I'd find a way to make it work.

"I know it'll work out too." I rubbed Asher's head between his ears and he let out a comforted sigh.

Silence fell between us for a few minutes as we both sipped on our coffees. I couldn't recall the last time I felt so... at home. When I was back in my apartment in Nashville, I had to keep the TV on no matter whether I was cooking dinner, working on sketches, or trying to fall asleep. The silence there had always felt like a void, as though there was something missing from my space and the meaningless sound from the TV kept the uneasiness at bay. But here, with Johnny next to me and Asher almost falling asleep with his head in my lap... yes. *Home* was exactly how this felt.

Which was *crazy*. Because it was only two weeks ago that I saw Johnny for the first time after twelve years apart still thinking he'd left me without a word. Maybe it was the mind-blowing sex that I refused to have with anyone else that had me losing my marbles.

"Are you planning on staying at the estate when you get all your stuff down here?" Johnny asked, breaking through my thoughts.

I blinked at him. I hadn't actually considered where I was planning on staying, but the idea of staying in that giant house all by myself had my heart galloping. "No," I blurted. "I don't know if I will ever feel comfortable staying there. It's definitely way too much house for one person and it has Adeline's imprint all over it. It would probably cost a small fortune to make it my style and I'm not sure that's how I want to spend this money."

Johnny took a sip of his coffee as he assessed me. "You could move in here. At least until you get things settled." He said the words so nonchalantly over the rim of his mug as though he didn't just ask me to move in with him after being apart for twelve years.

"I…" I clamped my mouth shut, stunned into silence.

Is this what I want? I asked myself and a resounding yes clanged through my mind. But that was crazy. Moving in with a man who, yeah, was my first love and my best friend for most of my life and who just gave me the most mind-blowing sex, and my God did I want more of that mind-blowing sex.

Focus.

I looked around the kitchen and out the window to the wrap-around porch and the beautiful front yard. Then my gaze trailed downward to the sweetest pup who was now staring at me with those big golden eyes. And finally, to Johnny who was leaned back in his stool, one arm stretched out toward the counter where he still had a grasp on his coffee mug. He was the portrait of serenity—my own safe haven—and I nearly screamed yes at him if it weren't for the nagging insecurity clawing at my gut.

"Can I think about it?" My voice was meek and I hated the disappointment that flashed in his eyes.

"Of course you can," he said, releasing his mug and rising from his stool.

Goosebumps rose along my arms as he stood behind me and swept my hair off my neck. He leaned down and whispered, "But just so you know, darlin', this house is meant to have you in it and there will be one day when I won't take no for an answer."

"What do you mean you told him you'd think about it?" Sarah squealed through the phone. "Willow, how many times do we have to talk about this? Stop getting in the way of your own love story. Give the poor man what he wants and just say yes."

Always the hopeless romantic, this one.

"It's been twelve years, Sarah. We're grown up now and have practically lived an entire life apart from one another. Don't you think it's smart for me to wait and make sure that we're even right for each other?"

Sarah blew a raspberry and I rolled my eyes even though she couldn't see me. "No. I don't think it's smart. I think it's pretty dumb actually." I groaned and she continued trying to make her point, "Since we were kids, everyone in this town could see that you and Johnny were meant to be. I've never witnessed anything like you two, Willow. It's like your both penguins, mated for life and all you need now is for him to give you a rock."

I shook my head. "Sarah. What?" I laughed.

"Just trust me. You and Johnny are penguins and you should totally move in with him."

"Okay, well, just like I told him before he left for the shop, I'll think about it."

She let out an exacerbated sigh. "Fine. But I need you to come by my house. Cal agreed to meet with you about your mom's journal."

"Oh! When should I get there?"

"He's already on his way, so probably now?"

"Noted. See you in a few."

Cal Weston was a short, stocky man with a serious disposition about him. But I had no doubt there was likely a feisty, fun side to him if he was best friends with Theo Williams. Theo was kind and had been the class clown, doing whatever it took to make others laugh. That was until we all grew up and his parents no longer saw the value in his humor, so they pressed him firmly under their thumbs and coerced him into going to law school.

Sarah told me he'd done it to keep the peace between all of them when she finally decided to open her bakery, but I hoped Theo was getting back to himself after deciding to quit law school and pursue his own dreams in the rodeo.

"Here's her journal. I tabbed all the pages where she wrote about Henry Carnelle and what he'd done to her." I handed the leather bound pages to Cal and he handled it gingerly, as though it were a snake ready to lash out and bite.

Sarah and I looked at each other and I wondered if they could hear just how hard my heart was pounding against my ribs. Cal took his time, carefully reading through each passage I tabbed and it took about forty minutes before he finally set the journal down on the kitchen island.

"What do you think?" I asked.

He raked a hand over his face and my stomach plummeted. "There's definitely enough there to open the case and investigate foul play on Mr. Carnelle's part. But…" he trailed off.

"But what?" I pressed. Sarah placed a hand on my shoulder and squeezed. I leaned back in my seat and took in a deep breath. Calm. I needed to stay calm.

"The Carnelles are a very powerful family and I'm only wondering that if nothing was caught during the initial investigation, then maybe there's a reason for that."

Sarah chimed in, "If I remember correctly, the initial investigation wasn't considering foul play at all. Mr. Carnelle claimed it was an accident and that was that."

Cal nodded slowly. "You're right. No one questioned him stating that it was an accident, so I doubt anyone even thought to gather evidence against him." He turned his dark eyes on me and asked, "Are you sure you want to do this?"

I wrung my hands together, realizing this was likely the last time I'd be able to answer no to that question before he re-opened the case and the entire town found out about it. Maybe this was a terrible decision that would upend my life for the worse, especially now that I was making Pebble Brook Falls my home again.

But there was no hesitation within me as I said, "Yes, I'm sure."

"Okay. I'll need to take this into evidence." He held up my mother's journal.

"Just please be careful with it. It's my only connection to her and…I don't want to lose it."

"Of course."

I sat at Sarah's kitchen island staring blankly at the veins in the marble while Sarah walked Cal to the front door. When

Sarah returned, she lifted her full glass of lemonade to me and cheered, "To becoming the talk of the town for something that's actually worthy of their gossip."

A feline smile pulled at my lips as I raised my own glass, clinking it against hers. "To karma."

CHAPTER TWENTY-NINE

hree days passed since I spoke with Cal and handed over my mother's journal. Sarah and Johnny did an excellent job trying to distract me while we waited to see if anything came of it. But now that they were both back at work, I was stuck with nothing but myself and my thoughts, both of which are pretty miserable right now.

I debated staying in bed all day, letting the anxiety of waiting and the weight of my decisions consume me. But it would have been the second day in a row I did that and I was tired of sulking, so I grabbed a to-go coffee from The Roasted Bean and was now sitting on a picnic table at the park downtown, determined to get some sketches on paper.

Though, my thoughts kept cycling through. Questioning if I made the right call in making an enemy of the Carnelles right as I decided to move back to town. Wondering what I was going to do with the gigantic estate that was sitting empty. I thought of Johnny's hands on me and how stupid I was for opting to wait on giving him an answer when I knew in my heart that I wanted nothing more than to start a life with him—to make up for lost time.

I groaned at the blank page in front of me and slammed the sketchbook closed before burying my head in my hands.

Frustration coiled tightly around my spine. *Why do I deny myself joy?* It was a habit, I realized, that started after Johnny left for the military. Instead of staying close to Sarah, my only lifeline at the time, I moved far away from her and only saw her once every few years. Most of my time was spent working myself into a hole of fatigue only to wake up and do it all over again. There was little true happiness I experienced in my twenties and no one was responsible for robbing me of that, except for myself.

I didn't want to live that way anymore. Feeling so dragged down by the comforts of my despair that time flitted by until I was old and gray with nothing left to show but a cage made by my own fearful decisions.

No.

I certainly did not want that.

I wanted to live unapologetically. I wanted my days to be filled with joy, kisses from my man, and listening to Asher's happy barks and my best friend's laughter.

And maybe I deserved those things. Maybe it was finally time for me to let go of my own self-loathing because I was a good person and yes...I decided whole-heartedly in this rare moment that I did deserve happiness and there was no reason for me to feel guilty or unworthy of that anymore.

The sound of children chattering floated to me on the warm summer breeze and I lifted my head to find Ms. Mosely across the park, her new gaggle of children following in line behind her. She looked consciously over her shoulder every few feet, making sure none of them strayed off. The three girls I saw in the living room during my visit were walking hand in hand toward the middle of the line. I felt the strength of their bond, remembering how Johnny and I were inseparable all those years.

As the group made their way along the sidewalk, I couldn't help but notice how most of their clothes looked like they were either too big or a little snug. The consequences of hand-me-downs from the local charities.

I hadn't noticed it during my visit because I was too consumed with thoughts of my mother when I saw Ms. Mosely at the orphanage, but thinking back now I recalled how worn down the house was on the inside. The ornate rug in the living room was the same one that had been there when I was at the orphanage. Sofas and chairs were sagging in the middle and the staircase wood had chips in it on almost every step.

It was a roof over their heads and I knew they all had a place to rest at night, but there were consequences to living in such a place. All the years I spent there, Ms. Mosely had always allowed us to have friends over, but I never once asked Sarah to come stay with me. I was embarrassed and maybe that was my pride showing, but kids were cruel. One look at the inside of that place from someone who grew up in a regular home and there would be judgment.

But for these kids...maybe I could change that. Maybe I could give them the life I was owed, but never had a chance to live.

As I watched them round the corner, likely headed for the ice cream parlor, a smile graced my lips and some wounded part of my heart patched over.

Yes. I can give them something pretty great indeed.

Excitement bubbled through me as I headed back to my car. A simple shift in perspective—in how I saw *myself*—and I was already feeling like the weight I carried for the past twelve years was sleuthing off of my shoulders. It was like the sun was finally shining through rain clouds that had followed me around for a long, long while and I was basking in the warmth of the rays.

Johnny was still at work, but I couldn't wait for tonight to tell him about my idea. I knew he would love it.

Fishing my keys from my purse, I rounded the corner of the street I parked on and stopped dead in my tracks when I noted the empty store that had flitted through my mind over the past few days. Seeing the beautiful ivory shiplap walls, the stunning wood floors, and the Eddison lightbulb chandelier made me laugh at the old version of myself who first saw this corner store and scoffed at the idea of someone wanting to open a shop in Pebble Brook Falls.

That girl had been broken by a series of bad events and she had a sour attitude to match. The reflection that stared back at me through the glossy windows made me smile because there were no more traces of that girl—afraid, tired...lonely. The woman in that window was now a force to be reckoned with. She owned the humble beginnings of where she came from, stood up for herself when others sought to tear her down and fought for the ones she loved.

I was proud to be her and for the first time—maybe ever in my life—I felt *love* for myself.

Every. Single. Piece.

Love for the girl who was orphaned and whose pants were always a little too big and shoes too small. For the girl who was bullied for wearing those same clothes and was too worn down to stand up for herself. The girl who was kind enough to find a friend in Sarah even though our lives were so wildly different. The girl whose mother loved her maybe a little too much that she shielded me from the tangled mess of her world. And…the girl who fell in love with a boy and spent a very long time thinking she lost him, only to find him again.

It could have been a whim that led me to grab my cell phone from my purse and dial the leasing number posted on the window, but some part of me knew it was fate. That Adeline's decision to put me in her will led me to come back to Pebble Brook Falls to find that Johnny had been here waiting for me to come home to him. And that this beautiful storefront was still empty and it was the perfect space for me to plant roots and open my first boutique.

"Hello?" A woman answered the phone, her voice laced with that Southern twang.

"Hi. My name's Willow Mae and I saw that your storefront in downtown Pebble Brook Falls is available for lease."

"Oh, yes. Are you looking to lease it?"

I chewed on my bottom lip before replying, "I'm actually looking to buy it outright."

"Oh, honey, you would have to front quite a lot for us to be willing to part with it."

"Name your price."

"Johnny!" I called through the front door of his shop. I didn't notice any cars parked out front except for his.

"Back here!" he answered. I followed where his voice had come from the far corner of the store. More than two weeks had passed since being back home and this was the first time I'd been inside of his archery shop. All the walls were lined with various types of bows: longbows, recurve, crossbows, and a few more I didn't know the names of yet. In the center of the floor space were three aisles filled to the brim with arrows, grips, sleeves, and other bow-related trinkets.

I found Johnny on a small ladder hanging a beautifully carved recurve bow that had vines covered in flowers etched into the surface.

"Wow," I breathed. "That one's really stunning."

"You like it?" He stole a glance at me over his shoulder.

"Mmhmm." I nodded, smiling.

"It was handmade by a guy out of Marietta. His name's Brendan and he puts out about one or two of these a year. Each one with different carvings, so there are no two alike in the entire world. And they're not just for decoration either. His pieces are some of the best shooting recurves I've ever shot."

He placed the bow gently on the spokes protruding out of the wall before stepping down from the ladder. I wrapped him in a hug, slipping my hands into the back pockets of his Levi's giving his butt a squeeze.

"That's certainly one way to greet a man," he laughed,

pressing a kiss to the top of my head.

I shrugged, looking up at him innocently. "What can I say? I really like your butt."

He reached around and gave mine a good smack, yielding a squeal from me. "I really like yours too, darlin'." When his lips met mine, I immediately opened for him, relishing in the gentle sweep of his tongue over mine that had my toes curling in my sandals.

When he pulled back, his eyes were hooded and swirled with a desire that matched the heat pooling in my core.

"I came to tell you a few things," I said quietly.

"Oh yeah? Why don't you tell me over some sweet tea out back? I'm sure Asher is dying to see you. I think he's been having withdrawals the past few nights since you've been back at Sarah's."

"I have to admit, I've been having withdrawals from him too."

Johnny tucked me under his arm, leading me to the back door of his shop and when he opened it, Asher was sitting on the stoop of the steps. He almost tackled me to the ground as he jumped up, sweet little happy whimpers piercing the air between us.

"Hi, boy! Oh, I missed you too!" I knelt down and he nearly slobbered my entire face with his wet kisses as I gave him scratches behind his ears and along his spine.

"Easy, boy," Johnny laughed as he bent over and held onto Asher's waist so I could stand without him toppling me over.

I walked out to the picnic table with Asher while Johnny grabbed us a couple of sweet teas from his mini fridge. When he sat across from me extending the bottle over I untwisted the cap and took a long swig.

"Alright, baby girl. Let's hear this news you're so excited to share."

With a turn of my wrist, the cap was back on the bottle. "Okay. So, you remember how run down the orphanage was when we were there?"

"Yeah," he chuckled. "As soon as I learned how to turn a wrench I was constantly fixing the bathroom sink downstairs. And it didn't matter how many times Ms. Mosely vacuumed, those carpets were always filthy."

"Oh my gosh, I totally forgot about that sink. I'll never forget that one time I was watching you try to fix it and you got sprayed in the face." I couldn't help the laughter that bubbled from my chest. "I don't think I've ever seen you look that surprised."

"Yeah, well that's because *someone* forgot to turn off the water main." He glowered at me.

"Oops." I shrugged my shoulders and he shook his head before taking a sip of his own tea.

"Anyways, when I went to visit Ms. Mosely after finding my mother's journal, I noticed that the place is in even more distress than it was when we were kids. Honestly, I don't know how long the house will even be safe for her and those kids to stay there and I doubt there's enough funding in the charity for her to buy a new house."

Johnny looked at me expectantly as I paused. When he noticed that I was wringing my fingers together, he reached across the table and took both my hands in his, and rubbed his thumb over the top of my palms.

I looked into his eyes finding a kaleidoscope of chestnut brown, sunrise yellow, and tiny flecks of pale green. Warmth and comfort shone in those beautiful irises reminding me of home. The tension in my shoulders loosened knowing that there was nothing I could say, no idea I could share that Johnny would balk at.

"So, I was thinking of how I doubt that I will ever feel comfortable living in that big house. It holds too much pain knowing it was a place I could have shared with my mother and never had the chance to. But I don't want to just sell it to the highest bidder, I want to do some good with it." I took a deep breath in. "I'm going to donate the estate to the *Hope for All* orphanage and give those kids a dream home to grow up in."

Johnny just blinked at me.

"Is that a stupid idea?" I whispered, suddenly feeling very self-conscious.

His hand raised to cup my cheek and I swore those were tears lining his eyes as he said, "Not even in the slightest, Lo. I think that's the most generous thing I've ever heard." I blushed at his compliment as he leaned across the table and brushed his lips across mine. I didn't think I'd ever get used to the way my body soared every time he did that.

"I'm so damn lucky to call you mine."

Mine. One simple word that held so much meaning. The truth was that I had always been his.

"I feel like I'm the lucky one. I mean you have the biggest biceps I've ever seen. You look sexy as hell when you pull a bow string back. And your ass in those Levi's. Mm-mm-mm." He gently flicked the tip of my nose and I stuck my tongue out at him.

"Well, darlin' you're going to have to wait for me to reveal my favorite parts of you until tonight when I run my tongue over every last inch." He shot me a wicked grin. I clamped my legs together trying to ward off the pulsing heat his words had evoked.

"Bastard."

His head tilted back and he let out a wonderous laugh that didn't do anything to help the burning fire he'd started that now had my toes curling. I looked down at Asher who'd taken residence at my side. He gave me a sympathetic look as if to say, "*I know. He annoys me too.*"

"So, what's the other thing you wanted to tell me?"

I cocked my head at him.

"You said you wanted to tell me a *few* things."

Realization dawned on me. "Right! Yes. I…um…kind of bought something today."

His brows raised. "Oh yeah? What did you buy?"

"I'm not sure if you've noticed that there's an empty store-front downtown. The one that's on the corner with the white shiplap walls."

"I've seen it." He took another swig of his sweet tea.

"I called the owner and put an offer in to buy it for my first boutique location and she accepted it."

Johnny's eyes were bright with excitement as his lips slowly tilted upward, that dimple tugging on his right cheek. "So, it's official then. You're really staying here. Putting down roots."

"Yeah," I looked at him through my lashes.

"Well damn if you didn't just make my day, darlin'. I want to celebrate this with you. Take you somewhere special this weekend."

"I'd like that," was all I said before I met him halfway across the table and kissed him breathlessly.

CHAPTER THIRTY

Gravel crunched beneath his truck tires as he pulled into the driveway. The cutest little log cabin I'd ever seen was nestled between two giant oak trees. The front door was Candy Apple red, a stark contrast to the dark wood the rest of the cabin was made from. Various flowers spilled from two window boxes hanging from the pair of windows on each side of the door and two oversized wooden rocking chairs sat on the small front porch, as though he'd planned for this very day to happen all along.

After he parked, he came around to my side of the truck and opened the doors for Asher and me. We both laughed as Asher darted from the back seat and hopped around the oak trees like a bunny rabbit, stopping to sniff for some poor squirrel every few feet. Johnny grabbed my waist and hoisted me from the truck. My breath hitched when I landed on my feet and he reached for my chin, tilting my head back to look at him. "Welcome to The Lookout," he husked before planting a kiss on my forehead.

Taking my hand, he led me up the small path to the front

of the cabin. Something deep in my heart ached with joy as I noticed smaller details of the serene place. A small dog statue with strikingly similar features to Asher stood proud in the garden bed in front of the porch. Hanging on the wall behind the rocking chairs was a sign made of driftwood with crackling white letters that said: *Home is where the heart is.*

I'd seen the saying written out several times throughout my life on similar signs in stores but seeing it here, on the outside of Johnny's cabin, seemed to hit differently.

"You really own this place?" I asked.

It was more of a rhetorical question but he replied, "Mmhmm. It was the first place I bought when I got out of the Marines. There were still a lot of things I needed to work through and being in town was too much. It was...difficult to be around civilians after having so many tours overseas. Honestly, I was afraid of myself. Of what I might do if someone accidentally provoked me. I didn't want any more blood on my hands, so I looked for a place in the woods and came across this cabin."

His voice had grown more distant with each word he spoke and I could tell his mind was in a different place, another time, as we cleared the steps and took a seat in the rocking chairs.

"I could see why you would choose this place to heal. It's really special, Johnny."

"It took a lot of TLC to get it looking like this. When I first bought it, the thing was a death trap. I had to replace all the flooring and patch some holes in the roof. But the work kept my mind busy. Distracted from everything that happened over there."

"Can I ask you something?"

Those brown eyes slid over to me. "Shoot."

"The dog tags hanging on your mantel...whose are those?"

He shifted his gaze back to the trees and when he went quiet for several minutes I wondered if I'd overstepped. "Remember that night I told you about? The suicide bomber?" he finally asked.

I nodded, feeling too afraid to speak and risk saying something stupid or upsetting.

"One of the guys who died that night was my closest friend in the Marines. I met him on the first day at basic and somehow we made it all the way to the same squad. His name was Bradley Taylor."

I wanted to reach for his hand but years of knowing when he needed his space stopped me.

"You would have loved him, Lo." Johnny let out a strangled laugh as though the happy memories of his friends were still difficult to think about. "He was a giant pain in the ass. Always getting into trouble with our commanding officers for the stupidest shit. Mostly playing pranks that had him cleaning our toilets for weeks on end. But he didn't care about the punishment because the joy he brought to our squad was all he wanted. Especially during our deployments. He was the one who kept my mind straight when I was fucking terrified.

"I remember our first deployment like it was yesterday. We all talked a big game, but most of us were still kids, petrified out of our minds. That first week we were in Afghanistan, our base was attacked with mortars. It felt like the entire earth was shaking and when I took cover, Bradley was right beside me cracking jokes between each attack like it was a walk in the park." He scraped a hand over his face and I noticed the tiny worry lines etched around his eyes. The wariness that had his shoulders slumping forward like he was carrying the weight of the world on them.

And maybe that was because for years he had carried the weight of his country on them. And his need to prove himself to me. That he was a good and stable man who could provide a life for us—for me. Because he was told his entire life that he was going to end up just like his parents. That he would become a menace to society because of the blood that ran in his veins.

Anger rose in me. At Ms. Mosely. All the townsfolk who sneered at him when he walked by. The kids we went to school with who said awful things about him. And at myself... for giving in to the assumptions of others and believing that he truly was a rotten apple, breaking the only promise he ever made to me.

But I stomped it out. Anger wouldn't serve either one of us and I was tired of retreating inward. So tired of running away.

"It sounds like Bradley was really special. I'm so sorry you lost such a good friend, Johnny."

He nodded slowly. "The guilt is the worst part. I spent years, after that night, wondering why it wasn't me. Why it had to be him when there was so much good in him. So much light."

My heart squeezed and panic had my throat tightening at the mere thought of him being the one to have died. I got up from my chair and kneeled in front of him, taking his hands in mine. Deep sorrow carved a river between his brows and dragged those lush lips into a frown. I placed a kiss on each of his knuckles. "I can't even begin to imagine what it must be like for you. Having gone to war, faced death and the loss of people you cared deeply about. But please...don't for one second think that it should have been you. Because…" I tried to choke back the tears and failed as they spilled over, running down my face. "Because you make this world so much better, Johnny. And I'm so damn thankful that fate brought me back to you and we have this second chance to make things right. And I can't imagine it…can't even think of what I would do if I had to exist in this world without you. So, please. Please don't ever think that."

He looked at me for a long while and I didn't back down from the heat of his gaze, instead, I let it wash over me. Cleansing any remaining doubt that I was exactly where I was meant to be. And so was he. Together. On the front porch of the cabin that brought him peace, and helped him heal from the trauma of his past.

"I don't deserve you, Willow Mae." His voice cracked and a piece of my heart went with it.

Leaning forward, I grasped his face between my palms, whispering, "Yes you do." Then I kissed him. Wrapping my arms around his neck, I buried my fingers in his hair and pulled him closer. He sucked in a deep breath, stealing the oxygen from my lungs and I gave it willingly. I realized that I'd give him everything if it meant he'd be happy. My heart, my love, my *life*. I'd take a bullet for this man and I only wanted him to know how worthy he was. How *good* he was.

So, I showed him that through the sweep of my tongue against his. The fervent grasp of my hands on the back of his neck as I deepened the kiss, letting him consume me until there was nothing left in this world except for our souls intertwined.

When we pulled back, I witnessed the subtle change in him. How his eyes shone with hope and the ghost of a smile played across his lips, chasing away the grief that was haunting him only minutes ago.

"Thank you."

"For what?" I breathed.

"For loving me."

"Always, Johnny. I will always love you."

We spent the rest of the day exploring his property and playing fetch with Asher, who was currently pouting in the dog bed next to the fireplace because we came inside way before he was ready.

"Mmm, yes," I mused as Johnny handed me a glass of red wine.

The leather sofa dipped as he sat down and draped his arm behind me. My pulse quickened when his thumb met my bare shoulder, rubbing casually in slow circles. A loud pop sounded from the fireplace where flames danced and embers floated gracefully up the chimney. It didn't make sense that we were having a fire in the heat of Georgia's summer, but I'd always loved having fires in the grand hearth at the orphanage. The ornate stone of the fireplace was the most beautiful part of that house and something about it made me feel like— for once—I had something just as cool and fancy as the other kids at school.

So, I asked Johnny if we could have a fire tonight and his only response was a wide knowing smile before he set up some logs and kindling.

I shifted my body so I could face him and said, "It's strange how so much time has passed and yet, it feels like I still know exactly who you are and you still know me."

He tucked a strand of hair behind my ear, letting his fingers trail along the edge of my jaw before he gave my chin a little squeeze. "We spent every day together for over half our lives, Lo. I don't think it's strange at all."

"But parts of you have changed. And same thing with me." He just smiled at me. I playfully shoved at his chest and he wrapped his arm tighter around my shoulder, bringing me into him.

"Of course we've changed in some ways. But this"—he placed his open palm on my chest above my heart—"hasn't. To me, that's all that matters."

I placed my own palm over his and held it there. "Do you ever wonder what our life might have been like if you hadn't left?" It was the question I'd asked myself every day since I watched him walk away from me in that field. The same question that turned his memory into a haunted nightmare for so long.

His nostrils flared as he inhaled deeply. "Every day. Especially when I didn't hear back from you. There was a lot of regret in those first few years, but eventually, I found peace in knowing that I'd find you again one day. I've always known that our lives would be intertwined. That there was no way I could be without you for too long."

Looking away from him, I blushed. I didn't think I would ever get used to being loved by him. Hearing how I was wrong for all those years in believing that he didn't care for me and had left me. His words were like a lullaby for my soul —comforting in a way that only sweet nothings could be.

"Now that I have you in my arms and see the incredible woman you've become, I wonder if maybe those years apart really did make us better for each other. Like maybe we needed to grow into ourselves before we could make it together in the way we're meant to be." He took a sip of his wine, notes of berry, chocolate, and smoked wood wafting through the air as the burgundy liquid lapped against the side of his glass.

"It doesn't mean those years weren't hell though."

"Hell, indeed." We both laughed. "I think I like that perspective. Somehow, it takes the sting out of being apart from you for all those years. Feeling like we missed out on so much time when maybe, you're right, we needed those years to grow up. Become who we were both meant to be so that when we came back together, we would meet as the best versions of ourselves."

"Exactly." Those molten chocolate eyes were on me and I could see our history reflected in them. All the tiny and monumental moments that made up our lives and the love she shared for one another. Yes. I wished I could have been with him to celebrate making it through basic training. I wished that I could have been an anchor for him when he deployed during the war and especially when he lost Bradley and other brothers in arms.

There was nothing I could do to change that—to turn back the clock and figure out a way to be with him. But I could do something now. I could choose him, just as he'd chosen me every time he put pen to paper and wrote a letter to me even though I never wrote one back.

"Yes," I whispered.

His brows furrowed for the briefest moment and then

understanding gleamed in his eyes. "Yes," he said back to me with a tilt of excitement.

I nodded with a smile. "Yes. I'd like to move in with you. That is, if the offer still stands."

His voice was raspy, "Of course it still stands, darlin'." The smile he gave me was one I hadn't seen since we were kids when we ran through our field on snowy days or the first time he pulled away after our first kiss and he saw the surprise on my face. It was so bright and genuine that it was contagious. I couldn't help but feel elated as I took in his handsome face and that smile he held just for me.

He took my wine glass and set them both on the coffee table before shifting towards me, coming in for a kiss. I placed my palms on his chest, stopping him. "I have to be honest about something, though."

"Let's hear it."

"I'm saying yes because I love you and I want to start building a life with you. But"—I dragged out the word—"I'm mostly saying yes so I can spend every day with Asher."

"Is that right?" He slipped his arm under my knees and around my waist and pulled me into his lap, my bottom was flush against his crotch where his cock was already growing. I wiggled my ass against him and he growled against my ear.

"Mmhmm," I responded.

His teeth grazed the cuff of my ear, sending shivers down my neck. "I guess I'll have to do a better job making sure your attention is trained on me, baby girl."

Johnny rose with me in his arms and we headed toward the back of the cabin. "Where are you taking me?"

"Now that you've decided to move in, I think it's time I showed you our other bedroom."

When we reached the door, I turned the handle and he kicked it open with his booted foot and closed it once we were inside. There was no time for me to take in the space before he set me back on my feet and turned me around until my back was to him.

"Take off your shirt," he commanded and I heard the rustling of fabric behind me and boots clattering against the wood floors.

I did as he told me and tossed my shirt to the floor. "Good. Now shimmy that little ass for me while you take off your shorts."

A satisfied moan sounded from behind me as I swayed my hips from side to side, letting my shorts pool around my feet.

He still didn't touch me and somehow that was making me crave him more with each command. "Kneel on the bed. Good. Now lay your face down and spread your arms out for me."

There was no hiding my body from him in this position as I lay there spread wide, my ass straight up in the air. Rough hands palmed my cheeks making my core clench and when the air rang with the smack of his hand on my ass, I groaned into the comforter my hands twisting into knots from the wild sensation.

"That's it, baby girl. I fucking love seeing your skin turn pink when I spank you." I bit my lip at his dirty words and how they made my tiny thong soak with desire. One thumb hooked around my panties and tugged them to the side while his other hand spread me wide and when his tongue found my clit I nearly came from the warmth of his mouth closing around me.

"You taste so fucking good," he murmured against me and

then his mouth was on me again. His tongue dove deep into my slit, plunging in and out as I reached for him between my legs needing to feel some part of him to ground me from the ecstasy that had me flying high. I found his forearm and gripped it hard as I moved my ass up and down against his tongue. His lips closed around me and sucked so hard I saw stars.

"Oh my fucking God, Johnny. I'm going to come! Please don't stop. Please," I whimpered into the comforter.

Two thick fingers pumped into me while his tongue rolled over my sensitive nub, driving me further and further to the edge until I finally toppled over, my legs shaking wildly as I rode out my orgasm and he lapped up every bit of my release.

He withdrew his fingers slowly and nipped at my ass cheek before he picked me up and rolled me over, coming to lay beside me on the bed. I curled into him, wanting to be close, and felt the velvet smooth skin of his erection against my hip. When I went to reach for him, wanting to return the favor he gripped my wrist and said, "Not a chance, darlin'. This was all about you."

"But I want you to feel good too."

He pulled me into him and pressed a kiss to my forehead. "I'm sure I'll get mine later tonight. Right now I just want to bask in the glory of making you come so hard your legs nearly gave out."

I giggled into his side. "Bask away, handsome."

"And I need you to say it."

"Say what?"

"That you want to move in with me because I'm awesome and give you mind-blowing sex and not because you're more in love with my dog than me."

I sighed dramatically. "Sweetheart, a lady isn't supposed to lie."

"Hmmm. I didn't realize ladies were such screamers. Or that they enjoyed having their pussy licked so much."

Heat crawled up my neck and I knew my face was a deep shade of crimson.

"But if you won't say it, I guess I'll just have to try harder," he growled.

By the end of the night, I told him exactly what he wanted to hear.

CHAPTER THIRTY-ONE

My entire body—and especially my sex—was sore. Johnny spent the entire weekend showing me just how skilled he'd become at pleasuring a woman's body. *My* body. Part of me wondered if he'd lied about being with someone else given the expertise he put on full display the past two days, but I knew that was something he'd never be dishonest about. So, I chalked it up to him watching a ton of porn and doing hardcore research on female anatomy.

Regardless, I was going to have to get myself into shape if I was going to keep up with him now that we would be living together.

"It's really great to see that Sarah was able to buy a house for herself so soon after opening her bakery," Johnny said as we pulled into her driveway. The plan was for me to pack all my stuff and spend one more girls' night with Sarah before I left for his place tomorrow. I'd need to head back to Nashville eventually to pack up the apartment and cancel my lease, but that would probably be after I heard back from Cal about my mother's case.

"Yeah, I'm really proud of how much she's done for herself. Especially given the lack of support from her family. I know it was really hard for her to take that leap of faith."

He nodded in agreement. Just as Johnny opened my car door, Sarah appeared on her front porch, but something seemed off because she didn't smile or wave or do anything except stare at me with a harrowed look.

Johnny must have picked up on it too because he looked at me with concern, a muscle feathering along his jaw.

"Is everything okay?" I asked Sarah as the three of us made it up to her porch steps.

Sarah crossed her arms and said, "Let's talk inside." My stomach constricted as worry crept along my spine. Johnny pressed a hand against the small of my back and some part of me felt more at ease from his touch.

"It's going to be okay." I looked up at him. His face was a mask of certainty and I knew in that moment everything would be okay.

Asher's feet clattered on Sarah's hardwood floors as he veered into the living room and found a sunspot by the window, leaving us to gather around her kitchen island.

"Do you want any coffee or sweet tea?"

My stomach was too sour to handle anything at the moment so I shook my head. Johnny followed my lead and said, "No, thank you."

"Okay, then. I guess I'll just get into it."

When Sarah took a deep breath, I did the same, realizing I'd been holding mine for too long.

"Cal called me today since you were out of cell service. He told me that your mother's case has officially been re-opened.

I'm not sure of all the details, but he said something about Henry Carnelle's phone records. Apparently, some of the evidence was buried"—she used air quotes—"and no one actually looked at his phone and texting records until now. They found enough to bring him in and press charges."

My heart hammered in my chest. "So, he's in jail?"

Sarah's bright eyes flicked to Johnny and back to me. "Tell me, Sarah," I said firmly, knowing she was holding something back.

"His bail was two million dollars, but he posted bail this morning. Apparently, the Carnelles had enough cash on hand to put up."

"Fucking bastards," Johnny seethed. "I can't believe the judge even let him have bail."

Sarah just shook her head. "The Carnelles are a powerful family. I think the court is trying to appease the town because everyone's already in an uproar. That's why I stayed home today and asked Stephanie to cover for me. I wanted to be here when you got back to let you know that you should probably lay low for a little while."

"But they found something," I said more to myself than to them. I felt like I was floating, unable to keep my feet on the ground. This whole plan was a long shot from the start and somehow it was unwinding into a situation that seemed far beyond my control. And I knew that was a possibility. I knew there was a chance of this happening when I asked to speak to Cal, but I didn't truly think they would find something significant enough to put Henry behind bars. And maybe that was my own naivety in thinking they were too powerful to touch even if something had been found.

"There's a little more to it, Willow." Sarah's voice cut

through my thoughts. I grabbed Johnny's hand, needing a tether to this world as I slowly looked at her.

She ran a hand through her brown hair, the layers of her curtain bangs cascaded along the sides of her face. "Apparently, there are text message exchanges between Adeline and Henry that suggest Adeline may have been an accomplice in some capacity or that she at least knew Henry's plans."

"What?" I blurted out, my breathing growing more and more erratic. Johnny moved to stand behind me, placing both hands on my hips to steady me. Dizziness swarmed my senses and I wavered backward into his embrace.

"How?" I cried out. "How could she have done something like that to her own daughter?"

Tears lined Sarah's eyes and her voice cracked when she said, "I don't know. But I'm so so sorry, Willow."

With Johnny's arms wrapped gingerly around my waist, I braced myself against the island counter, sucking in deep breaths.

"Slow, darlin'." Johnny started rubbing circles on my back. "Slow your breathing down." Through the clanging of thoughts in my mind, I heard Johnny taking slow deep breaths. An anchor for me to hold onto so I wouldn't float away. I swatted the raging thoughts away, trying to find enough clarity to focus on the sound of his breath—to match it with my own.

I closed my eyes, fighting with everything I had to conquer the rising anxiety and just...*listen*.

In. Out. In. Out.

Slow.

Slow.

In. Out.

You're okay. You're safe. A voice somewhere deep within gently guided me back to myself, weaving through each tumultuous thought that tried to attack.

"That's it. Good," Johnny crooned, continuing to rub my back in those slow pacifying circles. I opened my eyes and finally, the dizziness ceased. I blinked at Sarah, her image coming back into focus.

"Okay," I croaked, straightening my back as I found Johnny's hands around my waist and intertwined my fingers with his. "Is there more?" I asked her.

"Like I said before, I think you should lay low for a while. If everything we're hearing is true, this will be the first murder Pebble Brooks Falls has ever seen and just the idea of it being true already has the townsfolk in an uproar."

"I'll take you back to my place tonight," Johnny said.

"But—"

"No buts. I know you wanted to spend another night with Sarah, but if the entire town is already up in arms over this, I want to keep you safe from anyone who might get a wild hair and start pointing fingers in the wrong direction."

"I agree," Sarah chimed in. "Especially since Henry made bail and is free to wander around town. There's no telling what he's capable of."

I snorted. "I think we all know exactly what he's capable of." The weight of that statement sat heavy in the air between the three of us. As the seconds of silence ticked by an overwhelming feeling of fatigue washed over me like a crashing wave.

"I'm going to go pack," I said to both of them before heading to Sarah's guest bedroom.

It didn't take me long to fill the large suitcase I brought

and wheel it down the hall toward the front door. Asher's ears perked up when he saw the suitcase and I wanted to tell him that I was going to be staying with him from now on. That he'd have a life filled with ear and belly scratches. But I couldn't muster the energy to feel excited.

Today was like living through a tornado. Everything was going so well and then a violent storm came and swept everything away. The worst part was that it was of my own making. Of course I knew there was a risk that I was right about Henry Carnelle. That he truly was the monster my mother painted him out to be in her journal. But finding out that I had, indeed, been right was an entirely different experience than I thought it would be.

The Carnelles were a beloved family in this town. Respected by everyone for how many jobs their stud ranch created and the townsfolk loved seeing all the winning horses that came from their ranch. Pursuing this case was surely going to make me public enemy number one. Especially if Henry Carnelle had some tricks up his sleeve, and knowing just how awful he was, I didn't doubt he'd do everything in his power to win the jury over in his favor if this went to court.

And Adeline...*no*. I couldn't go there or I would spiral out of control. There was enough to think about already. I didn't need the possibility that my own grandmother had played a part in my mother's murder hanging over my head. Not now, at least.

I heard Sarah say, "Please watch over her, Johnny," right before I rounded the corner into the kitchen.

"You know I will," he replied before shifting toward me. "Ready, darlin'?"

"Yup."

Sarah bounded toward me, pulling me in for a tight hug. When she pulled back, her eyes searched my face. "I'm going to miss having you around."

"Me too. Thank you for letting me invade your space and turn your guest room upside down."

She laughed quietly, as though she also didn't have the strength to be her normal peppy self. "There will always be a room for you here. And please let me know if you need anything."

"You've already done so much for me, Sarah. Thank you." I rubbed her back up and down before pulling away.

"That's what friends are for." Her smile was sweet and genuine as we parted.

"Ready?" Johnny asked as he picked up my suitcase, placing a hand on the front door handle.

"Ready." I let out a long exhale. "Come on, Asher." I patted the side of my thigh and he jumped up to follow Johnny and me out.

Sarah waved at us from her front porch as we pulled out of her driveway and headed to Johnny's house. It was still too soon for me to think of it as *our* house even though every part of me felt like I was headed home.

We rode in silence for a quarter of the ride. The only sound in the cabin was Asher's quiet panting in the back seat.

"Alright, Lo. I think I've let you stew for long enough. What's going on in that pretty head of yours?"

I felt his gaze slide over to me, but I kept my eyes fixed on the road in front of us, too afraid that if I looked at him my composure would slip.

Adeline—my *grandmother*—had played a part in this. And it was her blood that ran through my veins. Running my hands up and down my arms, I tried to ward off the chill that crept along my skin.

"I..." I blew out a long breath. "I guess I'm just wondering what kind of person this makes me. If my own grandmother had a hand in my mother's murder, does that mean I'm capable of something just as terrible?"

"Jesus, Willow. Is that really what you've been thinking about?"

I finally looked at him and something like heartbreak was carved into the planes of his face. "Yes." I drew my knees up and curled my arms around them, looking back out the windshield.

A moment later, Johnny's hand was on my left forearm tugging until I relented and gave him my hand.

"I'm going to tell you something that you've told me a million times over. You are not your parents. And you are certainly not Adeline. There isn't a wicked bone in your body, Lo. You are kind and generous and the entire world is brighter when you're around. So, no. There is no way that you could ever be capable of hurting someone else."

I closed my eyes, letting myself get lost in his words and the feel of his hand on me.

Adeline was always a cruel woman. The few times I saw her around town, I could see that cruelty beneath the veneer of propriety and a good name. And maybe there was a reason for her rotten core. We all harbored secrets behind closed doors and it wasn't above me to understand that there was a possibility Adeline had her own torturous past that shaped her into the snake she was.

"I just hate that I'm connected to someone like that. Even if she didn't actually play a part in my mother's death, she was still an awful person."

"It's our actions, darlin', that make us who we are. Not the blood in our veins or the name we were given or the family we were born into. It's how you treat people. It's living with integrity and trying your best to be a good person." He gave my hand a squeeze. "You know who taught me that?"

"Who?" I asked.

"You." He shot me a wink and I laughed, lightness starting to fill my chest in place of the heavy darkness I thought was going to swallow me whole.

I scrunched up my nose. "Yeah, I guess I did." For years and years, I'd told Johnny the same thing when he battled worries about turning into his parents.

"I think it's time that you take your own advice and realize just how wonderful you are."

"Wonderful, huh?"

He lifted my hand to his lips and pressed a kiss to the back of my palm. The simple gesture had me clamping my thighs together, memories of those lips on another part of my body chased away the remaining tendrils of self-loathing. There was only *him* and the life we both decided to share.

"Yes, darlin'. Wonderful."

And maybe I never truly believed that about myself. But hearing him say it. Knowing without a doubt that he truly believed it…maybe I could believe it too.

CHAPTER THIRTY-TWO

*T*hree days had slowly passed since Sarah gave Johnny and me the news about my mother's case being re-opened and I was told by my best friend to lay low. Apparently laying low entailed staying locked up in Johnny's house with hardly anything to do except have staring contests with Asher. I'd already made the payment transfer to the lady who owned the storefront for my boutique, but there was little more I could do without getting into the space to take measurements.

Johnny had to get back to work for the summer camp he and Deacon ran for children with special needs. I couldn't be mad at the guy for leaving me at home to do that even if the cabin fever was making me talk to myself.

By the third conversation I had with the blank wall in the kitchen, I said, "*Screw it,*" and left for *Joanne's Tavern*. It was only three o'clock so the likelihood of running into anyone but Michael was slim. So, I grabbed my purse and headed downtown.

There were a few familiar faces from the first time I wound up at *Joanne's Tavern*. Mostly weathered faces with sorrowful eyes that had probably seen too much of the world and needed a place to rest for a while. They all had their attention fixated on the TV hanging against the far wall, facing the bar entrance. It was showing the local news station with the weather forecast for the upcoming weekend. Another heat-wave, apparently.

Michael came through the double swinging doors at the far end of the bar as I slid onto one of the wooden stools.

"Look who we have here," he smiled widely at me.

"In much better shape I might add."

"It certainly looks that way. What can I get you?"

"Is it too early for a glass of Chardonnay?"

"Coming right up." Michael reached for a wine glass off the shelf behind him.

"That's not an answer you know."

His wide shoulders moved up and down as he chuckled. "It's not my place to tell people what they can and can't do. Well"—he tilted his head back and forth—"that's unless they're being an asshole. Then I usually intervene."

"Noted. I'll do my best not to be an asshole."

"I doubt you have to try very hard at that." He sat down the healthily poured glass in front of me.

"I appreciate the vote of confidence, Michael."

The coolness of the chilled wine was a welcome reprieve

rom the heat my body felt from the harsh summer afternoon despite the short walk from my car.

"Did you get everything sorted out with those letters of ours?"

I swallowed the second sip of wine and set the glass down. Actually, yes. It turns out that the guy I've been pining after ll these years feels the same way I feel toward him."

"Well, look at that. A happy ending after all."

I smiled at him before he left me to tend to the other atrons. I pulled out my sketchbook and went to work on ome of the ideas I had for a spring collection that played on nerging deep tones with pastels. When I opened the outique, most of the store would be filled with other fashion rands, but I eventually wanted to have enough of my own lesigns to fill the entire shop. Maybe even branch off into ewelry and home decor.

One day. One day everything will come together and I'll see this ream come to fruition.

After a while, I leaned back on the stool, taking a moment o acknowledge just how far I'd already come. The intensity f the past few days clouded the fact that I *owned* a storefront lready. I got lost in the logistic of getting all the paperwork ompleted on Monday amidst the investigation news that I ever really celebrated the fact that one of the biggest mile-tones was complete. I had a place to start and that was reaking awesome.

"Can you believe that guy got away with murdering that oor woman? And he was given the option of bail. What has his town come to?"

I looked up from my sketchbook to where two men were

sitting at a bartop table, one of them had a boney finger pointed at the TV where a large picture of Henry Carnelle was shown in the corner, next to the news anchor's face. Then, a picture of my mother appeared in place of Henry's. Blonde curly hair framed her heart-shaped face as she beamed at whoever was behind the camera. She was beautiful and so...*young*.

In a year, I would be the same age she was when she died and the thought left a heavy sinking feeling in my gut, like an anchor barreling toward the ocean floor.

"It's such a shame that someone that beautiful died so young," Michael said as he stared toward the TV, a damp cloth in his hand as he aimlessly wiped the bartop down.

"Yeah, it is." My voice was barely above a whisper, but Michael shifted his attention to me and something like recognition dawned on his wrinkled face.

"She was my mother," I said to him before he had a chance to ask. The first time I came in this bar I never gave him my name. Maybe that night I just needed some anonymity. A person to talk to who had no idea who I was...who my family was. Or maybe it was just the alcohol that kept me from engaging in proper manners.

Now, things were different. I wanted to stand strong with my mother's memory. I wanted people to know what Henry had done to her and to me when he took her life. The need for vengeance had become overwhelming ever since I got home from Sarah's. Some might have told me I was being ridiculous, petty even. To hope that Henry Carnelle got what he deserved for taking my mother and any future we might have had together. But I didn't care. Not when the pain of not knowing her was too much to bear at times.

"Willow," Michael said my name like a curious question. "Willow Baxley. You're Melanie Baxley's daughter."

"I am."

"Well, I'll be damned. I heard rumors about her daughter coming back into town, but I never thought she—you—would have wound up at my bar. You look so much like her. Same white blonde hair. Striking blue eyes." Suddenly, the corners of his lips tugged downward and then he shook his head. "I'm so sorry. Here I am rambling on about how much you look like her when the news is carrying on about her case being re-opened for murder. Stupid old fool," he murmured to himself.

"You're not a fool, Michael," I said softly. "Honestly, it's nice to hear someone say that I look like her."

"You don't just look like her, Willow. Now, that I put two and two together, it all makes sense. You sound just like her too. And the way you scrunch your nose...she used to do that all the time."

I leaned forward. "Wait, you *knew* her? You knew my mother?"

He nodded, a gleam shining in his eyes. "My younger sister was born ten years after me—a total surprise for my parents. But she was your mother's age and they became pretty close growing up. We'd all go to the lake together and your mother," he let out a chuckle, "she was a pistol. Never took shit from anyone and she always stood up for the underdogs. I remember one time when we were all at the lake and there were three guys, a few years older than her, and they were picking on one of her classmates. A nerdy looking fellow with glasses. Melanie walked right up to those guys and shoved them all in the chest, even though they towered over her by more than a solid foot. She was a force to be reckoned with, that's for sure."

"I wish I could have seen that. Seen that side of her. But I never got the chance to know her."

His head bobbed up and down a little, his eyes going glassy. Lost in memory. Then he said, "I remember when the news of her death was first released and they spoke of how she had harbored the secret of having a child when she was a teenager. How she'd given the child up for adoption. That child was you. I always wondered where she went. That story of her breaking her back and not being allowed to have visitors sounded like horse shit to me."

I didn't know why I felt so comfortable opening up to this man I barely knew, but there was something in his eyes. In the genuine curiosity behind his questions that made me feel safe. And the more I thought about it, the more I realized just how much I needed to talk about it all. Not just to Johnny and Sarah, but to someone who knew *her*.

"Yes," I nodded. "That was me. I didn't know everything until these past few weeks, but she gave me up so I wouldn't be forced to partake in her world. She wanted me to live freely. Without the expectations that came with the Baxley name. And I wish, more than anything, that she felt strong enough to remove herself from that world so we could have been together. So that I could have had the mom I always dreamed of having growing up.

"All I have now are her things. Pieces of her that don't give me much but a blurry image of what she was like. So, it's really nice to hear from someone who knew her. Thank you, Michael. Thank you for giving me that."

"I'm so glad I was able to put some of the pieces together

or you, Ms. Willow." The smile on his face was warm as he ilted his head at me before making his way over to one of the patrons who called for another beer.

I sat there, staring at nothing in particular as I mulled over what Michael had said about my mother. It was a gift, I realized, stumbling into this bar for the first time over a week ago now. Michael was a kind, gentle soul and maybe it was something I made up in my mind, but it felt like I was led to be here. To find this place. To find *him* so that I could have a few more pieces of my mother.

Yes, I decided. It most certainly was meant to be.

In the peace that seemed to settle over me, I reached for my pencil again and started on another sketch for a cotton crop top paired with matching shorts. Lost in my work, I almost didn't notice the door of the bar opening until I felt the heat from outside swirl against the skin of my exposed back and arms. Looking over my shoulder, I expected to find another elderly man, similar to those who were scattered in the bar already.

But the moment my brain recognized the man's face, my heart rate skyrocketed. Freckles splattered across his handsome face and bright blue eyes looked almost dazed beneath strawberry-blonde eyelashes that matched the wavy hair atop his head. He was tall. Probably the same height as Johnny and that made me nervous because a man that size could do serious damage if he wanted to.

Henry Carnelle.

He'd, somehow, ended up in the same dive bar as me in the middle of the afternoon. The one time I decided to go out in public when Johnny was miles away at his shop and the only people I had around me were likely too drunk to even notice if something went down and I needed help.

Michael. Michael was here. I tried to convince myself that everything would be okay as long as I had one person to help me if shit hit the fan.

My mind was whirling, my body shaking, as I watched him over my shoulder. He hadn't taken notice of me yet, those glassy eyes were fixed forward as he took a few stumbling steps toward the bar.

He's drunk.

The longer I looked at him, the more I noticed how there was a sheen to his pale skin. His long sleeve shirt was haphazardly rolled up to his elbows and crinkles indented his slacks from his hips, all the way down to his ankles as though he'd worn the same pants for several days.

When he picked up speed toward the other end of the bar, I slowly turned myself on the stool until my back was to him. Every bone in my body told me to flee, that I should run away from this monster. But I was frozen—unable to move from the stool because fleeing meant I would be all alone in the street as I looked for my car and what if he followed me?

My thoughts were buzzing at a rapid-fire pace. *Breathe, Willow. Just breathe.* One breath in, then out. Again. And again. I focused on my breath until I no longer felt the hard banging of my heart against my ribcage.

"Whiskey. Straight. No ice," Henry slurred.

"Are you sure—"

"Isn't your job to pour drinks? So, pour me a goddamn drink!"

While I kept my back to him and everyone else in the bar, I could feel the tension in the air. It was quiet too, the only sounds being the low murmur of the voices on the TV and Michael's movements as he poured Henry a glass of whiskey.

"That wasn't so hard, was it?" Henry snickered as I heard the glass slide against the wood of the bartop.

Heavy silence ensued for what felt like an eternity as I kept trying to come up with a plan to escape. Uneasiness gave way to rising panic and giving in to that was my one and only mistake as I chanced a look at Henry over my shoulder. Those icy eyes met mine and when they widened, I knew I was in trouble.

"You," he said with such disdain, it rattled my bones.

I wanted to look away, to gather my things and run like a bat out of hell toward the door, but I couldn't stop staring at him. The monster who killed my mother. And in those eyes, I saw a promise he held for me too. One laced with malice.

"I heard Melanie's orphan had come back to town to cash in the Baxley estate. I still can't believe Adeline would give everything over to you." He glared at me. "Then again, you can never trust a woman to make a decision best left for a man to make."

His words stung, hitting that exposed nerve that never seemed to fully heal over. I didn't deserve the estate, the money, or anything else that came with it. I was the forgotten one. The girl who was born as a mistake. Over and over, the self-loathing thoughts attacked, exacerbated by this man's words.

Tears burned the back of my eyes and when I looked at him—really looked—something started to shift in me. The self-doubt I lived with my entire life loosened its hold on me as I was filled with something much stronger than the hate shining in Henry's eyes.

Love. Yes. I had been loved. From the moment I was born and my mother chose to give up the chance of knowing me so I might have a better shot at escaping the chains of her world. Ms. Mosely had shown me love too in how she provided a home for me and put clothes on my back. And when everyone else at school had shunned me, Sarah had shown up. Made sure I felt like I belonged. Johnny…just his name alone brought butterflies to my stomach. The love we shared gave me power that was stronger than anything this man could say to me, no matter how dangerous he was.

And in that love, I found courage.

I straightened my back out of the scared, slouched posture and narrowed my gaze on him. "You can say whatever you want to me, Henry Carnelle. You can tell me that I'm not good enough. That I was never wanted. Or that my mother was stupid. In fact, I encourage you to get it all out now because in a short while the *truth* of what you did to my mother will put you exactly where you belong. Behind bars where you will spend the rest of your miserable life, eating peanut butter and jelly sandwiches, begging to be let out in the concrete yard so you can feel the sun on your face."

I slid off my stool and took a step toward him. "So go ahead. Say whatever you want to me because this will be the last chance you have before you get sent away to rot."

Splotches of red crept along his neck, rising into his flushed cheeks. When he spoke, droplets of spit flew from his mouth, the jowls of his cheeks shaking with fury. "You stupid little cunt!"

A flash of fear had me stepping back, but the notable sound of a shotgun being cocked had me turning to find Michael with a double-barrel shotgun in his arms. The barrels were lifted toward the ceiling, but the look on his face suggested he was about a millisecond away from turning them on Henry.

"No one speaks to a woman like that in my bar and lives to tell about it. But since I'm feeling generous today, I'll give you one chance to turn around and leave before I blow your ass sky high."Michael's voice was steady as he spoke.

I watched as Henry's blue eyes slowly darted between the shotgun and Michael's face. Assessing whether he wanted to risk the chance of Michael bluffing. But when Michael started to lower the barrels toward him, he threw his hands up and staggered backward a few steps.

"Fine," he spit out. Fear shone through the drunkness as he backed into one of the small tables and nearly fell over. Righting himself, he shifted forward and darted for the door like the coward he was. When the door finally closed and he was gone, I loosed the breath I'd been holding since Michael intervened.

"Oh my God," I whispered, drawing shaky hands to cover my mouth.

"Michael stashed the shotgun from wherever he kept it below the bar and looked at me. "Are you okay?" His tone was soft.

I shook my head, completely unable to speak because all I could think about was how my mother must have felt having to deal with someone like that for years when I was about to break down after just one encounter.

"I want to go home," I finally said. "I want to go home." I couldn't stop shaking.

"Is there anyone I can call for you?" Michael's eyes darted toward my cell phone laying next to my sketch pad.

"Johnny. Please call Johnny."

I plopped back onto the stool, propping my elbows onto the bartop so I could shield my crumpling face from view. Somewhere, I heard the muffled sound of Michael's voice as he spoke to Johnny through the pounding in my ears. I wasn't sure how long I stayed like that, letting my hair fall over my face. A curtain to hide from the prying eyes of the other patrons, until finally I felt the warmth of his presence behind me.

Scooping me into his arms, Johnny lifted me from the barstool, and in the safety of his arms, I finally let it all go.

CHAPTER THIRTY-THREE

*S*haking. My entire body was shaking like a leaf on a tree and I couldn't stop. I wrung my hands together in my lap as Johnny walked to the driver's side door of his truck and hopped in.

"Lo." His voice was soft but stern. I didn't turn to look at him. I just kept wringing my hands together, the image of Henry's beet-red face as he stepped toward me playing over and over in my mind.

He was going to hurt me. If Michael hadn't cocked the shotgun and threatened him, Henry would have hurt me just like he did to my mother. I knew it. *Felt* it. And I couldn't get the fear out of my mind.

"Lo," Johnny said again, placing a hand on my knee that I hadn't even realized was bouncing up and down.

I still couldn't look at him. Couldn't face him. He told me not to leave the house without him. That it wasn't safe knowing what Henry was capable of. I should have listened. I should have stayed home and none of this would have happened.

"Lo," Johnny's voice snapped like a whip cracking. I finally looked at him and the devastation written on his face was my undoing. My lips quaked as a sob racked through my body.

I heard the electronic motor of his seat backing up and in the next moment, strong arms hauled me into his lap. I curled against him, drawing my knees up and resting my head on his chest. The sound of his steady heartbeat was soothing as the tears rained down my face like a dam being destroyed.

He held onto me tightly and dropped his head low so I was covered in the shadow of his face. In slow circles, his hands moved along my arm and my thigh for a long while. With each haggard sob that rattled my chest, he held me closer. There were no words he could say that would match the comfort of being in his arms and he knew that. Johnny always knew what I needed and gave it freely. Without question.

Safe, I finally thought. Yes. I was safe now. Henry was gone and I was no longer being threatened by the man who killed my mother.

Safe. The word clanged through my mind. *Safe*. I breathed in the scent of cedar wood and knew that smell meant I was home. *Safe*. His strong body held mine with ease and when I lifted my head from his chest and looked into his deep brown eyes my mind cleared, the fear lessening a fraction.

"Talk to me, baby girl," he whispered before pressing his lips to my temple.

"Henry..." I swallowed against the knot in my throat. "Henry Carnelle showed up at the bar and I...didn't know what to do. I wanted to run. To get away from him, but when I saw him, I froze. And then"—I raked my hands over my face trying to wipe the dampness away—"I got so damn angry. All could see was my mother suffering at his hands and I told him that he was going to rot in prison for what he did to her."

Johnny's brows shot up, his mouth popping open like he wanted to say something, but I kept rambling on, needing to get it all out, "Then he tried to come at me and called me a cunt." I felt Johnny bristle beneath me, a growl rumbling in his chest, but I didn't stop, I couldn't. "He was going to attack me. I saw it in his eyes and how he came toward me. But Michael...he stopped it."

"Michael? He's the one who called me?" He continued rubbing those soothing circles against my skin, but I could feel the heat of his rage.

I nodded. "He's the bartender. The owner actually. He pulled out a shotgun and told Henry to leave. And he did."

"Fuck, Lo."

I thought, for a moment, that he was going to chastise me. Tell me that it was my fault for leaving the house and that I should have been more responsible. That none of this would have happened if I would have just listened to him.

But he didn't. He only held me closer and whispered into my ear, "I am so fucking sorry that happened to you. I'm so sorry I wasn't there to stop it before it started."

"There's nothing you could have done. It was my fault for leaving the—"

"No." He gripped my face with his hands, tilting my chin back so I was looking into those blazing eyes. "Don't for a second blame yourself for the actions of that piece of shit. What he said to you and what he did is on him, Lo. Do you understand me?"

Tears welled in my eyes again and as one escaped, sliding

down my cheek, Johnny brought my face to his lips and kissed it away.

"I have half a mind to take you home and go hunt that fucker down." His nostrils flared from the rising anger he so expertly controlled.

I gripped his t-shirt in my fists. "Please don't. Please don't leave me. I can't be alone right now." Fear sat heavy in my chest, making it difficult to breathe.

"Whatever you need, Lo. Whatever you need at all, just tell me and I'll do it."

Just as he'd always done, this man would walk through the fires of hell for me if I asked, and that alone was enough to shake some of the fear. I gripped his chin and placed a kiss on his lips, still wet from the tear he'd kissed away.

"Take me home." I looked into his eyes and saw some of the anger melt away, replaced with determination and contentment.

"Okay," he whispered. "I can do that."

After a few more moments, I crawled back into my seat and buckled myself in. When we took off for home, Johnny pressed the call button on his steering wheel and said, "Call Cal Weston."

"Why're you calling Cal?"

Johnny's knuckles turned white over the steering wheel. "Because, if I can't hunt that piece of shit down and kill him with my bare hands, the least I can do is try to get him off the streets so you can live your life until he's put away for good." Malice laced his every word and it was at that moment I realized Johnny really would kill Henry if it meant keeping me safe. Maybe it should have worried me—being in love with someone who'd killed and would kill again to rid the world of someone awful. But I wasn't worried because I knew his heart. Knew that he wasn't the same as Henry, who'd taken the life of a woman much smaller than him. Who'd beaten her down every chance he got, probably to make himself feel more like a man.

Johnny was different. He killed to protect what he loved and maybe it made me twisted, but I loved him for that.

"Johnny," Cal's voice boomed through the car speakers. Johnny tapped on the volume control to lower it a few levels. "What can I do for you, brother?"

Johnny paused and slid his gaze toward me, a question dancing in his eyes. I gave a subtle nod and he said, "I need to tell you something about Henry Carnelle."

It took most of the ride back to Johnny's house to fill Cal in. Johnny did most of the talking and I filled in some of the details as needed.

"Is there anything you can do to get him back in jail until his hearing?" Johnny asked, the tires meeting gravel crunched as he pulled into the driveway.

"It might take a few days because I have to go downtown and question Michael and anyone else I can get as a witness who was there when it all happened. But given what you've told me, I shouldn't have any problem getting his bail revoked. In a way, this is a blessing in disguise. The longer he was back in society on bail, the more opportunities he had to spin the truth and get people thinking he's innocent."

My heart sank at the thought of that happening, knowing just how easily some people could be influenced by a man with a powerful name. To hear that Cal had enough to revoke Henry's bail nearly had me crying again.

"That's a good way to look at it," Johnny said. "But I have

to say, the man is lucky I wasn't there or it wouldn't be iron bars and concrete holding him, it'd be six feet of dirt."

Heat flared at the base of my neck, but Cal just laughed. "I hear that. I have a feeling his court date will be pretty quick given this is the first murder trial Pebble Brook Falls has ever encountered. But I'll keep you both updated on his bail revocation."

"Thanks, man."

"Any time."

With the flick of his thumb, the line went dead. Johnny threw the shifter into park and turned to look at me.

"How you doin', baby girl?"

I blew out a long breath. "I think I'm okay. Or, at least I will be okay. It's good to hear that Cal has enough to revoke Henry's bail and I can just stay at your house until he's back in jail."

"*Your house?*" Johnny echoed, narrowing his gaze at me as his right brow arched.

I bit my lower lip. "Yeah." I gestured toward the front of his house. "That is your house, right?"

Placing an elbow on the center console, he leaned toward me. With a single finger, he lifted my chin. "When I asked you to move in with me this *house* became *our* home, not just mine."

He cocked his head to the side, those beautiful chocolate eyes dipping to my mouth and back up again. My breath hitched as he lowered his lips to mine, close enough I could feel the warmth of his breath as he said, "And if you haven't already noticed, this has been my plan all along, darlin'. I bought this house knowing just how much you wanted it. You ee, it was never my intention to live this life without you. I knew I'd find you one day and I'd win you back so that we could grow old together, sitting side by side in those rocking chairs every night."

My heart squeezed as he brushed his lips against mine. "So never want to hear you say this is my house again. This is our home, darlin.'"

"Our home," I breathed, getting lost in the intensity of having him so damn close and just out of reach as his grip on my chin was firm when I tried to close the gap between us.

Johnny closed his eyes at my words, sucking in a deep breath. "Say it again." When he opened his eyes, I swore every memory of the love we shared flickered in his molten irises. A lifetime of little moments that had led us here with his hand sliding from my chin to the nape of my neck where he twined his fingers through my hair.

"Our home," I repeated, and this time I truly felt it. Felt the gravity of what he'd done for me before he even knew for sure if I'd ever come back to him. All those years I spent trying to forget him and he'd done everything he could to keep my memory alive, to fight for our future.

"And it always will be, for however long you want it." His voice was thick with emotion, as though the weight of today and the last twelve years was almost too much for him to bear.

The stubble along his jaw scraped against the palm of my hand as I stroked his cheek with my thumb. I brought my forehead to his, closing my eyes for a moment so I could take him in. The sound of his breath, the warmth of his presence, and the fresh woodsy scent of cedar.

"Forever, Johnny." I leaned back to look into his eyes. "That's how long I will want this—want *you*. Forever."

Relief flooded those irises as he smiled widely at me, his dimple tugging at the corner of his mouth, giving me butterflies.

"I like the sound of that, darlin'."

CHAPTER THIRTY-FOUR

THREE MONTHS LATER

*J*ohnny held my left hand while Sarah held my right as I sat on the sofa, squished between the two. All of our eyes were fixed on the TV as one of the jury members for my mother's case rose from the jury stand and unfolded the piece of paper in her hands.

"We, the jury, find the defendant guilty," were the only words I heard as I nearly fainted from lack of oxygen. I'd been holding my breath for way too long.

"Yes!" Sarah cried out, jumping to her feet at the same time Johnny rose and yelled, "Fuck yes!" They both high-fived one another while I sat there, frozen on the sofa.

"We, the jury, find the defendant guilty," played in my mind again and again like a broken record while I stared at a random spot on Sarah's living room floor.

"It's really over?" I asked, to no one in particular, but Sarah answered, "Yes, Willow! He's going to prison for life. You never have to see that asshole ever again."

Johnny moved in front of me, blocking my view of the TV as he knelt down and took my hands in his. "Are you okay?"

The haze of shock cleared as his handsome face came into view. "We really won?" My own voice sounded as though I was underwater.

He nodded, his lips curling into a smile that awoke some part of me as that dimple appeared. "Yes, darlin'. We really won. Because of you, because of your courage, that man will never hurt another person again."

My throat tightened as tears began to fall. I'd done it. All the words my mother had written about Henry Carnelle abusing her flashed across my mind and I couldn't save her. But...I could save others. I *did* save others from suffering the same fate and I knew she was with me as Johnny took me into his arms, goosebumps trailing along my entire body.

A deep sense of peace washed over me like a gentle hand caressing my back as I drifted off to sleep. I'd spent my entire life not knowing my mother, but this journey of discovering what happened to her gave me something I never had before. I may never have spoken to her, but I *knew* her. I felt her guiding me every step along the way in revealing the truth about Henry and maybe it had been her all along who'd brought me back home to my best friend and the love that was meant for me.

Laughter broke through the tears as pure joy radiated from my heart. It didn't matter that Adeline had conspired with Henry to have her daughter killed for deciding to end her own engagement. My mother wasn't the type of person they could keep in a box and they were threatened by that. So much so, they decided to take her life and there would always be a part of me that loathed them for that.

But today I wouldn't let those thoughts drag me down.

Today was for celebrating because Johnny was right when he said Henry would never be able to hurt another person again.

I sniffed, pulling back from Johnny's embrace. I matched his smile as he rubbed my arms up and down. "I think it's time to pop the champagne."

"Hell yeah," he said, shooting me a wink.

"I'll grab the flutes!" Sarah threw her arms into the air and I couldn't help but laugh at her excitement. Not a day went by since I got back to town that Sarah hadn't shown her love and support for me. As I watched her skip into the kitchen and then turn back to Johnny, I felt gratitude swarm my heart in a way I never had before.

After Sarah gathered three champagne flutes and we popped the top off the bottle and cheersed, I sent a silent *thank you* to the heavens above where I knew my mother was looking down on me.

A month after Henry's trial had concluded, the town was still in an uproar. Not that I blamed any of them with it being Pebble Brook Falls' first murder trial and the fall of two prominent houses, the story made nationwide news pulling in reporters from all the neighboring cities. People wanted to know how such a scandalously awful thing could happen in such a picturesque town.

The first few days I tried to leave the house after the verdict was given, I was swarmed by everyone who'd ever known me and even some people I'd never met. With each encounter, I felt more and more overwhelmed and just needed to take a step back from it all, so I buried myself in my work: calling interior designers to schedule consultations for my boutique, working on sketches for my own designs, and finding other Southeastern designers to showcase, and thinking up name ideas for the boutique.

Everything was going so well that I had to keep pinching myself that it was real and I wasn't living in some kind of delusional fantasy world.

As good as things had gotten, I still couldn't shake the feeling that something was missing. For almost a week, I moped around the house, drowning in melancholy before Johnny finally told me that I needed closure.

Not even six months had gone by from the time that I first arrived in Pebble Brook Falls, to learning more about my mother and giving in to the love I felt for Johnny. Then I found out my mother had been the victim of domestic violence and there was more to her death than anyone could have imagined. Even after Henry was sentenced, I never took a moment to say goodbye to the woman who, in a way, sacrificed herself for my betterment.

Johnny told me that it took him almost a year after Bradley died for him to visit the gravesite and say goodbye, but when he finally did, it brought him the closure he needed to fully move forward. So, I'd taken his advice and we stopped by the local florist to get a bundle of white roses before we headed for the cemetery.

I wrung my hands in my lap as Johnny's truck came to a stop in the cemetery parking lot. I looked over at him and that same smile that always made me weak in the knees tugged at his lips. Placing a hand over both of mine, he arched an eyebrow at me. "There's no reason to be nervous, darlin'."

"I know," I said with a laugh, shaking my head. "I know I'm being ridiculous, it's just that this is the first time I've actually spoken to my mother." When the words came out, I laughed again at how stupid they sounded spoken aloud. "Not that I'm actually going to be talking to her because she's gone, but... ugh. You know what I mean."

His hand moved to cup my cheek and I leaned into his touch. "I know exactly what you mean." A muscle ticked along his jaw. "I've never told anyone this before, not even you. But I talk to my parents all the time. I don't know if they're still here or if they've moved on from this world, but I talk to them every day. Sometimes, I tell them how mad I am that they chose drugs over me. And sometimes I tell them about how my day went and how badly I wish they could see where I ended up. How far I've come in life. So yes, Lo. I know exactly what you mean."

My mouth popped open to say something, but I closed it immediately, knowing there was nothing I could say to ease the hurt their absence caused him. It was the same hurt that had led me here to this cemetery.

I held his hand in mine and opted for the only thing that mattered. "I love you, Johnny."

The pain in his eyes shifted. Love, it turned out, was the only thing that mattered to him, too. "I love you, baby girl. Now, go give your Momma those flowers. I'll be waiting here for as long as you need."

"Okay," I whispered and gave him a quick kiss on the

cheek before I hopped out of his truck and headed through the tall iron gates of the cemetery.

It was the first time I'd been in a cemetery and while I'd seen a few of them as I drove by, I never gave them much thought. Now that I was here, I found the grounds to be startingly peaceful. Towering oak trees were scattered across the acreage, each providing shade for a concrete bench with swirls carved into the edges.

Since I had no idea where my mother was buried, I'd called ahead and gotten the information that her resting place was toward the middle and there would be a large tombstone shaped like an angel made of marble. It didn't take me long to find it because it was the second largest one in the middle of the cemetery.

When I made my way over to the area, I saw Adeline's first. Atop the marble stone was the most beautiful sculpture of an angel and I couldn't help but think of how undeserving she was to have something so beautiful mark her grave. I stared at the engraving and wondered who would have thought to put *'In loving memory'* when there was no one left to love the memory of her. And even if there was someone left, the woman was vile and wicked. It would have taken an equally wretched person to love her.

I could feel the scowl on my face deepen the longer I stared at her name and I hated how it felt. The anger. The resentment toward her...toward *myself* for having a grandmother who was so fucking awful. My stomach turned to knots and with a deep sigh, I closed my eyes.

This isn't about her.

When I opened my eyes again, a Monarch butterfly darted

cross my line of sight and landed on the tombstone next to
Adeline's. Etched into the stone read:

Melanie Baxley
Beloved Daughter and Friend
1975-2004

Above the headstone was the same exact angel sculpture
that Adeline had for hers, but it was a few inches shorter. I
moved to stand in front of it, already feeling a swell of
emotions swirl through me.

"Hi, Mom. Or Melanie." I cleared my throat. "To be honest,
I'm not exactly sure what I'm supposed to call you."

Silence. And then a gentle wind had the tree branches
above rustling. I looked upward, noticing how bright streams
of sunlight burst through the gaps in the branches. When they
hit my face, I closed my eyes and let the warmth soak in for a
few moments before I took a seat in front of her headstone.

"I think I'd like to call you Mom," I whispered. "I've spent
most of my life mad at you. Honestly, I think that's a trend for
me. When I feel hurt, I tend to get mad at the person who I
think hurt me without even considering if they meant to do it
on purpose. But I'm trying to be better about that now."

I picked at a blade of grass in front of me, needing to do
something with my hands. "But that's not why I came here—
to tell you that I spent a lot of time mad at you. I came here to
tell you thank you. Thank you for writing our story in your
journal and for giving me the gift of knowing just how much
you loved me." My voice cracked as I tried to hold back the
tears from spilling over. "Because...because as mad as I was at

you, I've always loved you, Mom. And I just wish…I just wish I could talk to you. Hear your voice."

There was no stopping the tremble in my lips or the tears that escaped as I dropped my head low and squeezed my eyes shut.

The pain of that truth had me trapped in sorrow for a long while. Wave after wave of sadness pushed through me until there was nothing left to give. Nothing left to let go of. Face taut from dried tears, I rubbed at the skin on my cheeks until I felt them loosen enough for me to peel my eyes open again.

When I did, the beautiful butterfly that flew past me earlier was resting on top of my right knee. Its wings opened and closed slowly as it took a step forward. And there was no mistaking the certainty in my heart that my mother was there with me and the beautiful winged creature was a symbol of her presence.

A smile split my lips and a choked laugh came out of me as I placed a finger in front of the butterfly. It slowly crawled onto my finger and I lifted it into the air, the sunlight illuminating the butterfly's fragile wings. It was so beautiful and the longer I looked at it, the more at peace I felt in knowing that while my mother was physically gone, she was still here with me. Wanting to know me. Loving me.

And so I spent a long, long time telling her about my life—my hopes and dreams. I told her about Johnny and Sarah and the plans for my boutique. I told her *everything*.

"I forgive you, Mom. I forgive you for giving me up. For not knowing how to make things work in a way that would keep us together. And I think maybe this was all meant to happen. Because if you wouldn't have given me to Ms.

Mosely, I wouldn't have found Johnny. So, I forgive you. And...and I love you, Mom."

The butterfly stilled for a moment and then its glorious wings spread wide and it flew from my finger into the bright blue sky, taking the last bit of my pain with it.

EPILOGUE

ONE YEAR LATER

"*I* can't believe it's been three months since the last time we came to the cabin. That's way too long, Johnny. We need to start coming up at least once a month."

Johnny's laughter floated around me as he placed a hand on my bouncing knee. "I agree, darlin'. But that's going to require you to step down from some of the tasks you've assigned yourself."

I scowled. "Which ones?"

"Well, let's see here. You volunteer at the orphanage once a week, as well as the animal shelter. And that's on top of you being at the boutique every day. Oh, and you're also working on fashion lines for the next two seasons."

"Okay, yeah. When you lay it out like that it does sound like a lot."

I looked over at him in the driver's seat and he cocked a brow at me. I stuck my tongue out at him. His shoulders shook with the deep rumble of his throaty laughter that had me trading in my childish gesture for a wide smile.

When he pulled into the gravel driveway and I caught site

f what had quickly become my safe haven as much as his, the tightness that had lingered in my chest lifted. Life had gotten busy lately and while it was all good—no, *amazing*—things, the busyness was starting to wear on me.

"Thank you for forcing me to take a break and bring us up here. I know you have a lot going on with the shop as well."

A few famous bow hunters had come through our small Georgia town and found *Far Away Archery*. They were all military guys and when they got to talking with Johnny, they took a liking to his story of going from orphan, to being in the Marines, to finding solace in archery. A few weeks after their visit, he'd gotten a call that changed his entire life. Apparently, one of them knew an editor at *Outdoor Life* magazine and he'd called Johnny, asking if he would be interested in having the magazine run a feature on his store.

My heart warmed at the memory of seeing his face light up like a kid on Christmas morning with dozens of presents under the tree. When they ran the feature four months ago, his shop went from being the local archery supply store to a well-known gem in the Southeast. People from all over flocked to his store, many of whom also loved hearing his story.

"Any time, darlin'."

We unpacked the truck and headed inside. "I just have a few emails to answer about a new jewelry designer I'm bringing in next month and then I'm all yours." I cracked open my laptop at the small dining table in the kitchen nook.

"No rush." He pressed a kiss to the top of my head. "Just head out back when you're done. I'm going to get a picnic set up for us so we can have dinner outside."

"Okay." I tilted my head back, giving him access to my lip before he bounded for the back door.

Fifteen minutes later and I was a free woman. I shut down my laptop, not wanting any more distractions for the rest of the weekend. Johnny hadn't come back in to start dinner yet so I grabbed my sweater from the back of the chair, slipped it on, and went for the back door.

When it swung open, my heart clenched at the sight of him and Asher standing atop a black and white plaid blanket under the biggest oak tree on our property. Dozens of candles surrounded them both and when Asher saw me, he gave a little bark in greeting.

Johnny shifted, extending a hand out toward me. "Come over here, darlin'."

My hands shook slightly as I walked over to him. He grasped my hands and took a step toward me as he brought them up to his lips and kissed the back of my palms.

"I want to show you something." His voice was gravelly, thick with some emotion I couldn't quite place.

He turned toward the trunk of the oak tree and what saw almost brought me to my knees. A large heart was freshly etched into the tree and within it, our names were carved:

Willow + Johnny
Forever

An homage to the carving he'd made in the tree downtown the day after we professed our love for one another. That first heart with our initials was small, like a budding flower. But this heart, it was large, taking up space, just as our love had done over the years. And I knew it would only grow bigger from here.

I trailed my fingers over the etched bark, tracing the outline of the heart. "It's beautiful, Johnny." When I looked back at him, he was down on one knee, Asher sitting tall and proud next to him. A sob broke through my chest as he took my hand in his, my other hand covered my trembling lips.

"Willow Mae, I have loved you before I even knew what loving someone meant. You have been my shade in the blistering heat of summer. The rock to my crashing waves. And the light to my darkest sorrows." Tears glistened in his brown eyes. "You have been with me my entire life, even when we were apart, I held you in my heart. You are the person I want to grow old with, to fall even more in love with each passing day."

My heart thundered wildly in my chest as I watched him untie a bright red bow that had been tied to Asher's collar. When Johnny looked back up at me, he held a beautiful diamond ring between his fingers.

"Would you do me the honor of becoming my wife?"

"Yes," I whispered as tears streamed down my cheeks. "Yes!" I jumped into his arms and we fell to the ground together, landing on the soft blanket. Johnny rolled me over until I was laying on my back and he was hovering over me, his body pinning mine beneath him.

His voice stammered as he asked, "Can I put this on your finger?" He held the ring between us and as I got a closer look, my mouth popped open in awe. The center diamond was a large oval nestled between twin pearls that sat atop a white gold band. It was the most delicate and unique piece of jewelry I'd ever seen.

I lifted my finger and when he slid it over my knuckle, butterflies swarmed my stomach. "It's so beautiful, Johnny. I've never seen anything like it."

"Neither have I," he whispered. But when I peeked up at him, he wasn't looking at the ring, he was looking right at me. And when he kissed me, it was so tender it nearly broke my heart. His fingers wove through my hair as he pulled away and said, "You're going to be my wife."

"Yes," I cried, nodding. "And you're going to be my husband." I placed both hands on the sides of his face and kissed him again.

Bark! Bark!

We pulled away, laughing as Asher told us just how upset he was for being left out. Johnny sat us up and I crawled between his legs, letting my back rest against his chest. "Come here, boy," I called to Asher who was too happy to oblige.

He booped my cheek with his nose and gave me a little kiss. Those big golden eyes held such wisdom and love, it nearly made my heart crack.

Johnny reached around me and gave him a scratch behind his ears. "She's ours forever now, buddy." Asher seemed to understand him because he let out a gleeful whimper before he scooted closer, laid down, and rested his head on my leg.

I leaned back, feeling the incredible weight of my engagement ring on my finger and the strength of Johnny's arms around me.

Home. I'd finally made it home.

Ingram Content Group UK Ltd.
Milton Keynes UK
UKHW050222240623
423807UK00022B/549